Avalon One
(Fidelien Knights Book 2)

By Daniel (DG) Shipton

The Fidelian Coat of Arms

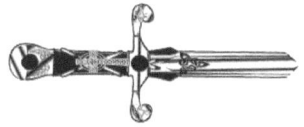

Front Matter

Avalon one
By Daniel G. Shipton

https://dgshiptonblog.wordpress.com

ISBN 978-1-7322607
Library of Congress Control Number:

Approximately 73,000 words

This is a fictional account. Names and places depicted are not based on anyone in real life, but flow from the author's imagination. The views expressed are meant to entertain and should not be taken in any other way.

Limits of Liability and Disclaimer: The author and publisher are not liable for any misuse of the material.

Unless otherwise noted all images have been used with public information laws, through Pixaby

Prologue

After surviving their struggle on Hyperborea, Nash Braveheart and his young crew were assigned to a new Triton Bomber. The Pegasus was a mid-sized ship that could carry a crew of six. There were small living quarters at the rear of the ship. It was equipped with front and rear auto-turrets and upper and lower personnel turrets. The ship had a rounded triangular-shaped reflecting panels to give it radar and sensor cloaking abilities. The weaponry included both rechargeable pulsar bombs and six mega-ton conventional bombs.

The four young members of the crew had been together for almost one year. They were now nearly inseparable. They were on their way to Avalon One, the headquarters of the Fidelian Knights. The Fidelian Abbey housed the center of their faith, the Academy of the Knights, and the leadership of the Council of Twelve. For over three hundred years since humanity arrived in the Elysium System, Avalon One had been a haven of peace for the Fidelians Knights, as they tried to protect humanity's faith and most precious knowledge.

Twelve-year-old Skylar Knighthawk, a Fidelian Pledge had been recalled to Avalon One to face the Pledge's Quest. It was the next step in advancing his training from Pledge to Squire. His cousin and mentor, Halie Ambrosius had to accompany him to the lush moon where they had grown up. She was there to see that he faithfully completed the test.

1

Arrival

"Avalon One, this is the Pegasus, requesting permission to land south of the Olympian Forest," First Lieutenant Nash Braveheart called in. He guided the mid-sized, Triton Bomber toward the lush, first moon of Avalon. Nash was twenty-two, well-built, with sandy-blonde hair, and in need of a shave. He had been in command of his crew of two soldiers, and one Fidelian Pledge for just over a year.

"You're clear for landing, Pegasus. Please continue on your present trajectory in a southeasterly direction."

"Acknowledged," Nash said shutting off the communication link and adjusting the spacecraft's pitch. "Well, it looks like we're almost there. I suppose you're looking forward to getting back home."

"Yes, in a way," Halie, the beautiful seventeen-year-old copilot, and Fidelian Knight replied. She pulled her long auburn hair back into a hair tie, as she watched the green forest below.

"I wish we weren't coming back at all," the grumpy voice of twelve-year-old Skylar came from his seat behind Nash.

Nash glanced over his shoulder, "What's this Pledge's walk-about thing you're going on anyway?"

Halie waited for her younger cousin to answer. After a few moments of silence, she glared at the boy answering for him, "Since, he's not going to answer you. It's called the Pledge's Quest. It is a testing of a trainee as they approach becoming a full Pledge, within the Order. They must be tested and then Pledge allegiance to the Order of Fidelian Knights. The Quest requires the Pledge to find their way from the far side of the Central Mountains back to the Abbey and Academy."

Corporal Ariel Pembroke, the navigator, leaned over from the seat behind Halie. She was twenty, having short hair, and wearing a tan military shirt and green cargo pants. She smiled at Skylar, "So kiddo, do you think you're ready for this test?"

"I don't know. I just wish it was all over. I didn't ask to come back here," Skylar grumbled turning back to stare out the window.

Nash grinned as he glanced back at the younger boy, "This should be a piece of cake for you, kid. I mean you've ridden on dragons and helped to rescue a planet from a whole legion of the Varangian Guard. This little hike through the mountains should be as easy as taking a swim for you."

"I sure hope so," Skylar pouted. "I just don't know why we have to do this stupid test anyway. I've been learning a lot from you Halie. This test isn't going to prove anything. It seems like a big waste of time to me."

Halie looked back at her younger cousin, "It helps to show that your training has prepared you and that you're ready to move on. It's also a part of our tradition, and every Pledge has been through the same test when they were about your age.

However, Nash, it's a bit more than a hike. He can only have what he takes in with him, and he really doesn't know what he's facing. Even though I'm with him, I'm not allowed to help him. He'll be going over some extremely rough terrain, and there are real dangers along the way."

"But you will stay with him all through the Quest, right?" Ariel asked. "I mean he isn't alone, so he's kept safe through the journey?"

"I'm just there to make sure he doesn't get himself killed. But I'm not supposed to help him, unless it's a serious emergency. In fact, I'm supposed to follow his lead through the entire quest. It's to see how his skills in wisdom and leadership are developing as well."

Ariel grimaced, "How dangerous is this quest, Halie? And, remember this is me you're talking to. Don't try to lie."

"Well, people do get hurt going through the trials of the Quest. I remember, I had several bumps and bruises when I went through. In the end, I was able to make it safely through. That's why I'll be accompanying him on his journey. The Order doesn't want anyone killed on the Quest. It's to develop character and perseverance, not to kill anyone."

"I'm not worried about the hike through the wilderness," Skylar growled, looking up at his cousin. "I'm more worried about the gauntlet than I am about crossing the mountains."

"The what?" Nash asked.

Halie sighed and looked to the ceiling, "Skylar it's not the gauntlet."

"Well, that's what Joel and Sidney always called it. Back at the academy they always told me that the quest through the mountains was the easy part. Then we would have to face the gauntlet, in front of the full Knight's Council."

"I know that's what some of the trainees call it. It's just an examination before the Council of Twelve, to be sure you're ready for your next step toward knighthood. They need to make sure you have the knowledge you need to be a proper knight one day. They also need to be sure your skills in fighting and survival are strong enough to carry you through life physically, emotionally, and spiritually. The training you've had has prepared you for the examination, and you'll be fine. In the end, this is all for your good."

"I know this is all for my good. I just don't understand why we have to do it right now. I wish we could've just gone back to the Excelsior and continued fighting the Varangians," Skylar argued.

Halie put on an encouraging smile, "I don't really think your father, or the rest of the council gave us a lot of choice in the matter. When we met with the Counsel of Twelve last month, they made it clear that we had thirty days to return to Avalon One and start the Pledge's Quest."

The boy rolled his eyes and looked out the window once more, "That doesn't mean I have to like it, you know."

He was irritated and didn't care who knew it. He didn't want to return Avalon One, the closest of three moons in orbit around the Large planet of Avalon. He and Halie had been born on the lush moon and had spent their childhoods growing up at the Fidelian Knight's Abbey.

Skylar had been enjoying his travels throughout the Elysium System, with his cousin for over a year. He'd been assigned to learn from her, since she was older and a full Knight, in the Fidelian Order. They'd served with Nash and Ariel as part of the pulsar bombing division assigned to the Star-cruiser Excelsior. Even if their recent travel to Hyperborea had nearly gotten them killed. The adventure of serving on a starship was far more exciting than staying on the peaceful moon of Avalon One.

"Ariel, see if you can find us a nice open field to land in," Nash requested, as he looked out over the Olympian Forest below.

"There is a large open field about five kilometers southeast of the central mountain range. It should be coming up straight ahead of us," Ariel replied, studying the navigation maps on the computer in front of her.

"Oh goody, I can't wait to get on with this," Skylar mumbled.

"Mind yourself, young man. I may have to follow your lead through the wilderness, but I don't have to put up with the attitude," Halie gave a stern look to the boy causing him to sink into his seat. "That field would be fine, Nash."

"All right then we'll put down there."

Nash flipped switches as the ship slowed to a stop in midair. The turbo engines in the wings slowly turned to allow the craft to descend in a straight motion. The sound of the landing spacecraft caused two Furlinks, large weasel-like animals, to scurry off toward the three hundred-foot high trees of the Olympian Forest. The wide palm ferns in the field blew around from the force of the engines, as the landing gear touched the ground. The whining engines soon came to a stop, and the dark spacecraft sat silently in the tall grass and ferns of the open field.

"All right Sky," Halie said turning her seat to face the boy, "Let's get our packs. I put them on the seat by the table in the back. Then it's time to head out. I'm sure these two would like to get onto their furlough."

"Yeah, they're lucky," the boy whined.

"Knock it off. I've had just about enough out of you," she snapped at him. "Now, get your butt moving."

He took a deep breath and looked down, "Yes, Halie. I'm sorry." He stood up and walked toward the rear of the spacecraft, where the small living and sleeping quarters of the ship were located and grabbed his backpack.

"Sorry guys," Halie said, standing to join Skylar.

"It's all right," Ariel replied. "We understand how he feels. We're going to miss you guys too."

"Sure, I get it," Nash smiled, "I wouldn't want to go through some test either."

"It's a necessary part of our training. If he's going to continue toward knighthood, he has to pass the test and pledge his allegiance before he turns thirteen. I just hope he gets through all of this the first time through."

"I didn't mean that it wasn't necessary. I just meant, after hanging out amid action and adventure, it would be hard to return to any kind of test," Nash replied. "You've done a great job training and working with him, so I'm sure in the end he'll do great."

"That's right," Ariel smiled at her friend, "He couldn't have had a better mentor than you. I'm looking forward to having you guys back and getting back to some adventure myself."

"Thanks, we'll miss you guys too. Remember you're invited to the Pledging Ceremony after the Quest is over. Sky's expecting you to be there."

"Don't worry, we wouldn't be anywhere else," Ariel stood and gave her friend a hug.

"I've got my bag," Skylar said stepping back into the cockpit.

"Well kiddo, you go give it your best," Ariel said giving the boy a small hug, "We'll see you at the ceremony in a few days."

"That's right, kid. We're looking forward to it," Nash smiled at him.

"Thanks. I appreciate that a lot. Now can we get this over with?"

"Well, let's get going then," Halie said, as they walked back to the rear of the ship together. She grabbed her backpack and started toward the ramp leading out of the ship.

"Wait," Ariel shouted studying the screen in front of her, "Something's wrong."

"What is it, Ariel?" Nash asked.

"Are we expecting anyone? I mean I wasn't told anyone would be joining you?"

"No," Halie replied. "Why?"

"I'm picking up a ship approaching from over the mountains, no wait two ships. One is coming from over the mountains and another is south of us quite a way out."

"Try to identify them, or raise them on the Com," Nash ordered.

"This is the Pegasus to the approaching craft, please identify," Ariel said into her headset.

"Pegasus this is the Fidelian transport ship, Franklin. We're planning to rendezvous with you momentarily."

"We weren't told about this," Ariel replied.

"Council Leader, Knighthawk is aboard. He wishes to see his son before he departs on his Quest."

"Understood, Pegasus out."

"What does he want?" Skylar glared at his cousin.

Hallie looked puzzled, "Don't look at me. I wasn't told that he wanted to see us."

"What about the other ship?" Nash interrupted.

8

Ariel studied the screens, "It's gone."

"What do you mean gone?"

"It's not on the radar any longer. I don't know where it went. Must have been another transport or something."

"Well, we'd better go find out what your father wants, kiddo," Halie said pointing Skylar toward the ramp of the ship.

2

The Quest Begins

The Triton Bomber sat in the open field of tall ferns and grass just south of the Olympian Forest. The larger transport-ship landed about fifty yards away. The ramp of the Pegasus slowly dropped down from the rear of the spacecraft. Skylar walked down the ramp first. He wore dark green cargo pants, a tan military shirt, and a long black overcoat appearing a few sizes too large. His hair stuck out, in an unkempt way, beneath a small olive-green knitted hat. The hilt of a Fidelian plasma sword protruded from his open coat, which blew in the breeze as he walked.

Haile followed her younger cousin. She was dressed in similar clothing, except her coat fit her form much more appropriately. She reached out and pulled the small knitted cap off the boy's head and tossed it playfully into the air, as she passed him on the way down the ramp.

"Stop it, Halie," Skylar yelled, jumping trying to get the hat back.

"Fine," the young woman said tossing the hat into his hands and stopping to take a deep breath of the fresh forest air. "So, Sky, even though you were forced to come back, you've got to admit it's kind of nice to be home, isn't it? I know I've been looking for a break from the battles with the Varangian Guard, especially after Hyperborea."

"I think I'd rather have gone back to Caspian for a break. I still don't know why we had to do this right now. There's a lot more to do on Caspian. If we would have gone to New Athens, we would have been able to see Aunt Dara and maybe we could've gone to the Caspian Cup."

"Sure," Nash replied, as he followed them. "But then you would miss out on all this great silence, wonderful wildlife, and simply awesome fresh air."

"Thanks for the support," Halie chided Nash.

"Glad to help. So seriously, are you sure you want Ariel and I to leave you here for week or two? Maybe you'd like us to hang around a while?"

Halie smiled and nodded at Nash, "Since I'm responsible for him and his training, I'm required to follow him on this quest. But you can't hang around. Skylar knows that this is a necessary part of his training. Don't worry, we'll be fine."

"All right," Nash replied. "If you change your mind, we'll be on Avalon Prime, we are staying at the Grand Hotel for our R and R. Ariel and I can get back here in about six hours if you find that you need us."

"I thought you said yesterday that you were going to Caspian?" Skylar glared at Nash.

Nash smiled and rubbed the boys head, "I was just giving you a hard time, kid. I knew how much you wanted to go. I'll be thinking about you while I'm playing games at the Videoplex and watching the Caspian Cup on the video stream."

"Stop it," Skylar snapped.

"Please," Halie begged Nash, "This is hard enough without you picking on him and making things worse."

"Sorry," Nash replied.

"Good afternoon," the deep voice of Justin Knighthawk broke the playful banter.

"Uncle Justin," Halie said approaching the tall man, in the dark blue cape. She hugged him.

"How are you, Sweetheart?"

"Very well, Sir. But we weren't expecting to speak to you until we were back at the Abbey."

"Skylar, how are you son?"

"I'm fine, father," Skylar said standing next to Nash.

"Well, we were planning to drop off one of your friends for their Pledge's Quest, and I thought I'd say hello and wish you luck."

"Thank you, Sir," the young boy replied. "You said you were dropping off one of my friends?"

"Yes, Sidney Morgan. I believe you were in classes together at the Academy."

"Yes," Skylar replied, smiling for the first time since they'd left the Excelsior.

Sidney was also twelve-years-old, had light brown hair, fair skin, but was a few inches taller than Skylar. She wore the dark pants, tan shirt, and brown cloak of a Page enrolled at the Academy. She had a small knapsack and carried her Fidelian Sword at her side.

"Hi Skylar," the young girl said grinning, as she walked up to them.

"Um, hi," Skylar stuttered. He hadn't seen her in over two years, and she was growing into a beautiful young lady.

Halie looked at Sidney and then to her uncle, "I didn't know I'd have two people on this trip. I thought we only allowed one Pledge and one mentor?"

"You don't. Sarah Michelson is accompanying her."

"Sarah, my old classmate from the Academy?" Halie said excitedly.

"That's right," a taller young woman approached and hugged her. "How have you been, Halie?"

"I've been great. I haven't seen you in a long time."

"I know," Sarah grinned, "Not all of us get the privilege of going off on a star-cruiser and get to be the hero fighting the Varangians. Some of us must stay here and help train the next generation of Knights. "

"I'm only doing my part to serve the Fidelian interest within the Commonwealth," Halie replied.

"Sure, helping your cousin, while seeing all the sites in the solar system," Sarah teased.

"If only," Halie laughed. "This little monster is more than a handful most of the time."

"Hey!" Skylar slapped her arm.

She smiled at him, "All right, he's not that bad. Most of the time. We've had to help in some negotiations at times. And of course, in fighting Varangian forces."

"I know your work is important. And, as for your little cousin, I remember him trying to tag along and bugging us when we were kids. He could be kind of annoying as I recall," Sarah said smiling at Skylar.

"Funny," he sneered. "I kind of remember you guys being the ones picking on me all the time."

"Whatever, kiddo. It's good to see both of you," Sarah said giving the boy a quick hug.

"Well, I hate to break the reunion up," Justin interrupted, "But, all of you need to get on this Quest, and I must return to the Abbey. Godspeed and be safe. I look forward to seeing all of you in a few days. And Nash, thank you for getting them back here on time."

"Your welcome Sir," Nash replied.

"Good luck to all of you, and be safe on your journey," Justin turned to walk back to his ship.

"Father," Skylar said.

"Yes," Justin turned back.

"Thank you for coming."

"I wouldn't have missed it for anything. Go with blessings, my son," Justin hugged him before turning to walk to his ship, which quickly flew away.

"Well, I'd better get going too. I'll see you in a week or two then," Nash said heading up the ramp of the Pegasus.

"Safe journeys. May mercy and grace be yours," Halie said, as they watched the ramp fold back into place.

"So. Who was that?" Sarah teased.

"That was our commanding officer, Lieutenant, Braveheart," Halie stated.

"Braveheart? Wow, he couldn't have a better name to go with those beautiful blue eyes."

"Knock it off."

"Why? Do you have dibs on him or something? I mean flying around in space all alone. I can see why you'd rather be there, than here on Avalon One," Sarah grinned.

"You're just as boy crazy as ever, Sarah. I would've thought serving as a Knight might have given you some maturity. Nash is my comrade. I'd die for him, but we are not romantically involved. He's a lot more like a big brother or close friend," Halie explained.

The engines began to whine as the air blew leaves, dirt, and loose ferns up around the foursome. They turned away from their small home away from home, as the ship lifted above their heads and flew over the three-hundred-foot trees rising into the atmosphere.

Skylar watched the ship disappear, wishing he was on board.

Halie picked up the two backpacks from the ground. She tossed the smaller pack toward her cousin, "Take your stuff Bub, we've got a lot of walking to do, and nightfall will be coming soon."

Skylar caught the bag and rolled his eyes, "O boy, I'm so excited. I'm so glad to know how much the Council cares about my future and training. Dropping us in the middle of nowhere to learn from the great wilderness."

"No, they do care," Halie insisted. "That's why we landed right here, where they wanted us to start this Quest. Now, get your butt moving!"

Sidney was smiling at Skylar, as he turned away from Halie, "So Skylar should we stay together?"

"Sorry Sid," Sarah answered. "We may bump into one another along the way, but each of you must make your way through the Quest. That means you have to choose your own path and make your own decisions."

"So, Sarah, what are you doing at the Academy?" Halie asked.

"I teach science and botany, and I've been mentoring Sidney and four other girls for the past two years. I chose to go with her on the Quest because I see some great potential in her."

"That's awesome. Sometimes I miss the Academy and the peace of this moon."

"But you'll learn more working with the military and the diplomatic departments than I'll ever know. Science has always been my thing; people have been yours. I heard the stories of Hyperborea. I don't think I could've handled things as well as you did. You're so much like your mother which is great."

"Thanks," Halie smiled thinking about her mother, who was probably leading the Commonwealth Senate after all that's what Prime Minister's do. "You know your work is very important too. We need to pass on the ways of the Order so that we can preserve our work and the Commonwealth."

"Skylar," Sidney said running up to walk alongside him, "Why are you so hard on everyone about this Quest? I mean once we move up in our training, we can do more in the work of a knight. We get more freedom to explore things and even get out to make more friends."

"It's not the Quest that's bothering me. It's being a Knighthawk. I'm expected by everyone to be the best fighter, the best student, the best everything. Sometimes I just wish I could leave it all behind and do what I want for a change."

"Are you saying you don't want to be a Knight in the Fidelian Order? I've known you since we were little and all you've ever talked about is being a Knight."

"I don't know. But, I'm tired of everyone thinking I have to do this because my dad is the leader of the Knights. Everyone assumes because of my family heritage that I should be growing into a leader within the Order. Everyone's watching everything I do, so there's never going to be any freedom. Not for me."

Sidney reached out and took Skylar's hand, as they walked, "I guess I never thought about all of the pressure that would be put on you. I'm sorry. I forget sometimes that your father and his father were both Chancellors of the Council of Twelve," she smiled at him trying to get him to smile back.

"It's not your fault. It's just the life I've been given. My dad, and his dad. The Knighthawks go back about fifty generations in serving the Fidelian Knights, and their predecessors from the Templars on down."

"For what it's worth, I still think you're going to be a great Knight. And, not because of your father or your birth line. I think you're the smartest and kindest kid I knew at the academy. I've always admired and liked you."

"Thanks. That means a lot coming from you. I always thought you were the best plebe at the Academy. However, I must do what I must, what's expected of me."

"Well, good luck," the young girl said leaning over and kissing Skylar on the check.

He swallowed hard with surprise, "Uh, yeah. Good luck to you too."

"All right you two," Halie said walking up between them. "Enough of the chit chat. You both need to get focused on this Quest. It's time to start thinking about which path to take into the forest, and how to get back to the Abbey safe and as quick as possible."

"Good luck," Sarah smiled at Skylar.

"Thanks. Good luck Sidney, see you at the Abbey in a few days," he grinned at the young girl.

"See you, Skylar," she replied as they walked toward the woods.

"Let's get going, Bud," Halie said.

"Fine," Skylar said stopping to examine the monstrous trees ahead of them. "So, which way are we going anyway?"

"I don't know. Which way are we going?" she said smiling at the frustrated boy.

His eyes grew larger, "What? You don't even know where we are, or where we are going?"

She began to snicker, "I know exactly where we are, Bud."

"Then where do we go?"

"You tell me."

Skylar stood a moment in disbelief before answering, "No. Let me guess, this is part of the test."

Halie threw her pack onto her shoulder and smiled, "You got it, Bud. So, where do we go?"

"Just for the record I hate these life lessons and tests they're always giving," Skylar sighed. He then turned toward the woods dropping down to one knee and sitting on his turned foot, as he studied the tree line.

Halie knelt next to him, put her arm around him, and her face next to his looking hopefully toward the woods ahead of them, "So, what do you really think? Into the woods, or along the edge?"

He turned his eyes slightly toward her, "No clues even?"

She fought a smile and turned to look the boy in the eye. She felt his pain but knew he was very capable of surviving the lesson of finding the Abbey on his own, "You can do this, Sky. I know it. Your father knows it. The Fidelian Order knows it. And, you know it too."

Skylar's eyes dropped. He then took a deep breath and looked back into her eyes, "Okay, the woods. We go to the woods, because we are somewhere south of the Olympian Forest, which lies south of mountains and the Abbey."

"Then I guess we'd better get started," she said smiling and giving the boy a reassuring hug.

They began to walk into the giant Olympian Forest which towered high above their heads. Now and then a Furlink would scurry from the underbrush and up the sides of the great trees. The screech of a Zephyrhawk broke the silence, as its ten-foot-wide black and white wings crossed in front of them, grasping a furlink in its talons, before flying high into the treetops.

"Speaking of dinner," Skylar said. "What did you pack for us to eat on this trek? I didn't see any food set out in the galley when I was getting my clothes packed, so I figured you must have packed some."

"Nothing."

Skylar took a deep breath trying to control his temper, "What do you mean nothing? You didn't bring any food? The Great Forest is at least two days south of the Abbey. We're going to need food and water to get us home."

"You have a canteen of water."

"Great two quarts of water will only last part of a day. What do we do for the rest of the trip?"

"Sky, the idea is to live off the land or whatever you have at hand. To survive on what you can find around, and what you should always keep with you."

"Can I use technology at all?"

"You can use anything that you have access to. That means your plasma sword, hand laser, and of course your wits are allowed."

Skylar shook his head slowly, "Except there are some problems with your plan. Like the fact that I'm not allowed to carry a hand laser without your permission, and you never told me to grab one off the Pegasus. I may not have brought everything I should have either since I didn't think that you'd allow us to be dropped in the middle of nowhere without any supplies. I mean who does that?"

"Fair enough, but you should have some basics with you at all times, for survival. You've been taught that since you were born."

"I have a change of clothes in my bag, my emergency bandage pack, a small sewing kit, and flint lighter. I've got my laser sword and my multi-tool. And of course, a rope."

"See, you are all set. You have everything you need to survive."

"Let's just get moving," Skylar continued to walk into the woods ahead of them.

3

Varangians in the Woods

A sleek, black, Varangian yacht class ship glided over the lush forest of Avalon One. It slowly cruised over the Central Mountain Range, coming to a stop over a waterfall. The yacht descended beside the rushing water, landing in a clearing at the base of the falls.

A ramp lowered from the side of the yacht, as four small drones flew out and began slowly patrolling the clearing where the ship sat. Two small track-driven robots rolled down the ramp. The robots were box-shaped with two arms on each side and a raised round headpiece for observation.

Several dark dressed soldiers walked down the ramp. They were dressed in black cargo pants, heavy black flack-jackets, and wearing black helmets. Their helmet visors were raised, but when dropped allowed night-vision, thermal-vision, and electronic trajectory measurements. These were the elite guard of the Varangians usually assigned to officials and leaders of the Juntonian League Corporation. The soldiers formed a small perimeter at the foot of the ramp.

A tall woman wearing a dark purple cloak over dark blue pants walked down the ramp. She was carrying a walking staff, with a silver snake headpiece. A younger female office accompanied her. The officer wore a dark blue dress uniform with several badges and medals. She also wore a blue beret with a small silver bar pinned to the front.

"Most honorable Myra, are you sure this is where you want us to make camp?"

"Yes, Lieutenant this is where I want your soldiers to make our base camp. This location is invaluable to my plan," Myra, the Witch of Tintigal lifted the scepter in her hand and pointed over the area, as she instructed the younger woman. She'd been helping the Juntonian League in their attempt at controlling the seven planets of the Elysium System, for nearly nine years.

"If I may, what exactly is your plan for my troops while we are here, Ma'am. When we were assigned to your detail, I wasn't given any specifics. I only want to be sure the squad is clear in their orders."

"We are here on a very important mission to the Juntonian economy and hopeful control of Avalon Prime. It's also a very important mission to me personally. And, we need to be in this very spot for my plan to be completed."

"Yes Ma'am," the Lieutenant replied, as they stopped in the middle of the troops waiting at the end of the ramp.

"Very good," the beautiful middle-aged woman replied with a smile. "Have your troops set camp here at the base of the Pledge's Falls. We are in search of some herbs that are only found here on Avalon One. I am looking for the Avalonian Night Shade and a very special variety of Hemp, which only grow here on this moon. They are invaluable in funding some of our future projects. They may help us to gain control of the entire system as well."

"Yes Ma'am, I understand completely," the young Lieutenant answered, looking over her soldiers.

"You have no questions about my interest in Avalon One then?"

"We were assigned to you. To carry out your bidding Ma'am. I'm in charge of this detail and my command was to do whatever you may need. I plan to lead my troops to do whatever we can to help you out."

Myra smiled at the young officer, "You may be one of the best-trained people I've ever worked with Lieutenant. I look forward to working through this journey with you. However, to alleviate any concerns on your part I would like you to know that I have personal interests in Avalon One. We need to be in this very spot because I have a special purpose at this very time. Everything should come together in the next few days"

"Yes, Ma'am. I'll make sure the troops set up the camp immediately. We'll make sure everything is exactly as you wish."

"Very good. I'll need all the scientific and experimental equipment placed in my tent. I will need the entire lab set up right away, so we can study the specimens that your troops will help me gather from the surrounding woods."

"Very well Ma'am." The younger woman turned to her troops, "Jones, Thompson you move ahead of us and stand watch. I want a wide perimeter of protection because while we should have been able to avoid the Fidelian security system we can't be sure. The rest of you have your assignments. Let's get this camp set up and make sure that Myra's entire scientific lab is set up immediately."

The troops separated and began their various tasks to get the camp set up. Boxes and equipment were quickly unloaded from the Intrepid, Myra's yacht. Some of the men used lasers to burn debris and flatten areas for the tents to be placed. It was only a short time before the troops finished setting up their camp. The lieutenant started them on a rotation to guard the camp, as the sleek ship slowly ascended to the treetops and flew away disappearing over the mountain range.

Myra called the lieutenant into her tent, "Lieutenant Reed, I'd like to see a few of your troops immediately."

"Yes Ma'am, and what would you like them to do?"

"I would like them to come in here so that I can show them exactly what we are looking for. Then I will be sending them into the woods to search for the items that we have come to examine."

"Yes, Ma'am. I'll have my people here immediately, could I ask why we wouldn't use the droids to collect the specimens?"

"This requires a very delicate touch. That means I can only trust it to humans, and not to machines."

"Yes, Ma'am. I'll get some of my best people right away."

A few moments later she returned with four soldiers. Myra stood at a lab table with holographic images, of the two plants she was looking for, floating above the table. She looked at the soldiers, "I have a special task for you. I am assigning you to look in the Woods around us for these two very special plants. It is imperative that you find both varieties, as they are valuable beyond all measure. There are several possibilities for their uses, and we need them gathered with efficiency and care."

"We understand," the Lieutenant replied turning to face her troops. "I want you to study these holographs carefully. Be sure you know what you are looking for. I am sending you out in groups of two to gather these items and return to Myra. You're to remain at her beck and call for the duration of this assignment. Now, you have your assignment."

The Lieutenant remained with her soldiers as they examined the holographs to be sure they would find what Myra wanted. They soon departed the tent in search of the plants, as she turned to leave, "Will there be anything else Ma'am?"

"Miss Reed, have the rest of your squad prepare for a visitor to arrive in a few days. I must go to the river's edge and try to summon a Zephyrhawk."

"Ma'am?"

"They are large raptors that live in the woods of Avalon One. I need help from one of these majestic creatures in my other plan. You make sure the camp is fully ready and tell your troops to keep an eye out for anyone that might happen to come by. I don't want them killed but brought to me. I'll personally determine what to do with them."

"Understood. Do you want anyone assigned to protect you?"

Myra grinned, "I assure you that I don't need any protection. Now, carry out your work. I have my own things to attend to."

"Yes Ma'am," the Lieutenant answered, as she left to pass on the orders to her troops.

4

A Walk in the Woods

Skylar and Halie walked through the tall forest for over an hour, neither one speaking. Skylar stopped now and then when the trees allowed him to see the sun to check their position making sure they remained headed in the right direction. He knew they would have to find a place to rest for the night, but he wanted to move as fast as they could through the Quest to get it over, as quickly as possible.

After a couple of hours, they stopped to rest on a fallen log. Skylar looked around and checked their bearings once more, as he drank from his canteen. He leaned back against a nearby tree to rest a moment. The hairy hand of a Lemorkee reached down from the branches above and took his stocking cap. Lemorkees are mid-sized long brown-haired primates that inhabited the forests and lower mountains of Avalon One.

"Stupid Lemorkee. Give my hat back!" Skylar shouted at the fury hand, which disappeared into the foliage of the tree above.

Halie couldn't help but laugh at the creature, which only exasperated Skylar.

"Ha, ha. It's really funny. How'd you like it if they took something of yours?"

"It's just a hat, Sky. Besides it's not like he's going to wear it or something."

"Then why would he take it?"

"Because they're curious creatures. They're also very playful. I mean it's not like you haven't seen them before."

"Yes, but playing in the water or chasing each other around in the forest outside the Abbey is a lot different than taking something of mine. I want my hat back, and I'm going to get it," he replied jumping and trying to grab the branches above him so that he could try to climb the tree. The large Lemorkee moved swiftly up the tree, and was three trees away, as Skylar managed to get his feet up to the first limbs.

"Skylar, get down here," Halie instructed, still smiling. "You'll never catch him. They may be big, but they move quickly through the trees."

Skylar jumped down beside her, "Fine, but it's still not right."

"Well, you should be lucky that you didn't catch him."

"No, he should be lucky I didn't catch him."

"Skylar, Lemorkee's can lift three times their weight, and when provoked they will attack. They have sharp canine teeth. They're also strong enough to can break a large man's bones easily."

Skylar rolled his eyes at his cousin, "Fine, so I guess my hat is lost. Enjoy my hat your stupid monkey!"

"So, now what?"

"We keep moving," he replied, starting to walk through the woods again.

They walked for over four hours through the woods, and the shadows were beginning to grow longer. They came into a large clearing within the woods. Two Lemorkees played on the branches of a five-trunked Silver Palm tree that grew next to a pool of water. The water bubbled from the flow of a freshwater spring rising at the center of the pool. A small river flowed out of the clearing away from the pool. Flowers of various colors and sizes grew around the edge of the pool, along with some berries hanging on vines near the water's edge.

"This looks like a great place to sleep tonight," Skylar said, dropping his backpack beside the palm tree, and kneeling to drink some of the refreshing water with his hands.

Halie stood back a few feet and examined the entire clearing. She could see several varieties of birds, more Lemorkee's, and the flowers and vegetation growing around the clearing.

"Look, your friend seems to have followed us through the woods," she said pointing to a Lemorkee across the pond from them, who held a green stocking cap in its hand.

"Funny," Skylar said scooping up another handful of water.

Halie continued to scan the area, as Skylar drew another scoop of water to his mouth. They both stared at the water, as he slowly dropped his right hand across his body and drew the plasma sword from his side. Halie seemed to move in simultaneous motion drawing her sword and igniting the plasma, which doubled the length of the sword. Skylar swung his weapon forward into the water, as Halie jumped over his kneeling form. Her laser sword was aimed straight down held tightly in her clasped hands. She landed in the knee-deep water, just where the boy had been drinking. She buried her glowing sword into the pointed head of a water dragon. The sword drove a hole through the animal's head, and its twenty-three-foot body floated to the surface.

Water Dragons looked a bit like the ancient Earth's Megalania monitor lizards, growing to over twenty-five feet in length, and with razor-sharp teeth, which they used to quickly tear into their prey. Their nostrils were higher up their forehead between their eyes allowing them to hide near the water's edge with only their eyes and nostrils rising just inches above the water. They often stalk their prey and strike with great bursts of speed and pulling their prey under the water to drown it before shredding it to pieces in a matter of minutes. Razor-sharp teeth fill the mouths of the monstrous lizards, and two rows of boney spikes run the length of their body and thick tails. The body of the animal slowly turned over, as it lost buoyancy, showing its muscular legs and piercing claws.

"I hate Water Dragons," Skylar cried shutting off his laser sword and sitting down in the mud.

Halie returned her sword to her side, and knelt wiping the tears from her cousin's cheek, "Are you okay Sky?"

"I hate those things. I thought they stayed in the swamps. I didn't think they came into the forest ponds," the boy's voice quivered.

"Well, I'm very proud of your reaction time. You were smooth and fully focused on your motions. You also kept yourself in complete control showing no fear until after the confrontation," she encouraged her young cousin.

"Sure, that's easy for you to say," he argued through his tears. "You have a laser sword powerful enough to kill. All mine can do, is give a small shock to the nose of something that big. I could have been killed if you weren't here."

"Your instinct was dead on, Sky. Hitting a Water Dragon on the end of the nose with a hard jolt should have made it turn away."

"Maybe, or maybe it would have made it mad enough to rip my leg off. I want you to remove the safety settings on this thing, so I can have a better defense," Skylar said tossing the handle of his plasma sword to Halie.

Halie sighed and gently placed the handle back in the boy's hands, "I can't do that Skylar."

"Can't or won't," the boy argued.

"I can't," she leaned in and placed her forehead against her young cousin's head and looked him in the eye a moment. "I am not allowed to do that. I am only allowed to interfere if it's serious."

"So, let me understand this. My father wanted you to let me get killed out here so that I could learn some lessons that he and the Fidelian Order think I need to learn. He never cares about me, only the stupid honor codes and lessons," he said standing and walking away from Halie.

"That is not true, Skylar!" Halie insisted. "He loves you very much. That is why I was chosen to accompany you through this Pledge's Quest. I would never let you get killed."

Skylar stopped and turned to face her, "Well you almost did."

"I'm sorry, but I have to let you try to work through all the things that may cross our path without interfering unless it's necessary. Your reflexes were just as fast as mine, which proves that you are growing in your perception abilities. You can do this, and you are going to be a great leader in the Fidelian Order one day. Just like your father."

Skylar looked to the ground and took a deep breath to calm down, "Fine. I still wish you would increase the power of my plasma sword. It's the only defense I have. The training settings are ineffective in the real world."

Halie stepped toward the boy and embraced him in her arms. She placed the sword back into his hand, "I'm really sorry kid, but I can't do that."

"Fine."

"So, where are we going to sleep tonight?" Halie asked stepping back and looking around the area.

"In that Palm tree," Skylar said. "We'll be up off the ground, which is safer. I also saw some vines with thorns on the edge of the clearing. We can take them and wrap them around the trunk of the tree for several feet. The two-inch thorns should deter any more of those Water Dragons from trying to climb up and eat us."

Halie laughed, "Sounds good."

The two were soon lying on separate limbs of the large palm tree, within a few feet of each other. The last of the daylight turned into darkness. Halie watched Skylar, as he opened the handle of his plasma sword and was working on the internal settings. She didn't say anything to deter him from his goal of readjusting the device. It was part of the process, she knew that she couldn't do the work, but he could use his ingenuity to make the sword more powerful.

After over an hour Skylar lit up his plasma sword and swung it toward a nearby limb. The laser sliced cleanly through part of the limb, which fell to the ground below.

"Now that's better," he said with a grin. "I suppose I wasn't supposed to do that though, was I?"

Halie gently smiled at him, "Actually you were. I said to use whatever you had to help you. Your intellect and ingenuity are skills that you always have with you. Just remember when you have power you also must have the restraint to know when and how to use it."

He shut off the sword, and nodded slowly, "I know. I promise I'll be careful. I'm sorry I overreacted earlier. I was just scared. I am glad that they sent you with me on this Quest. I am also glad that you've taken the responsibility for helping to teach and train me in becoming a Knight."

"What else is family for, if we can't help one another? Your father has a lot of demands from the whole Order, being part of the Council of Twelve and Chancellor of the Fidelian Order everyone looks to him for wisdom and guidance. You'll always be more like a little brother than a cousin to me, kiddo. Now we should get some sleep. We still have a day or two of travel to the Abbey."

"Thanks anyway. I do appreciate it. Goodnight, Halie."

"Goodnight, Sky."

When she was sure the boy was asleep, Halie carefully went down to the ground and walked several feet away from the tree. She pulled a communicator from her belt and turned it on, "This is Halie Ambrosius, to Abbey Command Center."

"This is Abbey Command; how can we help you?"

"I am reporting in. Can you inform Brother Lawrence that we are at a pool in the Great Wood? We are about two days from the Abbey. He is doing extremely well."

"Understood."

"Thank you. Halie out," she said before quietly working her way back to her perch for the night.

She looked over at her younger cousin sleeping on the branch across from her, "Great Father, help him to learn well to walk in your ways. Let him understand and grow into the mighty and honorable Knight I know is within him."

5

Evil Concoctions

Myra stood at the lab table examining the specimens of Avalonian Nightshade, and Avalonian Hemp laying in front of her. Bottles of liquid bubbled in flasks over burners and several vials were sitting in holders around the table. There were also two mugs and a plate with some bread sitting beside it.

Lieutenant Reed walked into the tent and quietly approached, trying not to disturb her work, "You called for me, Ma'am?"

"Yes," the witchy woman looked up from a microscope, "I need a couple of volunteers."

"Yes, Ma'am. Do you need more specimens gathered?"

"No, just three volunteers to help make sure I have these first recipes blended correctly."

The younger woman winced slightly looking at the lab table of chemical concoctions, "Yes Ma'am."

"Is there a problem Lieutenant?" Myra asked glaring at the woman across the Bunsen burners. "You and your troops are at my disposal after all."

"Yes, Ma'am. I'll return shortly," she replied turning to leave the tent. She couldn't believe that she was helping such an evil woman. It wasn't that she didn't believe in the Varangian's work or the Juntonian control of the Elysium System, but Myra was pure evil and brought fear to her.

She entered the soldier's tent, where several cots were placed along one wall. There were storage chests next to each of the cots, and a table and a small kitchen at the opposite end. It was one of two tents where the troops were housed during their stay on the moon of Avalon One. She was dreading her next order, but she knew there was no choice, "All right everyone, I am looking for three volunteers."

"For what, exactly?" one of the young men asked as he sat on his bed.

She swallowed hard and took a deep breath, "I won't lie to you. You are all aware that we are here to assist Myra in her research of some herbs and their chemical makeup. The greater good of the Juntonian control of the System is at possibly at stake. Myra is asking for a couple of volunteers to sample her current recipe created from the herbs."

"You're asking us to go and try some poison for the sake of the Juntonian League?" one of the women snickered. "That is insane."

"Nevertheless, we all knew what we were getting into when we joined the Varangian Guard," the lieutenant said sternly. "I am not sure that these are poisons. What I'm sure of is that Myra needs to test her concoction, and I'd prefer that you volunteer for the greater good of the League. However, I will not hesitate to order someone to help if that is needed. I'll leave it up to you. Now, I'll step outside and wait exactly one minute for three volunteers," she replied, turning and stepping outside the door of the tent.

In less than a minutes two young men and the young woman followed her to Myra's tent. They entered and stood at attention awaiting their orders, as the lieutenant stepped toward Myra, "I have three volunteers for you, Ma'am."

"Very good," Myra replied, as she pointed toward some chairs beside a table, "Please won't you each have a seat. Now, I am sure that you are a bit nervous about participating in this experiment. I can quite understand. You can be assured that this is vital to my plans, so your service is very appreciated."

She took a vile serum and stepped toward the young woman, "We shall start with you, my dear. Don't worry it will only prick a bit."

"Yes Ma'am," the young woman replied.

Myra smiled as she injected the young soldier. The woman's breathing became erratic, her eyes rolled back in her head, and she went limp in the chair. Her body slowly slid down to the floor laying in a heap. The lieutenant stepped forward and knelt next to her younger subordinate.

"Leave her Lieutenant," Myra instructed, as she returned to the table. "I haven't given her a fatal dosage of the Nightshade mixture. It would have been very easy for me to have killed her. However, I just needed to know about how long it would take to fully take over her body."

"Yes Ma'am," the lieutenant replied stepping back and wondering what was going to happen to her troops.

"And, now for you," Myra said stirring a steaming mug and turning to one of the men sitting silently next to the girl, "I have a special cup of cocoa for you. I would ask that you please move to one of the cots at the rear of my tent, as this is a very potent sedative. You'll have some wonderful dreams. Do you understand?"

"Yes, Ma'am," the young man said standing and walking to one of the cots.

He sat down, and Myra walked to him. She handed him the steaming mug and looked into his eyes, "Open your mouth and drink it in. Open your mind's soul, deep within. Time is past, and time has come. Know thy heart in full sum."

He took the steaming cocoa from her hands, as her long dark nails scratched him slightly, "Thank you, Ma'am."

She stepped away and took some bread from the table spreading what looked like green jam upon the bread, "And, finally for you my young servant. You get this special herbal jam that I think you'll find quite delightful. Speaking of which, did you enjoy the cocoa?"

The soldier at the rear of the tent was fighting the drowsiness, his head bobbing slightly, "It was quite delightful."

Myra smiled, "I'd suggest you lie down, young man because you will soon be sound asleep. We'll talk about your pleasant dreams when you awake."

"Yes, Ma'am," he replied as he laid back and passed out on the bed.

"Now, here try some of the herbal jam," she said handing the bread with jam to the last young soldier.

"Thank you, Ma'am," he replied taking it and biting into the bread. "This is very good."

"Not too sweet I hope?"

"No. It's very delicious."

"Perhaps some more then?" she asked with a smile as she sat a plate of bread and dish of jam in front of him.

"Thank you," he said taking a knife and spreading more jam onto the bread.

"Don't overindulge too much," the lieutenant suggested.

"Please," Myra said. "Let him enjoy the treat. You see this is only one of many ways the hemp can be prepared. It isn't that harmful. It does provide one with a very fulfilling euphoria though. He will not only enjoy the flavor but in a few moments, he will be happier than he's likely ever been."

"You said all of these things are temporary?" the Lieutenant questioned.

"I assure you that your people will be safe. This young man is merely happy for a time. He may want more latter, and that may need to be dealt with. The young man in the back has been given some mind-opening cocoa. It opens the mind to know deeper thoughts, memories, and other things that I may want to know. Meanwhile, the young woman will be waking up shortly and she will be quite susceptible to suggestion."

"I understand."

"Now guards," Myra said to two guards standing by the door, "Please pick the young woman up and return her to the chair."

The guards complied and lifted the soldier into the chair. Myra knelt next to her, "What is her name?"

"Stevens, Private Jill Stevens," the lieutenant replied.

"Miss Stevens," Myra said with a soft sweet voice. "Oh, Miss Stevens. Wake up, my dear."

The young woman opened her eyes slowly and stared forward clearly in a state of trance. She sat motionless staring out in front of her, as Myra grinned.

"Now, Lieutenant, please bring that candle and place it on the table in front of us."

"Yes, Ma'am," the young officer complied.

"And, now you will see just how powerful this drug is. Given in the wrong dose it is fatal but given in the correct amount it completely renders a person's will to my control. Miss Stevens, I want you to place your hand into the fire. Do you understand?"

"Yes, into the fire," the private replied lifting her left hand and placing it into the flame of the burning candle. She held her hand in the flame sitting silently as they watched.

"That is so awesome," the high young man said laughing at his comrade.

The smell and the sight of the burning flesh we almost more than Lieutenant Reed could bear, "Please Ma'am," she begged. "She's a good soldier."

Myra smiled, "Of course, ever the protective leader of your troops. Very well. Miss Stevens, you can remove your hand from the flame." The young woman pulled her severely burned hand from the fire. "Now, Miss Stevens you will accompany the lieutenant to the crew quarters to treat your hand."

"Yes, accompany the Lieutenant," she answered standing from the chair.

"Very good," Myra said. "Lieutenant, take the young woman for treatment for her burns. She'll not remember this, but the pain will become real when the treatment wears off. Take Mr. Happy here, with you. Your other soldier will be awake in several hours, and I'll want to hear his memories. I will return him to duty after that."

"Yes, Ma'am," the Lieutenant replied. "All right you two, please come with me. Let's leave Myra to her work."

"And Lieutenant, please tell your troops that our visitors will be arriving by tomorrow evening."

"Yes Ma'am," Lieutenant Reed replied, as she escorted the others out of Myra's tent.

6

Onto the Mountain

Skylar woke up and crawled down to the ground and began looking for something to eat for breakfast. He walked around the edge of the small lake and found the berries growing on vines. He began picking some of the sweet berries and placed them into his shirt, which he'd made into a small bowl.

"Hey Skylar," Sidney's voice startled him at first. "How's it going?"

Skylar smiled at her, "I thought we weren't supposed to be working together."

"We're not. We just happened to find that little stream and I followed it to this pond. We ended up at the same spot I guess," she smiled at him.

"When did you get here?"

"Just this morning. Sarah's over talking to your cousin. I saw the berries and thought it would make a good meal. The water's fresh, so we're going to fill our canteens before moving on."

"We spent the night here, but I'd be careful about getting water. We killed a Water Dragon last night. It was coming after me when I went to get a drink."

"I'll keep that in mind," she said, as she picked some of the berries, letting her hand gently touch Skylar's hand.

Skylar pulled his hand back slowly, "Well, I'd better get back. Good luck on your Quest."

"You too," she said batting her eyes at him.

Skylar walked around the small lake to where Halie and Sarah were talking, "Breakfast is served."

"Looks great," Halie said. "It looks like we're all on track and headed the right way."

"You mean you knew we'd end up here together?" Skylar asked.

"Not necessarily," she replied, "But there are only a few good paths through this section of the Quest."

Sarah smiled at them, "But, we would have met up by the time we came to the Pass of Courage."

"The what?" Sidney asked approaching them with her own berries.

"It's a narrow pass on the mountains, which everyone has to go through to get to the main mountain pass," Sarah explained.

"It's called the Pass of Courage because only the mountain goats can walk the narrow pathway easily," Halie added. "We'll probably see it before nightfall."

"Speaking of which," Sidney grinned, "Let's eat on the way. I don't want to lose any time getting back to the Abbey. Besides I want to stay ahead of Skylar."

"All right," Sarah agreed. "Looks like you'll be eating our dust, the way she pushes us."

"I doubt it," Skylar smirked.

"Really," Sidney sneered. "We'll just see who makes it back first."

She began running ahead, as Sarah stood up, "I'd better go. See you two back at the Abbey. Hey, remember it's still a long way back so pace yourself," she shouted to Sidney as she walked away.

"See you later," Halie said.

"I suppose we'd better get going too," Skylar said.

"Finish your breakfast. It's not a race to see who gets back first. It's about learning from the experience. If you go too fast you can get hurt or wear yourself out. We'll leave after eating."

"Sounds good to me."

They were able to make good time through the remainder of the Olympian Forest and soon arrived at the foot of the Central Mountain Range. The volcanic mountains separated them from the woods and plains that lay just south of the Fidelian Abbey. The entire range was tall and very rugged with only a few places to pass through to the other side.

Skylar stopped and sat down on a fallen tree studying the sharp mountains ahead of them. He was trying to assess the best route over the mountains to their destination. He figured a few minutes rest would be best, before taking on the uphill climb. He also figured that taking some time to meditate and pray might help him make a better choice along the way.

Several minutes later he pointed up the side of the mountain, "It seems to lead up toward that break between the two peaks. Maybe it's a pass through the mountains, which would be easier than going over the steepest part of the mountain."

Halie smiled and shook her head in agreement. She should be used to his strong ability of discernment, but somehow, she was always amazed at how clear he could see situations and people. "Your right, that is the easiest pass through the mountains. Just past the small path of the Koza sheep the path widens. It still takes some work and time, but after a few up and downs through the pass, you come out onto the plains a few miles south of the Abbey grounds. Your choice to follow the path of the Koza sheep is very doable, but keep in mind that they are far more sure-footed than we are, so we need to be very careful."

"As you said, we can do it," Skylar said standing to his feet.

They slowly made their way up the side of the
mountain following the path worn into the rocks by
the small Koza, the long-haired goats which dwelt on
the mountainside. The path at times narrowed to only
a few inches wide, and the edge of cliffs dropped
twenty feet or more to small outcroppings below.
They soon caught up to their friends, who were
working their way along the same narrow pathway.

Facing the cliff to keep their feet on the tiny
path they used their fingers to grasp cracks in the
rocks for balance and support, as they climbed higher
up the mountainside. A Zephyrhawk screeched above
their heads and began to quickly dive toward them. It
let out another piercing screech, as it tried to sink its
talons into Skylar's arm.

"Skylar, watch out," Sidney shouted, as he
pulled himself close to the rocks.

"I'm okay," he said. "But, watch it I think it's
circling back."

The bird again tried grabbing at Skylar, and he
swung at the bird. It flew back into the air once more.
He then grabbed his plasma sword from his side and
turned on its glowing blade, "Go ahead and try it
again," he shouted.

"No Sky. Birds like shiny things. I don't think
that'll be a very good idea," Hallie instructed.

"Yeah kid, be careful or it might try to take that
sword," Sarah added.

Skylar put the sword back onto his belt, but the
bird was already making a third pass at them. It
swooped just over Skylar and hit Halie in the head.
Her balance was shaken, and she fell toward Skylar.
He tried to grab her but swung around as she pulled
away from his grip. Sarah reached out for her friend
and lost her balance as the two young women fell
down the high drop to the ledge below. Sarah banged
her head on the side of the cliff as she fell. They both
lay sprawled on the stone ledge.

"Halie!" Skylar shouted to their motionless bodies below. "Halie, are you okay?"

"Sarah!" Sidney chimed in. "Sarah, answer us."

"We have to go down and help them," Skylar said looking at Sidney.

"But how? We'd have to work our way back down to where they are by following this small trail back."

"Then that's what we have to do," he replied. "They're going to need our help."

Skylar and Sidney crawled down to where the two young women still lay. He untied the red scarf that Halie was wearing and formed a pillow from the scarf. He gently placed it under her head.

Halie grimaced slightly and exhaled trying to fight pain, "It's okay Sky. I'm just a little bruised," she said forcing her head up from the rocky ground. She tried to move her feet but was overcome with pain, "I think."

"What do you mean, you think?"

"I can take the pain. However, I think that I might have broken my ankle, and I've at least sprained my arm. You may have to go on ahead for help. But, right now go help Sidney with Sarah."

"No. We're taught in the ancient texts not to leave our friends. I'm not leaving you here alone. I'll go help her, but then we are all getting out of her together."

"Look you, little clown, don't be quoting verses to me. I've helped teach you most of them. I think that I might be seriously hurt, and the best way to help might be for you to move ahead for help. Now, go check on Sarah, I'll be okay."

"Okay, but don't move until I get back."

Sidney was kneeling next to Sarah. She took her knapsack off to make a pillow. Sarah was still unconscious, and her breathing was very shallow. Skylar took off his coat and covered Sarah's feet. He pulled her coat tight around her.

"Sarah wakeup," tears were running down Sidney's face. "Please, wake up."

"How is she doing, Sky?" Halie asked.

Skylar put his head down by her mouth to listen to her breath, "Halie, it isn't good. She's barely breathing. I'm not sure what to do. I wish Ariel was her right now. She'd know what to do."

"Who's Ariel?" Sidney sobbed.

"She serves with us on the Pegasus. She's also our medic and saved my life, so she'd know what to do.

Halie pushed herself to sit up, "Come help me get over there, so I can help."

Skylar touched Sidney's arm, "She'll be okay. Halie will help her."

"I sure hope so," the young girl cried.

Skylar went to his cousin, who was now trying to push herself up from the ground. He placed his shoulder under her arm and helped her up. He helped her hobble her way to her friend, and she sat her next to Sarah. Halie forced the eyes of her friend open looking at her pupils and felt around her neck.

A tear ran down Halie's cheek, "God we need a miracle right now."

"She's going to be okay, right Halie?" Skylar asked.

"Skylar. Sidney," her voice was shaking. "I think Sarah's neck was broken in the fall. She's not going to make it, and there's nothing we can do, but try to make her comfortable."

Sidney fell onto Sarah's body bawling. Halie leaned over her and tried to comfort her. Skylar wasn't sure what to do, so he just reached out and held his friend's hand.

Halie looked up at Skylar, "Bud, I need you to be very strong and brave right now. You're going to have to go on ahead to the Abbey to get help. I can't make it back to the Abbey like this, and I'm not sure Sidney is in any condition to go on."

"We stick together," Skylar reiterated.

"Skylar, we are in a very bad place, and we need help fast. You have to go on ahead for help."

"You said we use what we have," Skylar replied raising his eyebrow. "I saw you last night."

"What?"

"I saw you on the communicator. You thought I was asleep. Since it doesn't help me, and since this is serious, maybe now is the time to use that communicator to call for help."

Hallie reached into her pocket, "I'd love to, kiddo, but as you can see it was crushed when I fell."

Skylar stared at the broken pieces of the communicator in Halie's hand, and he began to cry, "There has to be another way."

"Sky this is a bad situation. I need you to be the strong man I know your becoming. I need…" Halie's words were stopped as Sarah began coughing and gasping for air.

"Help her, please help her," Sidney begged.

"Skylar, get my backpack over there," Halie instructed. "I should have a small knife in there. I think I'll have to try to open her airway."

Sarah gasped again and then stopped breathing. Skylar dug quickly through the bag and found a small jackknife and handed it to his cousin.

"Don't you need a tube or something to make an airway?" Skylar asked.

"Yes," Halie said opening the knife and igniting her plasma sword. She stuck the knife quickly into the sword to sterilize it.

"I can't find anything," Skylar cried, as he started digging through Sarah's bag.

Halie leaned over her friend again, her hair fell around her friend's face. She listened for any sign of breathing and felt again for a pulse in her neck. Tears began running down her face again, "Oh Sarah. Why? You were my best friend growing up. I can't believe this is happening.

"Halie, I can't find..."

"Skylar, it's okay. We can't help her anymore," Halie wept.

"No. No, it can't be," Skylar sobbed.

Sidney fell onto Sarah's feet bawling. Halie sat up and pulled Sidney away from Sarah's body. She held her tight, as she reached out and grabbed Skylar and pulled him to her as well. They sat crying together for several minutes.

"All right Skylar, we need to get our friend buried so that the wild animals can't get to her. Then you are returning to the Abbey to get help."

"No!"

Halie took a deep breath, "Do not yell at me. Sarah is dead. I have a broken foot and injured leg. Sidney isn't in any condition to go anywhere. You will have go to the Abbey. You have to."

"No. There's got to be some way. I can't leave you here. There isn't any water or food. We have to get you off this stupid cliff. No one gets left behind."

Halie hugged the younger boy again, "I can't walk, Bud. There's no way to get off this cliff if I can't walk."

He looked past her at the brush hanging near the ledge. "Okay, I can make a splint from some of the sticks and try to find a long stick for you to use as a crutch. It may take some work up the cliff-side, but we'll be off this trail and into that pass soon enough. I can't leave you here. We need to stay together."

Halie bit her lip, "Okay, you get the stuff and make a splint. Then we'll need to gather some rocks and give Sarah a proper burial. I will try to go with you, but if it becomes too difficult, I am sending you two ahead of me. Do I make myself clear?"

"Yes," he answered staring down at his friend crying on the ground.

"Skylar Orion Knighthawk, look at me. Am I making myself clear?" Halie asked more sternly.

"Yes. We may still have to go on without you. I got it."

"Good."

It took a couple of hours, but Skylar managed to fashion a crutch and make a splint for Halie's broken ankle. Then the three of them carefully Wrapped Sarah inside of her cloak and moved her body next to the bushes on the ledge. Sidney and Skylar carefully placed stones over her body covering it in a couple of layers of stone. They stacked two large stones at the head of her body.

Halie took Sarah's Fidelian sword and knelt next to her friend's grave, "Great Father, from the dust of the ground we have come. And to the dust, we return. We come into life with nothing and coming full circle we leave this life to face eternity without anything from this life, but our soul. Bless Sarah as she enters the eternal dwelling.

Lord teach us to number our day that we may live them well. Sarah was a great friend and mentor. She was noble, honest, and good. She will be missed by all who were blessed to be touched by her life. We will always carry a part of her with us and keep her memory alive in our own lives. Bless us Father and help us to safely return home. Amen."

Sidney began crying again, and Halie wrapped her arms around her to comfort her, "I know it will be hard Sidney, but we need to move on. We must, or we'll all find ourselves in great danger. There is no food or water here on this ledge, so we must move on."

"But, I can't. She was so special."

"You will always have a piece of her with you. But she would want you to move on. She would want us all to continue back to the Abbey and finish what we have started. It's the only way out of this wilderness for us all."

"We can do this together," Skylar added.

"No, you can do this," Sidney said trying to smile.

"We all can," he repeated his effort to motivate her.

"I'll try."

Halie placed her friend's sword on her own utility belt, and they began to make their way up the narrow slope. The sun was becoming low in the late afternoon sky, as they reached the top where the main pass was. The main pass was a dry rocky riverbed. They tried to move forward hoping to make up time.

"I need to rest Sky," Halie said. "We are almost out of water too. I am slowing our progress terribly. We've made it off the narrowest part now, so find some water, and then you two can move ahead of us."

"Where am I going to find water?"

"This is the main pass through this part of the mountains. There is a stream that runs through this area that will lead to the Pledge's Falls. Several springs flow into the stream. You can fill up with water at any of the springs or even the stream.

"I'll go ahead and see if I can find some water," Skylar said picking up their canteens, "You rest here. Sidney, take care of her and I'll get back with some water as soon as I can."

"I'll do my best," Sidney said sitting down next to Halie."

Skylar carried their canteens and walked through the rocky pass ahead of them hoping to find some water soon. He was also hoping that maybe he might find some food for them to eat too.

7

Skylar walked for about fifteen minutes and came around a couple of large boulders and found a small spring flowing down a rock and forming into a small brook. He looked ahead and could see the small brook flowing into a larger steam. He filled the canteens with water and drank his fill. Then he looked where the brook ran into the larger stream and could see cattails growing. He knew their roots were edible, so he walked ahead to dig some of the roots.

Approaching the bulrushes, he could hear water rushing ahead of him. He knew it must be Quest Falls. He'd never seen them from the top before but remembered seeing the foot of the falls on a camping trip with his father when he was about four or five. He couldn't believe they were so close to getting out of the dangerous part of the Quest. He walked to the crest of the waterfall, which dropped nearly one-hundred feet to the valley down below.

He was finally filling with hope. Knowing that they were almost through the rough rocks of the journey. He knew the valley would soon open into the Great Plain and the safety of the Abbey.

He looked over the peaceful valley below and suddenly stopped, dropping to his stomach, staring down to the foot of the waterfall. He could see a small encampment next to the stream, and a couple of black-dressed soldiers standing near a fire. Behind the fire three tents were placed, a dark purple tent flanked by two olive drab tents on each side. Skylar knew the dark dress of the Varangian Guard very well. His mind filled with images of large Varangian soldiers pointing rifles at him when he and his friends were on Hyperborea.

He crawled back from the edged and gathered the canteens and roots. Then he quickly ran back around the large rocks and across the rocky landscape to where he left Halie and Sidney.

"Halie," Skylar said out of breath.

"Settle down," she said to the boy who dropped to his knees beside her. "What is it, Bud?"

"Varangian Guard."

Her whole body tensed with the words, "What did you say?"

"Yeah Skylar, that's not even funny," Sidney added.

"We are near the drop to the valley, just past those big rocks the stream goes over the waterfall. I was looking over the falls into the valley. Then I saw a small camp of Varangian Guards."

Halie pushed the stick she was using as a crutch into the ground, and Skylar jumped to his feet and helped pull her to her up, "Show me right away."

Skylar led her toward the edge of the cliff where he'd seen the encampment. They all laid down tight to the ground hoping not to be seen. Halie pulled binoculars from her backpack and began to study the camp below them. She could see a couple more soldiers further back near the tents. Then a figure emerged from the purple tent. A woman wearing dark blue pants and top covered by a purple robe that shimmered as the sunlight caught it.

"Myra," Halie said under her breath, rolling back from the edge of the cliff. She knew the woman well and was filled with fear and anger.

"Let me see," the boy asked reaching for the binoculars.

"No," she replied quickly.

"Who's Myra?" Sidney asked.

"A witch," Skylar answered. "We had a run-in with her on Hyperborea. But why is she here? Let me see the binoculars so I can get a better look."

"No, Sky!"

"Hey, you said that I was taking the lead. It's all a part of the Pledge's Quest."

"I also said only what you had, and not what I had was available to you. Besides, things have changed now. Sarah's dead. The Varangian's presence is far more worrisome"

"What does that mean? Just let me look. I'll be careful," he begged.

"I said no!" Halie snapped.

"Sorry," the boy said sitting back pounding the ground with his fist.

"What do we do now?" Sidney asked.

Hallie looked seriously at the others, "Look the Quest is over. This is far too important. You are going to do exactly what I say."

"But we have been outnumbered by the Varangian's before, so why worry now?" Skylar asked.

"First of all, I am not able to fight very well with this broken ankle. Secondly, the Guard isn't even supposed to be on Avalon One, ever. This moon is considered a sacred sanctuary, and all sides of the war have agreed to leave it as a place for the Fidelian Order to try and work toward peace. However, their presence here is a breach of that agreement and the peace will be broken."

"What do we do now?" Sidney asked

"I saw some caves near the boulders we passed earlier," Halie said. "Let's go there and rest for a bit and figure out what to do from here."

They crawled back away from the edge of the cliff and then worked their way to the large boulders where they found a small cave opening at the edge of the pass. Halie pulled a glow stick from her utility belt and activated it. The entrance to the cave was small, but once inside, the cave opened to a ten-foot by ten-foot area with about five feet of height. Halie used her plasma sword and set it to a lower setting to heat some of the rocks.

Skylar sat down beside his cousin and Sidney sat on the other side of her. Halie put her arms around them, "It'll be all right. We'll figure this out."

Skylar looked up at her, "When you were looking at the encampment you said you saw Myra. Why would she be here?"

"Who's is this Myra?" Sidney asked again.

"Like I said, a witch we encountered on Hyperborea," Skylar answered.

Halie looked down knowing she couldn't tell him everything, but knowing it was too late to keep silent. "Yes, she's a witch. Myra was a great leader within the Fidelian Order years ago. She helped your father and my parents at the Abbey. She was given the great ability of discernment, foreknowledge, and persuasion. She taught many others and was a great leader within the Order. She was a very extraordinary woman."

"Why is she with the Varangian Guard? If she is one of us?" Sidney asked.

"The Guard lured her away. Myra became enamored with power and wealth. She began to desire more and more for herself, and less to help others. She joined the Juntonian Merchant Guild and quickly helped them to take over most of the trade throughout the system. She was finally excommunicated from the Fidelian Order, for her broken promises and her help in an attack on the Abbey. She abandoned the Order and has destroyed the lives of many people, especially those closest to her. You see she helped to ignite the battles that led to the current war we've been fighting for the past eight years."

"I know we've been warned to be faithful and to beware of greed, but I didn't know people ever actually left the Fidelian Order or their faith," Skylar said a bit bewildered.

"Why would anyone do something so awful?" Sidney added. "How could they just abandon everything we hold so dear?"

"Yes, it's rare, but it happens. Myra is one of the worst to have ever left. She still uses her abilities and gifts. Only now she uses them for destruction and manipulation wherever she goes. The path of destruction she has caused is great indeed."

"So, what do we do then?" Skylar asked.

"You are going to rest for now. It will be dark soon. After dark, you need to work your way down the side of the cliff until you are past the encampment. The trail follows the stream through the valley and into the open plain. You'll be able to reach the Abbey shortly after dawn if you move quickly."

"I can't leave you. I'm responsible to care for you. We have to care for one another," Skylar said.

"I can stay with her," Sidney replied, "or I could go if you'd rather stay."

"Right now, your main responsibility is to get to the Abbey and let the Elders know that the soldiers and Myra are here," She instructed. "And, I mean both of you. We can't risk both of you falling into the hands of the Varangians, so you will both need to try to reach the Abbey as fast as possible."

"But Halie..." Skylar begged.

"Skylar this is serious. We must warn the Elders. Myra knows even the secrets of the Abbey. She could sneak in before they even realize she is there. You can do this, and you must."

"Okay," he reluctantly agreed. "But what will you do?"

"I'll stay here hiding in the rocks. I would slow you down too much. Now get some rest. I'll wake you up and send you after dark."

"Yes, Halie," Skylar said turning to face away from her trying to hide the tears he was fighting.

Halie leaned forward, wrapped her arm around the boy, and pulled him closer to her. She kissed the top of his head and held him close, as he slowly drifted off to sleep. Sidney sat beside her and leaned her head on her shoulder and was soon asleep as well. Halie knew that this was their only choice, but she was more than a little concerned.

She didn't sleep but kept watch over Skylar and Sidney as they slept. She also kept praying for the mission that she was about to send them on. She remembered how the two of them used to play in the woods of the peaceful moon when they were younger. They used to play games in the fields and woods of the lush moon all around the Abbey

She remembered the Abbey, where she'd grown up from her birth. Playing in the flower gardens and helping the families and monks of the Abbey in raising vegetables and fruit for food. There were also the many meals shared in the Central Fellowship Pavilion, with friends and family. Thoughts of her parents and her uncle Justin, who had taught her so much about how to live a life of commitment and love, also filled her mind.

She couldn't believe all the tranquility of their childhood home was now in such danger. Why were Myra and her soldiers on the moon? She knew that she wasn't supposed to be here, and anything she was up to was of pure evil. Even more concerning was the fact that they'd managed to make it through the Fidelian Security detection. The moon was surrounded by satellites, which should have detected any unknown ships. The planet of Avalon also was well guarded, so it was a huge risk to try to land on the moon. She couldn't imagine how they managed this atrocity at all.

Halie knew that Skylar and Sidney were the only real hope that they had of getting to the Abbey now. She felt sad that he was being forced to grow up so fast, since there was so much training that he still needed. She'd have to trust that he would get to the Abbey and bring help back somehow.

8

Halie looked out into the darkness, beyond the cave entrance. It was time to send the younger children on the way to the Abbey, "Skylar wake up. It's time for you to get going."

Skylar was sleeping on her arm, and slowly sat up to look around the dimly lit cave where they slept, "What time is it?"

"I don't know. But I can see that it's dark outside. It's time for you two to get moving to the Abbey."

"I'm not sure I can see to make the way to the entrance," Sidney said sitting up next to Halie

Halie, pulled her sword out, "Close your eyes, it's going to get bright." The cave lit up in bright blue light, as she ignited the sword.

"That will help," Sidney said trying to force a smile.

"I still don't like this," Skylar reiterated fighting the tears in his eyes.

"Skylar, we have to trust that you'll both be safe. We also don't have much choice in this. I don't like sending you alone in the dark, down a cliff, to the Abbey, but I know this is the only way. I know you two can make your way around that Varangian camp by climbing down the cliffs and making your way through the woods. I also know you can make it to the Abbey sometime tomorrow and get help."

"I'll go because I have to," Skylar said. "But I don't like it."

"Me too," Sidney added. "I'll be with you, and we can do this together."

"I want you two to stay away from the Varangians camp," Halie instructed. "You must stay on the cliff and try to stay on the opposite side of the river to avoid them. I'm not expecting you to confront them. But go get help from the Knights at the Abbey. Do you understand me?"

Sidney looked her in the eyes, "I understand. I'll do my best."

"I know what we're supposed to do," Skylar grumbled. "We work our way down the cliff slowly. Then when we get to the bottom we move quickly to the Abbey, by following the river. I promise I'll stay safe."

"Well you should get going," Halie said pointing toward the cave entrance.

"Right," Skylar said standing up to tighten his utility belt, before crawling out of the cave.

Sidney was close behind, as Halie followed them. They were soon sitting on the rocks at the edge of the cliff beside the waterfall looking down into the darkness of the valley below. The only visible light was the glow of the fire at the center of the Varangian camp below them.

"Come here," the young woman said as she wrapped her arm around her cousin once more. "Be safe and God protect you."

"You too," he said hugging her back.

She then put an arm around Sidney too, "You be safe too, and help one another."

"We will," she said hugging Halie.

The two younger children were soon working their way over the side of the cliff. Halie lay motionless at the edge of the cliff and continued to watch them as they slowly worked their way down the rock cliff and into the valley below. She could see that Sidney was only a few feet ahead of Skylar and that they both worked their way along the rough cliff side moving around the rim of the canyon. She was hopeful that both Skylar and Sidney would find their way quickly to the Abbey. Once she lost them in the darkness, she said a prayer and returned to the cave to hide and rest her injured leg and arm.

Skylar and Sidney crawled carefully around the rim of the canyon, staying in the darkness, they managed to work their way past the encampment. It was hard work finding their footings and handholds, but somehow, they kept moving along the rocky wall.

"Skylar, I don't see the fire from the Varangian's camp anymore. Do you think it's safe to go down to the bottom?" Sidney asked as they hung over the valley below.

"I think so, but we need to be very careful, so we don't attract any attention," Skylar replied, as they slowly made their way to the bottom of the canyon.

They sat next to the river and washed their hands and drank some of the cool water. Skylar looked at Sidney, "I don't think it will be too much further."

"I'm just glad to be off that wall. I'm not sure how much longer I could have held on."

"I know, it was a lot harder and took longer than I thought it would be. But I think if we follow the stream for a little while we should find our way to the Abbey."

"I just hope we can warn the elders in time," Sidney said looking down the rocky stream ahead of them.

"Well we won't unless we get moving," he replied.

"Right," Sidney replied standing up, beside Skylar. "You know, even with all the trouble and Sarah's death, I wouldn't want to be on this Pledge's Quest with anyone else."

Skylar smiled, "I know. You've always been a great friend."

She moved closer to Skylar and grinned, "You're really special, Skylar. I've known that for a long time."

Skylar swallowed hard and took a deep breath before stepping back a little, "You're pretty great too. I think you're going to be a great knight one day."

"Sure," she snickered, as she gave him a shove on the arm. "Maybe better than you." She took off running along the edge of the stream ahead of him.

They ran playfully challenging one another, as they moved along the bank of the stream. They ran for nearly twenty minutes before Sidney stopped in front of Skylar, "Okay, I give. I can't keep this pace up."

Skylar grinned at her, "Then I win."

"Fine, you win. But we need to set a better pace if we are going to have enough energy to reach the Abbey.

"It looks like there's a path ahead. It seems to run along the stream," Skylar said. "That should make things a little easier."

"I sure hope so," she said slowly starting to walk ahead of him.

He was just about to start walking again when a dark-robed figure stepped out into the path in front of him, stopping him in his tracks.

"Good evening children," the soothing voice of Myra caused Skylar's heart to begin beating fast. "It's a good night for a walk in the woods isn't it?"

Skylar took a deep breath to steady his nerves, "It was."

Sidney stopped and turned to face the tall woman in her purple cloak standing between her and Skylar, "Who are you?"

Myra turned and smiled gently at the girl, "I am Myra. And, I assume the two of you are heading for the Fidelian Abbey?"

"No," Skylar said trying to stay in the shadows to look for a quick way around the woman. "We live in the village of Harbordale, beyond the plains. We were separated from our parents. We were here in the mountains looking for Violet Berries."

She looked at the boy with a knowing smile and reached out to straighten the collar of Skylar's overcoat, "No, this is the coat of a warrior. The people of Harbordale are pacifists. They live an agricultural life and despise anything to do with the military. Your shoes and pants are like those of the Commonwealth Forces. No one from Harbordale would wear such clothing. No, I'm sure you're part of the Abbey. You're likely out here in the woods, for your ritual testing."

"Sorry," Sidney said shaking her head, "We were lost, and we're on our way home. What are you doing out here in the woods at night anyway?"

Skylar turned his shoulder away pulling the coat from the woman's hand and trying to hide his face. He slowly slipped his hand down his side to close his coat, trying to hide the hilt of the Fidelian sword at his side.

"Yeah, our father made a trade for some clothing with some men from the Commonwealth military. I guess I grew too fast for the clothes I'd been wearing, so he gave me these to wear."

"And what about this?" Myra's hand pulled the edge of the over-sized coat back revealing the handle of his plasma sword. "This is not the tool of a pacifist, but a weapon for a warrior. It's the weapon of Fidelian Pledge."

"A weapon of defense only," Skylar snapped staring into woman's eyes.

The woman grinned at his words, "Yes, of course, a training sword, of the Fidelian order."

She placed her hand upon the boy's shoulder and then moved it gently along his right cheek. She smiled trying to look closely at the boy's face. Skylar shrugged his shoulder and pulled away from her hand.

"Leave him alone!" Sidney shouted. "We're just trying to make our way through the woods. We don't want any trouble."

"Relax, Sidney. Don't provoke her. I'll be fine," Skylar said, coldly staring at the evil woman.

Myra pulled her hand back, "I'm sorry, but I cannot allow you, children, to travel in the dark alone. It wouldn't be right to leave someone so young alone in these dangerous woods. Who knows what animals might attack you in the dark? Come and join me in our camp for the night and you can be on your journey at dawn."

"Thanks, but no," Skylar said trying to side-step the woman. "Sidney, run!"

Sidney spun and began to run down the pathway, as Myra spread her arms opening her cape to block Skylar's way, "You, are so much like your father. I knew it when I saw you on Hyperborea a few months ago. You've grown to be so much like him."

Skylar stopped and glared at her, "You don't know my father. And, you definitely don't know me!"

She smiled and took hold of the boy's face by the chin gently turning his head, "Yes you have that same messy hair, that cute little nose, but those eyes are the dark brown eyes of your grandmother. I know you far better than you can ever imagine."

Skylar considered what he'd been told about Myra from Halie, but a part of him was curious about what she knew about his father, his family, and about him. Her words seemed inviting, even though he knew they were filled with evil.

"Thanks for the offer, but I really must go," he said pulling away again and stepping around the woman.

Two Varangian Guards stepped out from the shadows and pointed their laser rifles at Skylar. The boy stopped. He wanted to draw his sword, but knew that there was no chance against them all. The best chance for Halie and Sidney might be to go with the woman at this point. He hoped the diversion would help to give Sidney time to reach the Abbey and return with help.

The woman placed a gentle arm around Skylar's neck, "As I said, I must insist that you spend the night with me. Don't worry, I am sure your little friend will be found soon enough. But it wouldn't be kind to let either of you wander alone in the night. Now, why don't you tell me where your other young friend is?"

"My what? You just saw her run away."

"Please, your father wouldn't let you out here alone, even for some test. I suspect that you've been accompanied by someone a little older and far more experienced. Most likely, Halie, the young lady who was with you on Hyperborea. Now, where is she, my boy?"

"Okay, like you said I'm on my Pledge's Quest. But I would rather die right here than join you in your camp. Besides no one came to help us on the Quest, we were left alone to manage," he said starting to reach for his sword.

"Enough!" The woman demanded, putting a firm hand over Skylar's hand and the handle of his weapon.

"I'm not going to kill you," her voice softened, and she placed her other arm around his shoulder. "A mother chick longs to protect her chicks under her wings. You are like the little chick, my little one."

Skylar removed his hand from his weapon. Myra's use of an ancient verse surprised him and made him wonder if she had fully left her roots within the Fidelian Order. He decided to accompany the woman and her guards back to their camp. He hoped that Myra would leave Sidney alone allowing her to return to the Abbey for help. He would keep his eyes open for an opportunity to escape and join her at the Abbey soon enough.

9

Myra and the Varangian Guard escorted Skylar through the woods and back to their encampment. Four soldiers were standing guard at the edges of the camp. The guards walking with Myra stepped away as they stepped into the firelight at the center of the camp.

"You will join me in my quarters, my child," Myra said as they approached the large Purple tent. "I want you to enjoy the comforts of my hospitality."

Skylar followed her inside and quickly examined his surroundings. A table with four chairs sat in the center of the room. A bowl of fresh fruit sat on the table, and the aroma of cooking food filled the room causing Skylar's stomach to rumble. He decided not to eat or cooperate with the evil women, in any way. At the side of the tent was a table with scientific equipment, rocks, and plants that looked like they were being examined. Near the rear of the tent two cots with blankets and pillows were placed at each side of the tent.

Skylar's eyes came to rest on the side of the room where a large Zephyrhawk was perched watching their every move. The bird turned its head and looked deep into the boy's eyes. Skylar knew now that the attack of the Zephyrhawk earlier in the day hadn't been a coincidence but was part of Myra's evil plan. Somehow Myra knew they were on the mountain and sent her pet to cause them trouble. He knew she was capable of anything and could never be trusted.

"Would you care for some tuber stew," the woman asked, as she stirred the pot on a small gas burner beside the table.

Skylar was hungry, and the savory smell brought back memories of meals back at his home at the Abbey. The smell tempted him to eat for a moment, but the thought of Halie alone in the rocks above came into his mind and sealed his determination.

The anger of knowing the evil woman caused her pain-filled his mind, "No. You made me come here to rest, so that's all I plan to do. You're the cause of all of this, and you won't get any help from me."

"Fine, but you are missing out on a wonderful meal. I'm told that no one can make tuber stew as good as mine," Myra said, sitting a steaming bowl onto the table. "Please, at least sit down and rest."

Skylar sat down at the small table across from the woman, as she tasted her bowl, "It's not going to work. I'm not eating your food."

"Hospitality is one of the virtues that I admire about the Fidelian Order," she said continuing to eat.

"You don't value anything about the Order. You are the opposite of what they stand for."

Myra leaned back in her chair, "Oh my boy, there is so much that you don't understand. So, much that you have yet to learn about life."

"I'm fine with what I've been taught and am learning from my mentor."

She stood up and walked to the back of the tent, "You can sleep here on this cot for the night. There are plenty of blankets to make it quite comfortable."

"Why are you here on Avalon One, anyway? You're obviously looking for something," Skylar looked at all the beakers, microscopes, and other scientific equipment on the tables around the room.

"Curious, like your mother. That's a wonderful thing," Myra grinned at the boy. "We are researching the minerals, and plant life of the moon. There are some very valuable things found here. Some of which are found nowhere else."

"But, Avalon One is off-limits to mining and development. You can't just come in here and take anything you want. This is a sacred place," Skylar replied.

"Oh yes, they have taught you to fear the destructive forces of wealth and power. They are already indoctrinating you into their perfect idea of what peace is. Many medicinal things could benefit people that may only be found here. Their value far outweighs the need for protecting some contract that has no real meaning off paper. Now it's late my child, and you should get some sleep."

She turned the blanket on one of the cots down for him and walked toward one of the tables to gather some dried leaves. She dropped the leaves onto an incense burner. Smoke rose to fill the tent around them. The smell was musky like burning straw and it nearly knocked Skylar over at first. The pungent smell made him lightheaded, he started to relax, and his eyes started to grow heavy.

Myra then went to the table and stirred another pot adding some spices, "Perhaps some of my famous hot cocoa will help you relax. I believe it used to help you relax when you were a boy."

Skylar yawned and took a deep breath, hoping to snap out of the weariness that seemed to be overwhelming him. I don't want anything from you. Besides it smells different than the cocoa I'm used to."

"Well, I have a few of my own secret ingredients in my blend. Please try it, I'm sure it will delight you."

Skylar studied her long black painted nails, a skull-shaped ring on her hand, and a red mark on the inside of her wrist, as she sat the steaming mug in front of him. "No, I'm not giving into your plans. I don't want anything that you have."

"I wish you would reconsider," the woman said, pressing a small communicator, which she held in the palm of her hand.

One of the dark dressed soldiers stepped inside the tent. She held a laser rifle in her hand, as she escorted Sidney in front of Myra, "Here she is Ma'am."

"I suppose you thought your little friend managed to get away. But as you can see my assistant Jenna has managed to make sure her soldiers brought her along to join our little party."

"Are you okay Skylar?" Sidney asked as she stepped near the table between Myra and Skylar.

"Yes. What about you? Have they hurt you?" Skylar tried to hide his anger and fear.

"I'm fine," she replied. "What does she want?"

"And," Myra interrupted, "I want everyone to remain fine. Perhaps you might reconsider my hospitality and have some of my wonderful cocoa now. Then again, I would hate resort to more drastic measures. We wouldn't want an accident to happen to your nice young friend here. Perhaps we could start searching for your cousin somewhere above the waterfall?" The woman said, as she lightly brushed Sidney's hair with her fingers.

Skylar couldn't control his anger and snapped at the woman, " Leave her alone. And I have no idea what you're talking about being above the falls."

The woman grinned knowing she was wearing him down, "You have quite a strong mind, I know that no one goes on a Pledge's Quest alone. I also know that you were with your cousin on Hyperborea, so it's easy to figure out that she was with you."

"No!" Skylar shouted. "They sent the two of us here alone. It's a new testing method."

"Don't try to lie to me, my boy. You are wearing down and I know you care for your cousin very deeply. Why not just drink up and take a rest? Things will become far clearer to you in the morning."

Skylar was starting to succumb to the drug within the incense, as he struggled to stay focused. The possible threat to his friend's life and Halie caused him to decide to comply with the woman's wishes, "Fine, I'll drink your stupid drink. But you leave my friend alone."

"I promise she will be safe with Lieutenant. Now, I suggest you make yourself comfortable. I'm told my cocoa can make someone quite relaxed. After you've slept we'll talk again."

He removed his backpack, placing it on the floor next to his chair. Then he sipped the steaming drink. He started to become even wearier. Myra helped him to make it to the cot. He fought to keep his eyes open, as he lay down on the bed. He left his shoes and coat on as he lay down, hoping to somehow get a chance to make a run for it.

The woman pointed to the guard, who led Sidney out of the tent. Then she pulled a blanket up by Skylar's face. He forced himself to turn away from her facing the side of the tent. She placed a gentle hand on his head, "Open your mind's soul, deep within. Time is past, and time has come. Know thy heart in full sum."

She watched his body relax and smiled as she began to sing,

SLEEP NOW, MY LITTLE ONE, SLEEP.
PROTECTED SAFE IN HIS KEEP.
NO WORRIES IN THE DARK OF NIGHT.
SO, CLOSE YOUR EYES AND SLEEP TIGHT.

Her gentle voice and the words of the song seemed eerily familiar to him. He fought sleep at first but soon found himself enchanted by her voice and subdued by the drugs of the incense and tea. He couldn't fight sleep any longer, as even the worry of his friend's safety disappeared in the fog that filled his mind and caused him to drift off into his dreams.

10

Skylar's body was in deep sleep, he was paralyzed, but his mind was coming alive. The smell of the food and the song Myra sang carried him into the depths of his memories. He remembered back to the younger days of his childhood. Memories long locked away rushed in and filled his thought as he began to relive long-forgotten days

"Justin, I just can't believe our boy is growing so fast," Skylar could remember his mom holding him tightly to her shoulder. He couldn't see her face, but he heard her soothing voice and could see her wavy auburn hair.

"The day we had him was one of the greatest days of my life," his father said, as he wrapped his arms around both Skylar and his mom. Skylar felt engulfed in their love.

"Oh Justin, how can we be so lucky?"

"We are truly blessed, my love. I am the most blessed man in the universe. I have the most beautiful and supportive wife a man could desire. And, we have a terrific son."

"You're just happy because you're getting to show him all the things that you did when you were a boy," the woman joked.

"That may be true," Justin laughed. "Maybe we should think about having another baby. Maybe it will be a girl, so you can pass on all the things you always dreamed of passing on to a daughter."

"Maybe. Maybe I'll just have to be satisfied with getting time with our niece," his mother said, as a much younger Halie ran into the bedroom.

"Happy Birthday Bud," the younger Halie said as she reached out and pulled him away from his mother.

"Hold it right there," he recognized the loving voice of his aunt Dara, coming from the door of his room. Her voice always calmed him and even now it calmed him in his dream.

"But mom," the Halie started to beg. "I waited for him to wake up from his nap. I just wanted to give Skylar his present, so he can play with it."

"Why don't you let me help you. Besides, don't you think his aunt missed him while we on Caspian the past two weeks?" Dara joked as she reached out to take him from Halie.

"Mom. Please."

"Halie," the firm voice of her mother stopped Halie from begging.

Skylar knew that he must be two or three years old. This memory was from his birthday.

The two families shared the apartment complex, there was a common kitchen, dining, and living area. Two stairways lead to the sides of the home, where each family's bedrooms were. There were also guest rooms in these upper wings of the home.

The rear door lead to a hallway that connected three apartments, two across from their own, and one beside theirs. The hallway led out to one of the main roads that went through the Abbey grounds. The opposite side of the common area had large windows and French Sliding Doors leading to a patio. The hedge around the patio gave some privacy, before opening to the common gardens that ran the full length of the mile-and-a-half long Abbey grounds. Their apartment was directly behind the Council Chambers, which was connected to the Abbey Cathedral at the eastern end of the gardens.

At the opposite end of the gardens was a pyramid-shaped building that rose high above the grounds. This was the Fidelian Command Center, where classes of the Fidelian Academy were held, and where the Fidelian Command ran the directions and plans of the Fidelian Knights. Beyond the command center sat the tarmac of the Abbey spaceport.

He could remember the light smell of vanilla that was on his mother. He could see his father in his dark shirt and pants. The smile on his bearded face brought comfort to Skylar, it was a feeling that he rarely felt in recent years. He loved his father, but as he often felt his father was more concerned with passing on the ways of the Knighthood and the concerns of running the Fidelian Order, than being close to him.

He could see his mother's pale skin and a small birthmark on the lower part of her right wrist. He tried to see her face, but in his dream, her face was veiled by the light whenever he tried to see her, preventing him from making out the features of her face. Every time his mind tried to see the woman's face it was like a fog covered her and prevented him from seeing her clearly. He longed to know the touch and love of his mother, but he had nearly forgotten her.

Skylar woke up and looked around the empty tent. Everything was blurry, but he could see a single lamp burning in the center of the room, and the Bunsen burners were burning low. He thought about the vision of his early years from the dream.

He tossed and turned, and soon fell back to sleep as more visions came again into his mind...

He was laying on his bed, in his room. Now he knew that he was about four years old because he recognized toys around the room from when he was younger. He could see light shining under the door, from the hallway outside their rooms.

"Justin, why can't you see the power and potential that you have," his mother's voice sounded angry and cold. "How long will you work with the Council and give in to their demands. There would be no Abbey left if it were not for you and me. The others were never capable of seeing the need for expanding the homes and buildings around us. If they hadn't listened to you, they would still be living in small shacks in the woods. We are the reason the Abbey is so beautiful."

"Dear, please. You know that we're all created with a purpose. We're all here to help work for the greater good of everyone. I'm no more important than anyone else on the Council, and neither are you," his father calmly reasoned.

His mother's voice was moving away, likely going downstairs, "We've been trying to negotiate a contract with the Juntonians for weeks. I think there is some merit to what they are offering. You are worth so much more and so am I. Now I am going to call Skylar to come down for dinner. Skylar! Skylar, come and eat," his mother's voice called.

"Please, Dear don't throw away generations of peace for some offer of temporary gain," Justin begged.

"I'm not staying here and be taken advantage of by the others in the Order any longer. I'm going to speak to the Juntonian representative about his offer to join in their profitable plan."

"Please. What about Skylar? What about our son?" Skylar could hear the pain in his father's voice, as the patio door could be heard sliding open and then shut again.

A few minutes later he could hear his cousin's voice shouting from downstairs in the common room, "Skylar come on!"

Skylar ran down the stairs and to the dining table, where he could see Halie, she looked to be about twelve. She was sitting at the table alone. His father stood at the glass door overlooking the patio and the gardens leading toward the Council Chambers and Cathedral. His Aunt Dara and Uncle Bern stood just behind his father.

"Come on Bud, my mom said I couldn't eat until you got here," Halie placed some tuber stew in the bowl in front of him.

" Where's my mom, and when is she coming back?" Skylar asked, as he sat down next to her and began playing with his food.

Halie started to eat, "She's going to meet with the Juntonian again. She'll be back later. You'd better eat while it's hot. Then I'm supposed to play a game with you before we go to bed tonight. So, you'd better eat if you want to play a game with me."

"I'm going after her," his father started out the sliding door to the patio.

"Justin," his Aunt Dara said. "You can't force her to stay. She's my sister and I can't seem to get through to her either. She has become obsessed with power and hungry for the riches that the Merchant Guild has been offering us. Perhaps in time she will listen and come back. I know that when she's set in her ways there is very little that can change her mind."

"Dara is right," uncle Bern said. "All we can do is hope and pray that she comes back to her senses sooner than later."

"I know, but I can't stay here and do nothing. I know that the Juntonian Merchant's Guild is very powerful. They are destined to cause us trouble. However, I can't stay here and do nothing. I have to try," his father said as he waved his hand in front of the door causing it to slide open.

The glass door slid shut and he could see his father walking toward the garden in the courtyard. Then a flash of light filled his sight, and the entire house shook, with an explosion. Black smoke rolled outside the windows which were now shattered.

He could hear shouting, possibly his father. But what were they shouting? He strained to make out the words. Micah? Amanda? Could it possibly be, "MYRA!"

His Aunt Dara turned and picked up Skylar, as his uncle Bern put an arm around Halie and carried her behind them. They headed for the opposite door with the two children. Four guards dressed in black with silver crosses on the left breast of their shirts, and wearing black cloaks led them down the hallway toward a patrol vehicle. The Elite Guard, Skylar had seen them many times growing up. They often escorted his family to meetings.

"The Juntonians," his father's voice came from behind them. He was out of breath. Skylar could see two guards helping him along toward the vehicle.

"Justin, where is..." Dara shouted as another explosion shook them knocking them to the ground.

"She's gone. She was in the building, and she's gone!" his father began weeping, as the two men continued to direct him toward the waiting patrol vehicle outside the apartment.

The patrol vehicle drove them across the Abbey campus to the hanger behind the Command Center. They stopped at an armored transport ship. Several other Fidelian officials were sitting beside them on board the transport. Some were weeping. Others were sitting quietly, but all were shaken by the event.

It was quiet for several minutes before Skylar heard his uncle's voice again, "The Juntonians left the negotiations. David Lawrence said they stormed out of the meeting and went to their ship. He said he and Sarah Roland begged them to continue to keep the conversation open, but they shot President Sheridan. Then they stormed out of the room to their ship."

"What was the explosion? Did they bring a bomb into the Council Chambers?" Dara asked.

"No," Bern continued. "They one of the guards said that the Juntonian ship flew over the Cathedral on their departure, and they dropped a bomb as they flew away. I'm so sorry Justin."

"No!" he could hear the pain in his father's voice.

He heard the story of when his mother was taken from him before. He was about four years old, and he rarely could remember any details of that night. Now, these memories were flooding into his dreams and brining him great pain. He wanted it to stop, but they flowed freely, as he slept.

"Skylar... Skylar," a soft, gentle, yet firm voice drew him from the pain of his dream. The voice had spoken to him many times in his prayers, since his childhood. It guided him in his visions and dreams. "All may not be as bad as it seems. Search your thoughts and know the truth."

Skylar sat up in the bed shaking, sweat ran down his face, and he breathed quickly with fear for a few moments. His sight was clearer now, and so was his mind. The tent was dark. The light from the fire outside caused shadows of the guards to appear large against the side of the tent. He looked at the second cot across from where he slept, but it was empty. He wondered where the witch was hiding, and where they'd taken Sidney. Then he laid back down/ Thinking about the visions.

11

Skylar sat up again and stared across the tent at the low burning flame, which kept the pot of stew warm. His stomach was growling. The smell called to him. He knew that he would need strength to get away from the Varangian encampment and Myra's trap, so he gave into the smell. He slowly worked his way across the tent to the simmering pot. He put some in a bowl and sat at the table devouring the bowl. The witch had lied to him and enchanted him, but not about her cooking. He hadn't eaten such good stew since he was a young child. He finished two bowls and ate some of the freshly made bread that sat on the table.

After he'd eaten his fill, he packed some of the bread into his backpack to have for later. Then he cautiously walked toward the lab table. He watched the door of the tent closely, as he glanced at an electronic tablet left beside the experiments. He read notes about several plants and minerals, which included estimated values on the public market and medicinal and other purposes for which they could be used. He knew now, even more than before that he needed to find a way to get away from the encampment. Saving his cousin and Sidney was important, but warning the Elders of Myra's plans was even more pressing. He couldn't let her ravage the peaceful moon where he'd been born..

Skylar began to look over the chemicals and various things sitting on the laboratory table. He knew what some of them were capable of doing. Then he slowly took a cup from the table and began to mix several chemicals. It took several minutes to gather and mix the right amounts for his plan.

Then he worked his way quietly to the back of the tent. He knelt next to the edge and pulled fighting for several moments, before finally pulling one of the stakes out of the ground allowing him room enough to crawl out of the tent. He took the cup of chemicals, which he'd mixed and threw it as hard as he could across the tent toward the door. When the cup hit the ground, an explosion shook the entire encampment. The tent filled with smoke. The disturbance drew the troops and Myra to the door of the tent, and he used the diversion to roll under the tent into the darkness of the woods.

High above the encampment, Halie was unable to sleep her mind filled with thoughts of Skylar being captured. She envisioned them taking him into the camp. Myra was threatening her young cousin. Her visions and thoughts caused her to work her way back to the edge of the cliff where she could watch the Varangian encampment below. Throughout the night she prayed and waited for an opportunity to help her cousin escape from the terrible grip of Myra.

The explosion was the opportunity that She'd been waiting for, "Good work kid."

She used her crutch to push on some of the rocks above the camp. The rocks tumbled down the side of the cliff toward the camp below. Some of the guards turned and began shooting into the rocks around Halie, as she moved away from the edge. She continued to throw loose rocks over the edge attempting to draw fire, as she hid behind large boulders near the edge of the cliff. She hoped with every rock thrown that Skylar was making his way further away from the encampment.

Halie continued her barrage of rocks and distracting the guards for over half-an-hour. She then began to make her way back to the cave where they hide earlier. She crawled back into the cave, facing out, so she could fight anyone or anything that might come her way.

"Skylar, I pray you'll be safe, and that you can get help here soon. Lord, protect him and protect Sidney wherever she is, too."

Myra wasn't distracted long by the explosion or the falling rocks but went into the tent to check on Skylar. The smoke began to clear, and she quickly returned, "You fools, this is a diversion. You've let the boy escape. Now find him. Send out the drones and find him immediately. And, bring that girl to me, she may prove valuable yet."

"Yes, Ma'am," one of the guards said as they began to look around the outside of the tent.

A couple of other guards ran out of their tent and returned with drones and controllers, which they quickly put into the air to start searching for the boy. The Lieutenant escorted Sidney from one of the soldier's tents toward the fireside, where Myra stood watching her troops work.

"You will help me find the boy," Myra said peering at the girl through the flames of the fire. You'll bring him back to me."

"I'm not helping you," the young girl replied. "I do not serve you, and I never will."

"Oh, you will. I promise you will," Myra said as she dropped something into the fire causing sparks to fly and smoke to rise around the girl.

Lieutenant Jenna Reed stepped back from the girl, who fell into a trance. She wanted to run but couldn't seem to move. Myra looked across the sparks and flames staring into Sidney's wide-open eyes, "Child of faith and child of light, you shall leave this very night, to serve my purpose in my fight. You shall find the boy who does flee and help to bring him back to me."

Sidney stood staring into Myra's dark eyes across the flames of the fire, "I shall find him and bring him back to you. But, where shall I look?"

Myra smiled, "Go child search and find him. Use your power to sense where he is."

Sidney turned from the fire and walked silently into the woods.

Skylar ran through the dark woods at the edge of the encampment. He didn't want to follow the path they had been on, so he ran away from the river. He could hear drones approaching, so he hid in the brush as the forest grew thicker. The briars and smaller evergreens hid him, but walking was far more difficult. He wasn't too far from the camp when he came upon a different path leading away. Figuring the path would help him get away faster he decided to start running down the path.

"Skylar!" Sidney's voice startled him.

He turned and saw his young friend standing on the pathway, "How did you get here?"

"Your diversion worked really well. When the guards ran out of the tent where I was being held, I managed to run into the woods."

"I'm so glad," he was smiled with relief. "Now we can get out of here together. What time do you think it is? I mean I wonder how much time there is before daylight. We'll have a better chance of getting away in the dark"

"I'm not sure. It was about twenty-two--thirty when they took me away from you. That was a couple of hours ago. It could be about one now."

"I know it sounds crazy, but we need to go away from the river and then try to move north. In the morning we can cut back to the east to get to the Abbey. That might get us away from the Varangians. So, let's go this way," the boy said starting to turn back away from where he thought the camp was.

"Sounds great to me. I've had enough of them for one night. But you're going the wrong way."

"No, I've been going this way. I'm sure it's the right way."

The girl tilted her head and smiled, "I think the woods are messing with you, or maybe whatever that Myra woman gave you. I've been on this path a while, and that's the way I came from."

Skylar stopped and looked around. Was it possible that his skills of discernment were being affected by the drugs Myra gave him, "Are you sure?"

"Absolutely," she said tugging on his coat sleeve and grinning at him.

They walked for about ten minutes. The path made a large turn and opened into a small clearing. They started to cross the open space, as Myra stepped out of the shadows in front of them.

"Very good my dear," Myra smiled at the girl.

"Yes, Ma'am," Sidney answered standing still in front of the wicked woman.

"Sidney, what's wrong with you? How could you do this?" Skylar begged.

A tear ran down the girl's cheek, "I'm so sorry Sky. I couldn't help it. She's got control of me. Please forgive me."

"Now let's all get back to camp. It's the middle of the night, and tomorrow will be a big day."

"I won't do anything for you," Skylar growled. "I hate you"

"Guards bring the boy to my tent and lock the girl up again. We may need her later."

Two of the guards picked Skylar up under the arms and carried his squirming body back to the camp and into Myra's tent. The dropped him in front of the woman. She was holding the crystal in her hand again, as she sat her scepter off to the side of the lab table.

"Sit down, my child."

"I'm not sitting down. And I'm not your child," Skylar glared at the woman.

Lieutenant Reed pushed him toward a chair, and forced him to sit, "I don't think it was a request, kid."

Myra smiled and knelt to one knee in front of the boy, still holding the crystal in her left hand. She grabbed his chin and looked deep in his eyes, "The memories you experienced show that you really don't know who you are. But now you're going to help me find your cousin "

"Never!"

"You don't have to cooperate. Your connection is so deep I just have to hold you and my crystal, and we will see where she is," she smiled as the clear crystal began to cloud over.

Soon the vision of the rocks above appeared clearly in the crystal. Halie was crawling into the cave where she hoped to hide.

"No!" Skylar cried trying to fight, as the Lieutenant knelt at his side to hold him still.

Myra smiled, "You see it's so easy when someone's so close to someone else. But it will take time for our troops to reach her. Maybe I should send persuasion to help her come to us."

A large grey and white striped Avalonian Tiger appeared in the crystal. Avalonian Tigers stand 4-and-a-half feet tall at the shoulder, they are over ten feet long, have razor-sharp claws and long piercing fangs that protruded out of their powerful mouths. The muscular beast walked across the rocky riverbed near the cave.

"Oh, how wonderful, a pet," The wicked woman sneered. "Beast of wonder, hear my voice, follow my every choice, find the girl whom I seek..."

"Stop! Stop it!" Skylar shouted kicking the woman and knocking her away. The crystal shattered as it hit the table.

Lieutenant Reed pulled the boy back onto the chair, but he managed to pull his hand free. He reached inside his coat and pulled his sword out igniting the plasma. He swung in a circle, before bursting out the door of the tent. Two soldiers shot at him, but he deflected their laser blasts. He ran past them and dove into the rushing river.

The soldier shot several times into the dark rushing water, as Myra stepped out of the tent, "Go after him. Send the girl again. I'm going to finish what I've started."

Skylar started to swim toward the shore but heard the whine of the drones approaching. The drones would soon close-in, and their heat sensors would find him quickly even in the darkness. Then they would bring the Varangian troops upon him with a vengeance. However, in the cold river, he might be able to mask his heat and get further away.

Skylar heard another drone and knew that the time had come. He took a deep breath and dove under the water swimming back into the river's flow. He struggled pushed his head above the water, fighting hard against the current. He was pushed quickly downriver, bouncing off the rocks and boulders as he moved downstream. He tried to swim, but the water's pull was too strong, and it kept pulling him along the rocks.

After several minutes of trying to fight the current Skylar hit his head hard against a boulder and was knocked unconscious. His limp body floated over the rocks of the rushing river for over a mile, before the river finally slowed and he came to rest against a tree limb laying at the edge of the water.

Halie heard the blast from the encampment and crawled out of her hiding. The tiger roared startling her. She spun and pulled her sword in one motion, trying to keep her balance on her injured leg. The tiger lunged forward and roared again. She stepped back hoping to get back to the small cave.

"I have him, my sweet child," she heard the voice of Myra in her mind. "Make things easier my dear, surrender and I'll stop the beast."

"I'll never join you. Skylar will get away. You can't have him."

"I shall have you both," the woman laughed.

"Never!" Halie lunged forward with her sword, as the tiger swung its large paw toward her. She managed to turn and swing a second time severing the head of the large beast.

Halie knew that Myra knew where she was and would send her soldiers to try to find her soon. She couldn't return to the small cave where they had been. She limped across the rocky pass. There were dozens of caves further back near the narrow pathway but making her way that far would take time. She only hoped that she could find a safe cave to hide in before the Varangians came looking for her.

It would take time, but she found another cave and crawled inside. The opening was tight, but it opened on the inside. The small cavern was only about four-foot high but was about twelve-foot wide and fifteen-foot deep. She heard water running and lit her sword to look around the cave.

She smiled, "Well it isn't my bed, but having water will help."

She made her way to the back of the cave where a small trickle of water fell. She took a drink and filled her canteen. Then she crawled away from the water and wrapped up in her coat where she could watch the entrance to the cave.

"Great Father and Creator help Skylar and Sidney. Help them to make it to the Abbey soon. Help me, Great Healer I need your strength," she said succumbing to exhaustion.

12

Sunlight broke through the trees shining down onto the edge of the river where Skylar lay unconscious beside a fallen tree. Sidney traipsed through the woods along the river's edge. She sensed that Skylar was nearby and was studying the bushes and river's edge. She wished for some way to break free from evil pull which Myra held over her, but she continued to feel obligated to return Skylar to the evil woman.

She knelt beside a rock to rest a moment, as the river took a bend around the remainder of the mountainside. She looked at some of the fallen logs lying along the flowing water, "Creator of the Universe, why is this happening to me? What does that woman want with Skylar? I need your help. We need you to help us get out of this somehow. Please help us."

Just as she was about to turn away, she noticed a hand sticking out of the muddy ground beside a fallen tree, "Skylar! Skylar is that you?" She asked running toward the lifeless boy's body.

Sidney grabbed hold of his body struggling and pulling at his wet jacket to get him out of the water. It took her several minutes to pull his cold body on the muddy ground, but she managed, with only a few falls, to get him onto drier ground. She looked around to see if anyone else was nearby, or if one of the drones spotted her.

"Skylar, are you okay," the young girl began crying, as she knelt next to him, her long sandy brown hair falling over his muddy face. "Please, Skylar you have to be all right. You must go away from this place. I don't want to have to take you back to her. I don't want her to hurt you. I don't want you to go back to that evil woman. Please. Please"

She picked up Skylar's head and put it in her lap, as she continued to weep, "Please wake up Skylar. Please, I don't want you to be hurt. I don't want you to be hurt. Please..."

"What seems to be the trouble, Young One?" the gravelly voice of an old woman startled the girl.

"Who are you?" Sidney asked as she looked up to see a short older woman standing over her.

The old woman wore a brown tunic and dark brown pants. She held a gnarled walking stick in her wrinkled hand. "I was looking for truffles. They grow along the river's edge. I heard you crying and knew that someone was in need. How can I help you, Young One?"

"My friend and I," Sidney began to sob again, " He fell in the river. He's unconscious, and I don't know what to do."

The elderly woman smiled at her kneeling beside Skylar. She placed a hand on his face, "Where is your mentor, Young One?"

"Our what?"

"I suspect that you are about twelve or thirteen. You're here in the woods on your Pledge's Quest. They wouldn't send you without mentors to watch over you."

Sidney's tears stopped, as she realizes the woman was somehow connected to the Fidelian Order, "Yes. We were separated from our mentors. One was killed and the other is injured, up above the falls. We were trying to get back to the Abbey to get help. We ran... We ran into..."

"Yes, dear?" the woman gently encouraged.

"No. I mean. I can't. I mean," Sidney closed her eyes fighting the feelings and powers working within her. "We ran into trouble. My friend fell into the river. I can't get him to wake up."

"Perhaps I can help. I have a cabin nearby where you and your friend can warm up and rest. We can help your friend. There is food there, and you can rest before returning to the Abbey."

Sidney smiled, "How far is your cabin?"

"Not far. If you can help me lift your friend, I have a horse at the top of the riverbank. We can put him on it and get him back to my home."

"He's far heavier than he looks, especially with all these wet clothes," Sidney sniffled.

"Come, let's try," the old woman said placing her hands under Skylar's body. "Help me, Great Creator. Give us the strength we need to move this boy to a safer place."

The woman seemed to glow as she lifted the boy from the ground. Sidney jumped up and helped the woman carry Skylar up the bank, where a small chestnut horse with a long dark mane stood. They laid Skylar's lifeless form across the horses' back, as the old woman took hold of the reins and started to prepare to leave.

"I think I should try to head to Abbey now," Sidney stopped and looked away from the woman.

"Come, my dear, you need rest too. We can get your friend dried and start making him better. Then we'll all return to the Abbey together. Then they will send help to your mentor."

"No!" Sidney turned sharply, before taking a breath to calm herself. "I can't come with you must go. After all, it would be a waste of time to go with you. I can go and return with help soon, I'm sure."

The old woman's smile disappeared, as she studied the girl deeply, "Well then, you'll need to follow the river downstream several miles. You will come to the grassy glen, which lies south of the Abbey. Once you are there you should be able to see the spires of the Cathedral or the peak of the Command Center and find your way home."

"Thank you," Sidney replied, as she turned walking back toward the river.

"Go in grace and peace, child. May the Creator help you? May you find your way."

"Yeah right, grace and peace," Sidney mumbled continuing to walk without turning back.

The old woman watched Sidney turn near the river and begin walking back upstream, opposite of where she had told her to go. She wondered where the girl could be going, but she sensed that she was set in her plans. She knew that something was deeply wrong but discerned that she needed to get Skylar away from the river and back to her home as quickly as possible. Turning her horse away from the river she carried Skylar off into the woods hoping to somehow revive the boy quickly.

13

Sidney followed the river back to the encampment. She managed to fight Myra's powers to stop Skylar. However, she was drawn to return to the evil woman.

Lieutenant Reed and two guards approached the young girl, "You're back. Were you able to find that boy near the river where we sent you to look? Myra is expecting results you know."

Sidney stood silently watching everyone around her. She fought tears, struggling to withhold the encounter with Skylar from them. She struggled but was being pulled to speak up by the enchantment and drugs given her by Myra. She said a prayer and stood strong against the urge to speak.

"So, you don't want to talk, eh. Well, Myra will fix that," the Lieutenant grabbed Sidney's arm and dragged her into Myra's tent. "You should have cooperated willingly, but I guess you just have to be difficult don't you."

Myra gazed into the cracked crystal, as they entered. Lieutenant Reed pushed Sidney toward her, shoving her onto the ground at Myra's feet, "The girl is back, but she's refusing to offer any help."

Myra stood and went to her laboratory bench and took a vile from the table before returning to where the girl knelt on the ground, "Why don't you make this easy on us all, Young One. You don't understand the knowledge and power I have. It would be so much easier on yourself if you just cooperated. If not, I'll have to show you the power I have."

"I would rather die than help you in any way," Sidney boldly said staring at the evil woman.

"Oh, let's not be so dramatic. I would hope that it doesn't have to go that far," Myra replied. "Hold her. It's time for your medicine, my dear. Perhaps then you'll be a little more cooperative."

The guards stepped forward and took hold of Sidney, pulling her arms out to her sides. The Lieutenant pulled the girl's hair and tilted her head back, as Myra grabbed her jaw and forced her mouth open a bit. The bitter green colored liquid dripped down the sides of the girl's mouth, as she fought drinking the mixture. Myra covered her mouth and held her nose forcing the girl to drink the potion. The potion quickly made its way into her body and began working on her mind.

It took only moments for Sidney to relax and stop fighting the guards. She sat on the ground quietly and subdued. Her eyes glazed over, and her breathing began to grow slower, as she relaxed.

"Put her in a chair," Myra instructed the guards, who complied with the order.

She handed a damp cloth to the girl, "Clean yourself up, my dear. Now, you were telling us where Skylar was. You were sent to the river where the drones lost him. I know that you helped him out of the river because my crystal revealed that to me. But, for some reason, I couldn't see what happened after you helped to pull him from the water. How is he? Where is he? What happened to him?"

Sidney was in a hypnotic state, "He was laying in the water, beside a fallen tree, unconscious when I found him. I pulled him out of the water and tried to wake him up. But he wouldn't wake up."

"So, you came here to tell us where he is?" the Lieutenant asked hopefully.

"No," she softly replied. "A woman came and helped me pull him away from the river."

"What woman?" Myra tilted her head and stared into the girl's eyes.

"I don't know. She said she lived nearby and could warm him up. She put him on her horse to take him to her home."

"Where is her home?" Myra smiled with pleasure at the answers she was receiving.

"I don't know," the girl replied.

"What do you mean you don't know?" Myra demanded as the smile left her face.

"I didn't go with them. I came here because I drawn to return. I didn't want Skylar hurt. I..."

Myra slapped the girl knocking her off the chair, "Your stupid little brat. How dare you return here without even finding out where he was being taken. How dare you resist my power over you. Surely, you must realize that you're only going to be around if you're useful to me."

The Lieutenant picked the girl up onto her feet, "What do you want me to do with her?"

Myra turned around, "Lock her up in the guard's tent for a while. She hasn't earned any comfort or privilege." Myra stared into the young girl's eyes, "And, young lady, I would consider your choices in the future very carefully. Get her out of my sight."

Lieutenant Reed handcuffed the girl's hands behind her back and led her out of Myra's tent.

"Guards!" Myra shouted.

Two other guards came into the tent, "Yes Ma'am."

"Expand your search. There's a home near the river. The boy was taken there. I want him found. And, I want him found right away."

"Yes Ma'am," the soldiers turned and went out on their mission to try to find Skylar.

Lieutenant Reed escorted Sidney to the guard's tent and locked her to one of the center posts supporting the tent, "Look, kid, I don't want to see you get hurt, but you're going to have to be a bit more cooperative. You need to tell us more about where your little friend went, or things could get pretty hard for you."

Sidney fought tears, "I told you I don't know. The old woman said she lived nearby. That's all I know."

"Yes, but we aren't finding any homes near where you were last seen by the drones," the Lieutenant replied.

"Go ahead do what you want to me, I don't know anything more," Sidney said glaring at the woman.

"Fine, have it your way," the Lieutenant replied as she stood up, "Sam, Roger come in here."

Two of the soldiers entered the tent, "Yes, Ma'am."

"Last chance kid," the Lieutenant said looking sadly at the girl.

Sidney sat silently.

"Have it your way then," the woman turned to the soldiers. "I want two people in here at all times. You are not to hurt the girl. But keep questioning her until we have the answers she has, or we find that boy."

"Yes Ma'am," one of the men replied.

"Report anything you learn. If you start to get tired call for replacements. I'll be in the command center trying to see if anyone else can find out where that boy went."

"Yes, Ma'am"

"We'll see how long you can hold out," the Lieutenant said turning to leave Sidney alone with the guards.

14

Skylar struggled to wake up, but soon the savory smell of tuber stew and sweet bread filling the air woke him from his slumber. He couldn't believe that he'd been found and returned to Myra. All his efforts and the struggle in the river seemed worthless. He forced his eyes open and looked around. Instead of the tent, he found himself in a small home lying on a soft couch covered with a hand-sewn quilt.

A table with two chairs sat across the room next to an old cookstove where a cast iron pot simmered. There was a crystal powered lamp hanging over the table, which gave light to the entire room. Near the fireplace, a gray-haired woman sat under a wool blanket in a rocking chair. The woman's feet were propped up on a stool.

Skylar tried to move his arms and legs, but was overwhelmed with weakness. He had no idea where he was or who the woman was. He had no intention of staying here, wherever here was, for long. He tried with all his effort to sit up but was unable even to raise his head. After several minutes, he forced his eyes open further and started to lift his head off the couch.

"You took quite a beating from the river," the old woman's voice broke the silence.

Skylar looked at the old woman, who slowly turned to face him. She was dressed in plain brown clothing and wore an old tattered gray wool sweater.

"How did you find yourself in the river, Young One? You should have known not to play in the dangerous flow."

"Where am I?"

"I am Kendall Pastore. You are in my cabin. I was out foraging for tubers and leeks along the river. I found your friend sitting with you. You washed up onto some rocks and trees sometime in the night. I've been nursing you and hoping to help you back to health."

Skylar realized his clothes were gone as he reached to his side to check for his weapon.

"Don't you worry about your sword, Young One. Your things are over there on the chair beside the fire. You're with a friend."

Skylar finally forced himself up on the couch, "I guess I should thank you, for saving me. I apologize for my behavior. It's just that I've found that I can't trust a lot of people lately, even those who say they want to be my friend. Speaking of which, you said I was with someone when you found me. Where is she?"

Kendall stood up and went to the stove and stirred the cooking stew, "I'm not sure. I told her the way back to the Abbey, but she appeared set on going a different way, back toward the waterfall."

Skylar closed his eyes, "She's still under her spell. I wonder what else they did to her. This is all my fault."

"Why don't you have some food to help you regain your strength," she said, serving up a bowl of the stew.

"Again, I'm sorry," Skylar replied. "I don't mean to be rude. I do appreciate your kindness."

"No need to apologize. Always help a stranger in need," the old woman said with a smile. "That's a motto I learned when I was a Young One, much younger than you. I also understand that it's hard to trust others at times. That's why I'm living here. I know I can trust myself. In most matters anyway."

Skylar recognized the words from the code of the Fidelian Knights, "I do appreciate your help. But I must get going soon. I have to get to the Abbey as soon as possible."

The woman stood and gently pressed Skylar back onto the couch, "I know you need to return to the Abbey, but you need some food and some more rest before you do anything else. Then I will help you on your way back to the Abbey."

"Look you don't understand. My cousin is hurt, and I was being chased by Varangian soldiers. They are most likely holding my friend back near the waterfall. They have a camp there."

"Varangian Guard? Here, on Avalon One?" The woman was shaken at the boy's words.

"The witch, Myra is with them too. I think she's behind everything. She has some interest in me as well, but I'm not exactly sure why. She tried to trick me into believing that she knew me and my family. She wanted me to trust her. That was when I found a way out of their trap. However, the only way to get away was to go into the river."

"Now what would she possibly want with you, Young One?" the woman studied the boy carefully.

"I'm a little confused about all of that. She seems to know my father somehow."

"Your father?"

Skylar took a deep breath. He knew the woman was somehow connected to the Fidelian Order. He worried that if she knew who his father was it might cause her alarm. He also knew that he couldn't hold anything back, because it might make her help him on his way, "My father is Justin Knighthawk."

"Yes of course," the color drained from the old woman's wrinkled face, as she sat a bowl in Skylar's hands. She sat silently in the chair next to the bed for several minutes watching Skylar eat.

"Thank you for the food, it's very good. I'm sorry if my story has frightened you. It's just that since my Father's the..."

"Chancellor of the Council of Twelve," the woman finished his thought. "I knew when I saw your necklace with your family's crest that you were connected to the Knighthawk family. I just wasn't aware that you were his son. But, if you've seen Myra, and she is after you now, we must get you on your feet and to the Abbey right away."

"Is it very far from your home?"

"Well, when I was a young pledge I could have ran to the Abbey from here in a matter of hours. However, these old legs will not move that fast anymore. You are not going to be able to move very fast, with those injuries either. I promise you that I will help you on the way."

"You've said I've been here for over a day and it could be a couple more days to the Abbey? Is there anyone nearby who can deliver a message?"

"Not now. If Moses returns, I can send him ahead of us with a message."

"Is Moses a friend? Does he live nearby?"

"He is my pet raven, who keeps me company. He is off foraging, but he will likely find us as we travel. I can send him a message with him to the Abbey when he does."

"I sure hope he comes soon because they need to know that the Varangians are here. They need to send help to my cousin."

"We cannot rush but must take the time needed to move safely. Hold on to hope that everything will be all right in the end," the woman encouraged.

"I left my cousin on a cliff near the Varangian camp. We were attacked by a Zephyrhawk. She fell and is hurt and needs help. We have to warn the others a quick as possible, so they can send help for her and to rescue Sidney from their camp."

Kendall sat down at the small table, in thought a moment, "I have never heard of a Zephyrhawk attacking anyone unless they'd first been provoked. Were you near a nest by any chance?"

"No. I think that there was more to it than that. When I was captured by Myra there was a Zephyrhawk on a perch inside her tent. I don't think that the attack was a coincidence."

"I believe you are a very wise young man. There are rarely coincidences when Myra is involved."

"The only thing I don't understand is how she would have known that we were even on the mountain. No one outside of the Council was supposed to know that I was on my Pledge's Quest. She and my cousin had a run-in when we were on Hyperborea a little over a month ago. But I don't get how she would have known we were coming back here. I'm not even sure how she got on the moon without the Elite Knights being alerted."

"Myra is very cunning in her ways. She has always been able to manipulate situations to her advantage. It's possible that she still has a friend or two on the inside of the Order, although after she turned against us, I couldn't imagine why anyone would want to be a part of her plans."

"I still have a hard time believing that she was once a Knight, like my father and the others. And, why would anyone want to help a witch anyway?"

"She wasn't always a witch. She was an excellent Knight in the Order. Her spiritual ability was quite strong. Her beauty turned many heads, and a great astuteness in all that she did. Unfortunately, she hungered to know more and do more than anyone else. Her pride would be her downfall. The old saying 'be careful what you wish for', fits well to Myra."

"What do you mean?"

"She wanted more, and she found ways to find more, for herself. She didn't like the texts and Scriptures that we have followed since the earliest of times. She sought out her own ideas and support of her power within herself. She found in some ancient writings ideas and teaching in the ideas of Simonians. This led her to seek knowledge of inner wisdom and magic as a way of giving herself more power. She lost her way in the woods of her misunderstanding and desire for greatness, and found herself in pursuit of magic, power, and wisdom within and for her own selfish gain."

"So, she wanted to make herself great in herself."

"It is the ancient sin of all humanity. The desire to make ourselves, god. If we become our own god, then we feel we have no one but ourselves to answer to."

Skylar shook his head, "No one is greater than the Creator. How could she be so stupid?"

"Many lose their way and leave behind what truth they know. They soon come to believe the lies and even think they are greater than the one who created them. The lie becomes their reality, and then it's nearly impossible to turn them back. As we are taught 'it's impossible for those who have been enlightened and tasted the word of God to be brought back.' Myra, unfortunately, is one who is lost to us."

Skylar sat up on the edge of the bed, and handed the empty bowl to the old woman, "This was a lot like my aunt used to make. I know we don't have all the answers right now, but that may not be the most important thing, for now anyway. I need to get to the Abbey and warn them of what I've seen, and more importantly to send help to my cousin and Sidney."

"Then we shall prepare to go. We'll get you up, so you can dress, and I'll pack up some things to help us with our travel to the Abbey. I'll leave you to dress," she said as she walked into a small room in the back of the cabin.

Skylar forced himself to his feet and worked his way to the chair beside the fire. He slowly pulled his pants and shirt over his aching body. He put on his utility belt and pulled his laser sword out. He looked over the control handle to be sure there was no damage from his trip down the river, and then he ignited the sword. It glowed as he slowly waved it back and forth in his hand. After he was sure it was working properly, he hooked it back onto the belt at his side.

He was tying his boots as Kendall returned to the room. She was dressed in a black hooded cloak, with a black shirt and pants. She wore a vestment over her shirt having a blue Fidelian Cross, visible through the opened cloak.

"You were part of the Elite Guard," Skylar said recognizing the dress of the best of the Fidelian Knights. He knew that the Elite Guard were the protectors of the Prime Minister, senators, and his own family, as well as the other members of the Fidelian Council of the Twelve.

"A lifetime ago, yes," she answered with a small laugh. "But my vow has never ceased. Your father is a member of the Council of Twelve, which means I am promised to protect you. It's my duty to assist you in any way possible on your current quest."

She pulled an intricately carved plasma sword from her side and ignited it and shook her head, before placing it at her side, "Well, young Knighthawk, we should be off to return you to the Abbey. You'll have quite a tale to tell of your Pledge's Quest one day."

"I hope we all live to share this tale."

They walked out of the small home. A well-groomed garden sat inside a wooden fence surrounding the home. A small barn sat behind the home, and Skylar could see dried hay piled inside the open door. The small chestnut horse was tied to near the gate in front of the home, as they walked slowly out into the garden.

"She isn't much," Kendall said with a smile, "But, I think if we take turns Annie will help us on our journey to the Abbey."

Skylar smiled, limping down the path toward the gate, "She's very beautiful. I'm sure that she will be a great help."

"Have you ridden before?"

"Yes," Skylar said grinning, "My father made sure to take me to the stables at the Abbey quite often when I was young. He told me that the horses brought here from earth were a part of the Knights tradition and all knights should learn to ride. He also said it kept us in touch with our roots."

"Your father is a very wise man. Why don't you ride, and I'll walk for now? I feel quite strong and rejuvenated," Kendall replied directing Skylar to the horse and helped him onto the saddle before they headed out.

15

The morning sun shone over the mountains around the camp. Myra stood in the doorway of her tent, "Lieutenant Reed!"

She quickly ran out of the command center, "I am sorry, Ma'am. I've been up all night trying to keep the troops searching for this kid and integrating the girl."

"And, has she revealed anything?" Myra asked.

"No. She is still resisting. We haven't allowed her to sleep or eat in the past two days. However, she continues to resist."

"Well, I don't have time to wait. My senses lead me to believe that this woman who helped that boy is planning to go to the Fidelian Abbey. They'll know of our presence very shortly."

"Should we call for the Intrepid to return and make plans to leave then?"

"No," Myra grinned, "I believe it's time for us to act. I want your communications officer to contact the fleet. Get a coded message to Admiral Hendricks. Tell him, the rock of Excalibur shall fall."

"The rock of Excalibur shall fall?"

"Yes," Myra replied. "Those specific words will bring a division to take this moon for the Juntonian League once and for all. Then in no time at all, we will gain control of Avalon Prime. This victory should ensure our control of the entire System soon."

"Yes, Ma'am," Lieutenant Reed replied turning to leave.

"One more thing," Myra stopped the younger woman.

"Yes, Ma'am."

"I am tired of waiting for answers from the girl. After the message is sent bring her here to me. We will have to persuade her with a bit stronger medicine," she said looking at a vile of light green medicine in her hand.

"Ma'am, Private Steven's is still out of her head from the injection you gave her four days ago. What if the girl doesn't tell us what we want? What if..."

"If she manages to resist somehow then she'll be of no use to me any longer. It will no longer matter if she has a mind left. Remember Lieutenant, she brought this on herself, by resisting and refusing to cooperate with me. Now carry out my orders."

"Yes, Ma'am," Lieutenant Reed said leaving Myra's tent.

Half-way across the solar system, a large space station orbited around Meriopis, the sixth planet of the Elysium System. Meriopis was where the central rule of the Juntonian League called home. Large domes covered the center with communication towers rising from the top and bottom. It was large enough to hold two super-cruisers on the inside of the dome. The station was used to build new spaceships and as the headquarters of the entire Varangian Fleet.

A large man with graying hair sat behind a metal and glass desk reading a report on a tablet. The window of his office in the space station overlooked the super-cruiser, Retribution, orbiting the planet below. The newest ship in the Varangian fleet was nearly two miles long. It was in the normal triangular shape of most Varangian cruisers, with sixteen decks. The super-cruiser was able to carry twenty-five bombers, sixty fighters, and five transport ships. The landing troop complement was two hundred soldiers. The ship also was armed with four upper and three lower blast cannons. The on-board crew was another hundred troops, with a command crew of twenty.

Four smaller destroyers flew near the Retribution, as was typical of most Varangian fleet squadrons. These smaller destroyers each carried one-hundred-fifty troops, twenty-five fighters, and five bombers. Dozens of fighters and bombers were patrolling the space around the ships and a couple of transports were delivering troops from the planet.

"Admiral," a voice interrupted the elderly man's reading.

"Yes, Lieutenant?"

"Sir, we've received a coded holo-link from the delegation assigned to Myra."

"Thank you, patch it through to my com-station," Admiral Hendricks replied.

"Yes, Sir."

A holographic image of a young soldier's face floated above the desk in front of him, "Admiral Hendricks, this is Corporal Stanton. I am with the squadron accompanying Myra, on Avalon One."

"Yes, Corporal. Please continue," the Admiral ordered.

"Sir, I was told to deliver you a specific message."

"Very well, what is the message?"

"The rock of Excalibur shall fall."

The Admiral took a deep breath, "I understand. Thank you, Corporal. Let Myra know that I have received the message."

"Yes, Sir. Avalon One, out."

The holograph went out, as the Admiral leaned back in his chair in deep thought for a couple of minutes. He finally leaned forward pressing a button on the underside of the glass desk turning on his com-link, "Lieutenant Iota, patch me through to Captain Alvarez, on the Scythian."

"Yes Sir," the young man's voice replied. A few moments passed, and his voice returned, "Sir Captain Alvarez is ready for you on holo-link."

"Very good," the Admiral replied, as the figure of a tall thin man in a formal black jacket with several different colored markers on his shoulder indicating his rank. "Captain Alvarez."

"Good day Admiral Hendricks. How may I be of service?"

"Captain, there is no time for pleasantries. Myra has issued the call. Operation Excalibur is now enacted."

"I understand Sir. I'll move my troops into a staging area over Avalon One before the end of the day. We should be able to deliver troops in less than twenty-four hours."

"Very good. The surprise should allow an easy takeover of the moon. But remember, Myra wants the Abbey preserved, as much as possible. She says the wealth of knowledge they have is invaluable. Including the ancient plans for atomic weaponry, which could help us conquer the rest of the system. I'm trusting you and your Squadron to handle this. I'll send The Retribution's squadron to replace you at your current location, so that section of space can remain secure. Don't worry about the few days it will take for them to arrive things are quiet there right now."

"Understood Admiral. We will get underway within the hour."

"Very good. We'll update you with any changes."

"Thank you, Sir. Scythian out."

The soldiers kept pressing Sidney for information for about three hours. They didn't allow her to sleep or eat and allowed her only enough water to keep her conscious. She was completely exhausted. However, she continued to refuse to answer any of their questions.

"Well kid, it looks like your going to visit Myra again," the young officer said unlocking the girl.

"Wonderful, I look forward to seeing her again," Sidney whispered.

The Lieutenant shook her head, "Apparently you have a death wish."

They sat the girl in a chair in front of Myra at the center of the tent. She was barely awake. She tried to force herself to look around for a way to escape.

"Well my dear," the cunning middle-aged woman turned to face the girl. She held a syringe in her hand. "Apparently, you can't tell us any more about where the boy went. And, my guards are incompetent in their ability to find him or this home in the woods that you spoke of either. What you don't know is that there are more troops headed here. My plan is far bigger than you can ever imagine. And, there is no way some child will stand in the way of my greater plans."

Sidney fought to speak, "You'll never force anything out of me. And, you'll never win. Faith and truth shall prevail."

Myra smiled, "I've decided to ask you something else. Instead of where the boy went, I want you to tell me where you left the young woman who was with you above the falls?"

"I don't know. And, I wouldn't tell you if I did."

"Why do you insist on being so stubborn? This serum is stronger than what I've given you so far. You know where she was hiding, and you will tell me," Myra said motioning for the guards to hold the girl still, as she pressed the liquid into her arm. Sidney shook, foam ran down her cheek, as she passed out from all the drugs being put in her body.

"What do we do with her now?" Lieutenant Reed asked.

"Make sure she can't leave," Myra instructed. "She'll pass out for about half-an-hour or so. When she wakes up, she will tell us what we want to know. Then we'll find the girl who's somewhere on the trail above the Quest Falls. We'll use her and this girl to get to the boy. This isn't the way I'd wanted to do this, but it will work out in the end."

"Yes, Ma'am," she said pointing to two other guards who placed a lock on the girl's foot and chained it to the center pole of the tent. They left her in a heap on the floor Myra's tent.

Myra smiled, "Are you showing weakness, Lieutenant?"

"No Ma'am, I just wanted to be sure she was going to be able to speak when she wakes up."

"I've made this potion before and trust me it is very effective. Within the next few hours, we'll know what she knows about the old woman's home, and we'll know where the boy's mentor is hiding. For now, keep the patrols searching. I'm going for a walk to clear my head. I'll return in about an hour."

"Yes Ma'am," the Lieutenant replied leaving the tent.

16

Kendall led Skylar along a small pathway, as they began their trek through the forest. They were slowly descending further into the valley, but Skylar wasn't sure how long it would be to reach the Abbey. He was not familiar with this part of the forest, so he was trusting Kendall to lead the way. His mind remained focused on trying to move forward through the pain of his injuries, and with concern for how Halie was doing.

"So, you said you know my father?" Skylar asked as they slowly made their way through the woods.

"Of course, I know him. Any member of the Fidelian Order knows the members of the Council of Twelve, especially the Chancellor."

"I know that. I meant do you know him personally?"

"I worked for some time in the Abbey, as a guard to the Council. I've also had opportunity of accompanying your father and grandfather on some of their diplomatic missions over my years serving in the Elite Guard."

"Did you know my mother, as well?"

The woman looked away from Skylar down the path ahead of them trying to avoid eye contact, "Yes, I knew her. It's an unfortunate thing that she was lost to us so young. I and many others wept over the loss. She was admired by all at the Abbey, and very skilled indeed."

"Were you there when she died?"

The woman took a deep breath pretending to be tired, "These old bones aren't used to all this walking anymore. I guess it will take us a bit longer than I thought it would. We might want to find a place to rest soon. There should be some water up ahead where we can refill our canteens and water Annie."

Skylar stopped and looked sincerely at the woman, "Kendall, I really want to know. Did you know her well? Were you there when she died?"

The woman looked to the ground before turning to face the boy, "Some truths are hard to bear, and are better left buried that we may know peace to carry on."

"And, the truth can set us free," Skylar responded, "I want to know what you know about my mother's death."

"I admired your mother deeply. I was among the guards who were there the day the Chapel exploded, and your mother was killed. There was chaos throughout the entire Abbey. Some of my best friends were killed, and I bear wounds from the fire," she said pulling the sleeve of her right arm up to reveal the scars. "When your mother couldn't be found we had no choice but to accept that the fire had consumed her."

"That's all you saw then?"

The woman stopped to look at him again, "I watched her enter the Council Chambers. I also watched your father as he was knocked to the ground by the blast that destroyed most of the building. My concern at that moment was to get all of you away from danger. We escorted your entire family away from your home. Then we put you all onto a ship and flew you to Caspian, where we sought help from the Commonwealth Alliance military to protect you. The Knights and Elite Guards who remained secured the moon.   They also began to rebuild the Abby. Your mother's body was never recovered because the destruction to the Council chambers was so bad. Now please, let's go to the Abbey and seek help against the current trouble."

"Thank you. I know it isn't easy to share, but I need to know what I can about her. I never really got to know her at all. I was so young when everything happened that barely remember her."

Kendall turned back toward the path ahead and took a deep breath, "I understand. Sometimes it's best to let the embers of the past grow cold, or the fire of your enemy may rise from the ashes."

"So, how long have you been living here in the woods?"

"About five or six years, since I retired from guarding the Prime Minister's family."

Skylar thought about the timeline for a while before speaking, "You served my Aunt Dara and Uncle Bern when I was young then."

"Yes."

"She and my uncle lived here on Avalon One, with us in our shared apartment. They were here most of the time until about four years ago when she moved to Caspian to be closer to the Senate and government center. You would have been here when I was little?"

The woman smiled, "Are you asking if I knew you when you were a young boy?"

"I guess I am."

"Yes, I knew you when you were very young. Your Aunt Dara loves you very much, and I know your father does too."

"So, you served with my father and mother. You also have served with my aunt and uncle at the Abbey."

"Yes. I served for a long time in protecting members of your family. I served your grandfather when he was on the Council, and I knew your father when he was your age. That was why when you told me who you were, I knew I must help you to get to the Abbey."

"I thank you for serving my family. However, you owe me nothing. You can just point me in the direction of the Abbey, and I assure you that you can return to your peaceful life in the woods," Skylar encouraged the woman.

"I cannot leave you until I have seen you safely to the protection of the Abbey. I may be old and a bit slower than I used to be, but my commitment will never waiver. Now, let's follow this small creek, which flows toward the Abbey."

Skylar decided to put the matter aside, at least for the time being. He continued to follow the woman through the woods and heavy foliage of the forest. He knew there was more that he would need to investigate later, but for now, moving ahead was all that mattered.

17

Lieutenant Reed and three other soldiers returned to Myra's tent. Myra was dangling a fat mouse in front of her Zephyrhawk, as it shot its great beak forward quickly devouring the creature.

"Is there any word from the patrols?" Myra asked as she turned to walk back to her table where food sat from her breakfast.

"Nothing promising. They found a small shack in the woods a little while ago. Unfortunately, it was empty. They said some could have been there earlier, but they weren't sure. We've also been told that the first ships of the squadron are arriving. The larger ships are remaining in the nearby asteroid field. They hope the asteroids will help mask them until they are needed. Command, is hoping the fighters and some of the bombers can sneak around from the backside of the moon."

Myra grinned at the news, "Excellent. Contact Captain Alvarez as soon as possible. Remind him that stealth is of the utmost importance. We'll want to surround the Abbey as quickly and quietly as possible, for this plan to work."

"Of course, Ma'am. Jones, take the message to the command center immediately," Lieutenant Reed replied, as one of the soldiers left. She looked down at the Sidney still lying motionless on the ground. "What of your other concerns? The boy and his mentor haven't been found yet."

Myra looked down at the girl and then back to the lieutenant, "It's been long enough. Prepare her for further interrogation. I am going outside for some fresh air. Have her ready when I return."

"Yes, Ma'am."

Myra stood and walked out of the tent. The late morning sun shone through the door as she left. Lieutenant Reed knelt next to Sidney's lifeless body, and gently shook her shoulder. She tried several times to wake her from her sleep, but she lay motionless on the ground. The Lieutenant tried to move the girl into a sitting position, but she'd simply slump back over.

The officer looked at her guards, "It looks like I'll need some help here. Let me take off these chains, they're obviously unnecessary at this point. Then you can help me get her into a chair and try to wake her up."

"Yes Ma'am," the younger guard said as she approached.

The two guards put their hands under the girl's arms, as the lieutenant unlocked the cuffs on the girl's leg. They slowly picked her up and sat her in one of the chairs at the table. The officer knelt beside Sidney, as they held her up. "Kid, you need to wake up. Come on."

"What can we do to help?" the second guard asked.

"Just keep holding her up," Lieutenant Reed replied. She moved in front of the girl and gently patted the side of her face trying to rouse her, "Wake up. Come on kid, wake up."

Myra walked in, as they were continuing to stir the girl, "You're far too gentle my dear." She said as she stepped past the young officer. She raised her hand high above her head and slapped the girl nearly knocking her out of the chairs and out of the grip of the guards. "WAKE UP! You little brat. I want answers."

Sidney opened her eyes. She was under the control of the drugs and power of Myra's spell. She was trying to respond but couldn't make the words come to her lips. The drugs rendered her unable to speak.

Myra turned around and stepped back to her laboratory table. She picked up a vile of the potion and began filling a syringe, "I'll have my answers now. There is no way she can resist any longer."

"Ma'am, she seems unable to speak. Perhaps she's already had too much," Lieutenant Reed begged.

"Don't go, soft Lieutenant. There is no room for that here," Myra answered, as she turned to face the girl again. "Hold her still."

The guards held the girl's arms, and Myra knelt next to her, "This is your fault. You left me with no choice." She injected the potion into the girl's arms, causing her to writhe in pain. Her body twisted, turned, and began to shake. Foam rolled out of her mouth and down her chin.

Myra sat the syringe back on the table and then stepped in front of Sidney's shaking body. She grabbed hold of her hair and pushed her head back staring deeply into the girl's eyes, "You cannot resist my power. Speak to me about what you know. From the depths let your truth flow. You can't resist or fight it now. Show me what I want to know."

Myra remained locked eye to eye with the shaking girl for several minutes, as the guards struggled to hold her. Suddenly, Sidney stopped moving and Myra threw her lifeless head back. She stepped away from her, and took a drink of water, "Get rid of her."

"Ma'am?" the Lieutenant asked.

"Her mentor is right above the falls. There are some caves just to the east. She's hiding in one of them. I told you she would tell me what I needed to know."

"So, what do we do with the girl?" Lieutenant Reed asked again.

Myra glared at the young woman, "I said, get rid of her. She is of no use to anyone anymore. Do her a favor and put her out of her misery."

The young officer swallowed hard, and took a deep breath, "Yes Ma'am. Take her outside," she requested her troops.

"Wait," Myra replied. "Don't dispose of her quite yet. Just throw her in the guard's tent. Just in case your troops are incapable of capturing an injured woman in a cave. We may need her to get the boy to come to me. However, she won't likely live that long."

"Ma'am, please," the Lieutenant requested, "Please, just give her something to stop this. Like you said she's dying anyway. This is inhumane."

"How dare you question my orders Lieutenant? If you like your rank, you'll do as I say. Throw her in the guard's tent and let her die in her pain. She should have cooperated, and I would have let her live. She could have been an assistant to one of the greatest sorceresses in the history of time. Now, get this garbage out of my tent."

Lieutenant Reed sighed and looked down, as she turned to the door, "Yes Ma'am."

They carried the girl out of the tent. Several soldiers walked past them as they made their way across the camp to the guard's tent. Lieutenant Reed led them past the line of beds and the table, into the front of the tent where her private quarters were separate from the rest of the tent.

"Place her on my bed."

"Ma'am, this is your bed," the younger woman said as they laid Sidney's body on the bed.

"I know. It's the least we can do. I want you two to remain here and keep an eye on her. Let me know if anything changes with her."

"Yes, Ma'am," the man replied.

"Ma'am?" the young female guard asked staring at Sidney's lifeless form.

"Yes."

"How can someone be so cruel? She's just a kid."

"She is Myra, The Witch of Tintigal. And, unless you want to end up like her or even worse, keep your thoughts to yourself."

"Yes, Ma'am."

Lieutenant Reed squeezed the younger soldier's arm and looked sadly into her eyes showing that she understood. Then she left the tent to return to the center of the encampment. She knelt by the open fire at the center of the camp, as mist blew around her. She sat staring at the fire in thought. The rumble of a small ship overhead let her know that the reinforcements were starting to arrive on the moon.

She stood up and looked around the camp at the soldiers moving around, "GATHER IN TROOPS!"

A few moments later everyone left in the camp was gathered around the fire, "We still have not found the boy Myra is seeking. However, she said that his mentor is hiding in a cave at the top of the waterfall. I want six of you to work your way up there and find her. Myra will want her alive.   There are two patrols still out searching the trails between here and the open field near the Fidelian Abby. I want them to continue their search. The rest of you should prepare for the battle "

"Ma'am," one of the soldiers stepped forward, "I'll lead the group up to find the girl. I think it will take some time, but we can move around the edge of these cliffs and find an easier way up the side of the mountain. We can work our way around the western side where it seems more accessible."

"Very good, Richter. I'm putting you in charge of getting that girl. You all have your orders now get to it! This is the time to give your best. Let's make the Varangian Guard proud."

The soldiers shouted in unison, "OORAH! OORAH!" before returning to their tasks.

18

Skylar and Kendall walked slowly along for nearly five hours. The trees were starting to thin, but they hadn't quite reached the open plain of the valley. They were now following the trail that went along the river once more. They figured that they hadn't seen any of the Varangians in quite some time and that it would be foolish for any of the enemy forces to show themselves so close to the Abbey.

"We're nearing the edge of the forest," Kendall said. "There is a small clearing along the path ahead of us. I think we should refill our canteens and rest there a bit, before moving on."

"Sounds good to me. Do you have any idea how much further we have to go?" Skylar asked, as he made his way to a fallen tree and sat down.

The woman looked down the path ahead, "We should clear the woods in about an hour or so. Once we are in the plain the trail will be flat and easy. Even with our slow speed, we should arrive in about six to eight hours. However, it's starting to get dark. We'll need to decide if we want to try to continue or rest for the night."

"I don't see any reason to stop, if the trail is easier, we should keep moving."

"We'll need to clear the forest's edge, before nightfall then. We should manage well on the path of the plain in the dim night light. However, we need to leave Annie here and go forward on foot. Here, eat some bread and berries. You need to keep your strength up."

"Thank you. You're a very gracious woman."

"I'm happy to serve you. It's my duty and it wouldn't be neighborly not to help," Kendall said, as she stood to her feet and looked around them. "Do you hear that?"

Skylar listened a moment to the forest, "I just hear the water and some birds. It sounds like the forest has since we arrived."

"No. Listen carefully. There is a raven approaching. I think it's Moses," she said with a smile, as she let out a couple of caws and chirps.

A couple of minutes past and a large raven glided down and landed on a branch next to the old woman. She gave the blackbird some bread, and gently pet the bird's head.

"Do you think we can send a message ahead of us now?" Skylar asked with excitement.

"I believe it's worth a try," she said digging into her backpack. "Now, where is that paper and pen I placed in here. Here it is. I'll write a note telling them who and where we are."

"But if I write my father can verify that it's my writing."

"Do you know the secret code of the Elite Guard?"

"The what?" Skylar asked.

"Right. You see we can't risk telling Myra or the Varangians about our location just in case my raven friend here gets confused and takes the message to the wrong person. I'll tell them where we are, but we'll need to keep moving just to be on the safe side. I will use the secret code of the Elite Guard since I know Myra wouldn't know it."

Skylar sighed, "Okay, whatever it takes to get out of here faster."

"There we are," the woman said, as she tied the note to the raven's leg. "Now, my old friend fly to the Abbey and get us some help." The raven flapped its wings and flew off ahead of them.

"Well, at least he headed in the right direction," Skylar smiled. "I guess it's back to our hike then."

"Yes, we need to clear the woods soon. The forest path is rough in the dark. So, we'd better get moving."

"Wait," Skylar said. "I hear something."

The low rumble of a ship's engines could be heard far off in the distance. Soon the sound was joined by another ship moving over the treetops ahead of them.

"It sounds like transport ships," Kendall replied.

"Ours or theirs?"

"It's impossible to tell without seeing them," the older woman answered watching the sky above. "We may not have to warn the Abbey. If that's enemy carriers, they'll be aware of the Varangian's presence. A small ship might make it through our defensive detections, but no transport could make it through. I think we'd better get moving."

"Why don't you take the horse," Skylar said. "I have ridden most of the way, and it wouldn't be right for you to walk any further." Kendall agreed and mounted the horse and they continued their journey.

They traveled on for just over an hour when the woods began to clear. They could see the sun setting far across the large plain ahead of them. Skylar was never so happy to see an open field in his life. The hope of reaching the Abbey now seemed to become a reality.

"All right, this is where I get off," Kendall smiled patting her horse on the neck.

"What do you mean?"

"I don't think we should risk riding Annie in the open plain."

"So, what are you going to do with her?"

The wise woman stood in front of the horse patting her head, "You've been good, ol' girl. Now, go on home."

Skylar laughed, "Do you think she'll go back to your cabin all on her own?"

"Of course," the old woman smiled. "She knows these woods better than I do. She'll be fine."

"Well then I guess we move on by foot from here then," Skylar said smiling as he turned to walk on ahead.

They walked along the path for another hour. Darkness fell over the grassy plain. Soon the large rampart of the Fidelian Abbey rose above the grassy plain. The walls surrounding the Abbey were four stories high, covering the full mile and a half by mile and a half campus. The spires of the Great Cathedral could be seen above the walls at one end of the grounds. The large step pyramid-shaped Command Center rose at the opposite end of the walled grounds. Rounded guard towers stood at each of the corners and to the sides of the four main gates leading out of the Abbey in every direction.

Skylar had been on the main road leading into the Abbey many times, and even though the ordeal of the past days weighed on him, he was happy to be heading home. Skylar and Kendall looked quietly at the Abbey below the grassy knoll where they had stopped. They could see that large metal gates, normally left open, were now closed tightly.

"We won't be able to approach from this way," Kendall said pointing to an encampment of Varangians sitting outside the southern walls of the Abbey.

"We're too late then," Skylar cried dropping to one knee. "The Varangians are already here. There is no way to get inside now. The Abbey is locked down."

"Quiet," Kendall instructed, as she pulled the boy off the trail into the tall grass.

"What are you doing. It doesn't matter anymore. We're not going to get inside, and Halie is in big trouble."

"Young Knighthawk, you need to keep control. We haven't the time to mourn our situation right now. Now is the time of action," she whispered.

"Action? What are you talking about? We can't take on the Varangians alone, and we can't get inside the Abbey."

"I said be quiet!" the old woman insisted.

Then two laser blasts exploded on the path a few feet from them causing Skylar to roll behind a large rock.

"I warned you to be still. There's Varangian foot patrol on the path. We'll need to defend ourselves."

One of the Varangians stopped a few feet from them looking into the grass, "I'm sure I saw something go into the grass over here."

"It's probably an animal," a second soldier said. "That stupid kid couldn't have made it this far without someone seeing him."

"I'm still going to check it out," The first soldier said.

"What's the point? We still can't get inside. They won't just open the doors for us. When the Abbey is threatened and in lock-down nothing gets in or out."

The old woman smiled at the boy, "We'll need to dispatch this small group of soldiers. Then we can continue on our way."

"What do you want me to do?"

"I want you to run off to your right, toward the large rock on the other side of the path. Your diversion should give me time to move in behind these two soldiers."

"Are you sure about this?"

"If you're ready?"

"I'm ready."

"Then let's go."

Skylar jumped up to begin to run back to the pathway. He startled the soldier in the grass, and they both began firing at him. He jumped and rolled across the roadway behind a large boulder. He watched as the old woman swiftly came up behind them and swung her plasma sword against the sides of their helmets causing them to fall to the ground.

A third soldier continued to follow Skylar, and he came up behind the boy. Skylar ignited his sword and jumped as he swung and knocked the helmet of the large man.

"I knocked him out," Skylar said as the old woman approached.

"I saw. Now, we can't afford to have them report anything," the old woman said raising her sword and shoving it into the chest of the motionless man.

Skylar watched her. He'd seen people die in the battle of Hyperborea, but he had never seen anyone kill an unarmed and motionless person before.

Kendall knelt next to Skylar, as he stared at the body in front of him, "Some decisions, you are not ready to make yet. However, sometimes for the greater good, we must act."

"But the code of the Knights says not to kill a defenseless person?"

"Yes, we must always live by the code whenever it's possible. Respect of all life is preeminent to everything in the code, for all life flows from the Creator. I wasn't aware of the presence of all these troops at the time and felt there was no other course of action. However, now we face greater odds. We must get you inside the Abbey to your father right away."

"How do you propose we do that, with all these soldiers wandering around? Besides, we still can't get inside. They won't just open the doors for us. When the Abbey is threatened and in lock-down nothing gets in or out."

The old woman smiled at the boy, "I know. I was part of the Elite Guard, after all. I also know the shield will be in place to prevent an aerial attack too. However, everything isn't as desperate as it seems."

"I get that you're wise and probably even have some abilities I don't but unless you can make us invisible, I don't see how we're going to get past the soldiers and inside."

"Follow me and learn from one who knows the Abbey's deepest secrets," she said smiling as she led him into the tall weeds away from the roadway.

They walked through the tall damp grass toward the Abbey. Skylar couldn't see where they were, but he knew it was better to move through the tall weeds than to walk in the open of the road. Near the middle of the field, Kendall stopped at a large gnarled tree.

"Why are we stopping here?" Skylar asked, assuming the old woman needed to rest.

"I was looking for Pan's Oak," Kendall said grinning at the boy, as she studied the tree and moved her hand over the rough trunk.

"The what?"

Kendall on one knee, "Well, not everything is quite as it seems. Here you see a large ancient tree. It's been growing here since before humans came to Avalon One. It looks like a simple shade tree, but inside is our way into the Abbey."

She lifted her hand from the tree revealing a small carved cross. She pointed at the carving and then pressed hard on the design. The ground beside the tree slid open showing a stairway leading underground.

"A secret passage?"

"That's right," she smiled at him.

"Why did you call it the Pan's Oak?"

"Like in the ancient story of Peter Pan. Wendy lived in a tree, and we created a secret passage beneath this tree as an emergency exit to the Abbey. Over time some of us started calling it the Pan's Oak."

But, where does it lead?"

"It comes out at the heart of the labyrinth in the Central Garden of the Abbey. We'll be able to find your father from there."

"I've spent a lot of time in that labyrinth, and I didn't know there was a secret passage there."

"That's what makes it a secret. Few people know, and even fewer remember that the passage is even here. Several passages lead under the Abbey, built for emergency use. Once we are inside the dark passage, we'll need to use our swords to help light our way into the Abbey."

"Then let's get going. We need to get the message about Halie to the others," Skylar said igniting his plasma sword and stepping down into the dark hole.

Kendall ignited her sword, "All right, Young One. When we get below, let me take the lead, because we'll have some choices to make as we find our way inside."

"Choices?" Skylar wondered.

"As I said, there are many tunnels under the Abbey. Some are false tunnels leading to dead ends. They were made to prevent any enemy from quickly finding their way into the sanctuary."

Skylar shook his head, "Then I'll let you take the lead."

Kendall smiled at him, "You'll learn too. You're young, but in time you'll know about all the things you need to survive and lead in the Fidelian order."

"I'm not always sure that I'm going to make it through the training. There is so much to know, and the Knights are expected to perform and live honorably in all things."

"You worry about your father's opinions," the old woman said, as they descended into the dark tunnel. She pressed a stone in the wall closing the secret opening above their heads and ignited her sword.

"How did you know?"

"Your father is the Chancellor of the Council of Twelve. You come from a line of knights many generations old. It is only normal that you would question whether you will be able to stand as strong as those who came before you."

Skylar smiled at the woman, "You're very smart, but even you can't fix the family I am related to. I'll always be judged harder, simply because of the family I was born into."

Kendall stopped and smiled at him, "Your father wasn't always the strong, secure leader that he is today. He too had to grow into his gifts and become his own kind of leader. None of us is created to be exactly like another person. We are created to use our unique gifts and abilities to shine goodness into our universe. There is a time when we must stop living in the shadows of others and learn to shine in our abilities."

Skylar snickered, "You expect me to believe that my father, the great Justin Knighthawk has struggled? He always knows the right thing to do no matter what the situation."

Kendall laughed at him shaking her head, "When your father was your age, just after passing his Quest he and his father argued continually. Up to that point your grandfather, Andrew Knighthawk had mentored your father. He wanted him raised in the highest standards. Your father wanted to expand his training and wanted to see the Abbey become more than it was.

It was your grandmother, Alexis who intervened. She convinced your grandfather to allow the rest of the mentoring to be done by someone else. That is when Brother Lawrence became your father's mentor. He not only trained him but has been at your father's side to this day."

"I never knew any of that."

"Even when your father was asked to serve as a member of the council he and your grandfather remained at odds. Your father could see the potential of expanding the Abbey and the training facility. But your grandfather wanted things to remain simple as they had been for over three hundred years.

You see in time, you'll grow up and you'll live your life the way you're meant to live. In many areas of your life, you will carry on a piece of your father. However, your unique design and calling may lead you down paths he never would've understood. That may be why he chose to allow others like Brother Lawrence and your cousin to help in the process of mentoring you."

Skylar was silenced by the woman's insight, for the first time he started to realize that he didn't have to become his father. He simply had to learn to use the abilities he was given for the good of others. It was a freeing thought. It was also a bit frightening since he could no longer hide behind who his father was. He had to decide who and what he would be for himself.

Kendall waited a few moments to let him think, before speaking, "Now, Young One. It's time that we get going, so you can start your destiny." She turned around and started down the dark tunnel ahead of them.

The narrow tunnel was cool and filled with spider webs and dust from disuse. Now and then they would come to a turn and Kendall would point which way to go. Skylar was growing hopeful that the nightmare of the past couple of days might soon be over.

19

Kendall led Skylar through several turns in the dark tunnel system leading under the Abbey. They eventually arrived at another small stone stairway leading up toward the ceiling. Kendall looked along the wall and pressed another stone, as the ceiling slid open revealing the exit above.

They cautiously emerged from the tunnel, as the light from the starry night seemed much brighter than before entering the dark tunnel. Skylar looked around the center of the labyrinth trying to get his bearings. He quickly realized where he was and where the tunnel had been hidden all his life. Several statues were around the center of the labyrinth. There was a statue of the Messiah kneeling over a rock in prayer, which now slid back into place concealing the tunnel. They shut off their plasma swords and made their way through the twists and turns that led toward the eastern gate of the Abbey.

"Who goes there!" one of the several guards near the gate asked as Skylar and Kendall approached. The guard was wearing a tan shirt, dark blue flack-jackets, and dark military pants. He carried a laser rifle in his hand and a plasma sword on his belt.

"Skylar Knighthawk. I have been on the Pledge's Quest. I must see the Elder Council immediately."

"We've been watching for you. But how did you get inside? There are enemy troops all around the Abbey? Everything is locked down?"

"I brought the boy in through one of the secret passages," Kendall explained.

"Who are you? What secret passage?" the guard asked.

Skylar smiled, "The one you obviously, don't know about. Now, I'd like to get to the Council right away."

Kendall looked at the guard, "I served as a guard here at one time, and I know a few things that some of the younger guards haven't learned yet."

The guard looked closely at Kendall and recognized her attire, "You're part of the Elite Guard. I'm sorry, 'Ma'am. I didn't mean any disrespect."

"It's all right," Kendall smiled at the young guard. "Now, I think you'd better help young Knighthawk here to the Council. I'm sure that his father is concerned about him."

"We'll take you inside where you can get some food, while you wait to meet with the Council. The Council will be informed of your arrival, and I am sure they will meet with you soon," The guard said, motioning for another guard to come and join them.

"No, I must see them now," Skylar demanded as he began to walk past the guard toward a path, he knew led to the Council Chambers. "My cousin Halie is hurt, and..."

"Look, kid, it's part of the process. The Council's very busy at the moment, and they can't meet with you right now. They'll want to speak to you once things settle down. The plans for a ceremony will need to be made. Then you'll be an official Pledge and Squire Level One in the Fidelian Order. I get your excitement, but we have greater matters pressing us right now."

"You're not listening!" Skylar shouted. "Halie, my cousin who was with me is hurt. Sidney, one of my friends was captured when we ran into Varangian Guards. Now I must speak to the Council immediately about sending help."

The second guard stepped beside them, "What is it?"

"The Knighthawk boy has returned. He says his friend was captured, and his cousin is hurt out in the woods."

Kendall stepped forward and became more forceful, "I'm part of the Elite Guard. I live in the woods outside the Abbey. I found the boy and helped him to get inside. However, I do think you should listen to the boy's request. His father, the Chancellor, would probably like to see his son, and know that his niece is in danger."

"Right," the guard agreed, and turned to the first guard, "I guess that would make the matter a bit more important. Take him to the Elite Guard at the Council Chamber right way."

"Okay, follow me, kid," the guard turned toward the pathway leading to Cathedral and the Council Chambers.

The small streets were laid out like the offset spokes of a bicycle, flowing out from each of the ends of the grounds. The Cathedral and Council Chambers at the center of the eastern spoked streets, and the Command Center at the center of the western center. They walked toward the red sandstone Cathedral, following the guard who led the way.

Two of the Elite Guards standing at the door approached them. One of them stepped ahead, "The Council is in session. You can enter the Cathedral, but the Council is off-limits."

"I've got the Chancellor's son, Skylar Knighthawk. He was on his Quest, and his father has been worried about him," Their escort explained.

The Elite Guard look Skylar over and then to Kendal. He stopped and stood at attention, "General Pastore, I apologize I didn't know it was you, Ma'am."

"Enough of this formality," Kendal waved the man off. "Please let the boy inside and tell his father he's here."

"Yes, Ma'am. Right this way," he answered turning to escort them into the Cathedral.

They went quietly inside the reverent structure, which had several holographic projectors along the wall displaying pictures of the stories that Skylar had been taught from the Scriptures since he was born.

"Wait here," the guard said, as they stopped near the front of the sanctuary. He left them going through one of the side doors near the front.

Skylar knelt in front of a stone Celtic Cross at the altar, "Thank you Great Father-Creator, for helping me to get home here safely. Please keep Halie safe, and help us to get to her soon. Protect us from the evil that is coming. Help the Elders to guide and protect us please."

Kendall sat on one knee next to the boy, "Very fitting, and I think it sums up my sentiment up fully."

"I just hope they meet with me soon. I can't stand not being able to help my cousin."

"Patience is a virtue. And, it is best to remain calm in the toughest of times"

"I know, but sometimes it's hard to just sit and wait."

"Indeed," the old woman smiled at his words. "But, then again some of the best things in life come from waiting. The fruits of our gardens must grow to maturity before we can eat the most flavorful crops. Waiting has brought humanity some of the greatest gifts and blessings."

"It's still hard," he said watching a flickering candle near the cross. "Do you think I'll be able to convince the Council to rescue Halie and Sidney? I mean they have to protect the whole Abbey and they are just two people."

"Speak with your father, and the others with honesty and they will listen," she encouraged.

"That's easy for you to say. You have years of experience. They have to respect you. I'm just a Pledge trainee. They have no reason to listen to anything that I have to say.

"Skylar," the woman said touching his hand gently and looking into his eyes, "Your father leads the Council. Speaking to them is no more difficult than speaking with him."

He rolled his eyes and sighed, "Then I am in real trouble. I've always had trouble speaking with him about anything. He so important and so worried about the affairs of the whole Fidelian Order, and I am just his son."

"No," the woman said sternly, "You are not just his son. You are your father's son, his child, and the hope of his future. You are the most important thing in the universe to him."

"You don't know anything about my father or our relationship. Not anymore."

She smiled, "No, but I know your father. I know his heritage, both the roots of his lineage and the foundation of his faith. His heart is deeply good, and you would be very close to the center of his heart. The only thing above you in the universe would be Creator. Your father will listen to you. You are a Knighthawk, and a faithful knight already. You can go in there with the same boldness that made your father and grandfather great. They will listen to you. Now, ask and you shall have the Spirit upon you as you go to see them."

"Thank you," Skylar smiled at her, and turned back to face the cross again in prayer.

20

Skylar and Kendall remained in prayer for several minutes before the guard returned to the sanctuary. He was accompanied by one of the monks who remained always on the grounds of the Abbey. He was dressed in a dark brown robe and had his hair cut very short. The monk motioned for the guard to leave.

The older man knelt beside Skylar and Kendall, sitting silently for a moment, before speaking, "Skylar Orion Knighthawk."

"Yes," the boy said quietly, as he remained on his knees, with his head bowed.

"Come with me," the monk said standing to his feet.

He escorted them through the heavy wooden door at the side of the sanctuary. They followed the man down a short hallway, which led to the Council Chamber. Three large over-sized, throne-like chairs were at one end of the room, and six similar chairs lined the sides of the room. The chairs were all raised on a short platform so that even seated the Council members would be slightly taller than anyone standing before them. At the opposite end of the room, where they entered was a large round wooden table with fifteen chairs.

There were only a few people in the room, as they entered. Kendall remained standing beside the door, as their escort directed Skylar toward the front of the room. The three chairs at the end of the room were occupied, as well as a couple of seats at each side of the room. All the knights were formally dressed in dark clothing and royal blue cloaks. Justin Knighthawk, Skylar's father, sat in the center chair. A short, balding man, obviously many years older than Justin, sat to his left. To Justin's right a middle-aged woman, with long blond hair wound high in a bun, sat silently studying the boy.

"We apologize," Brother Lawrence, the short man to the left of Justin said to Skylar," the full Council original had planned to see upon your return, young man. We had hoped to have a ceremony to honor the completion of your Quest. We were informed that you have an urgent message for us, so we've gathered all the members that we could at this time. Many of the members are busy with security concerns."

Skylar stood with his hands clenched at his, trying to remain calm and serious. He had known all the men and women in the room since he was a child. He'd grown to respect them all. Brother Lawrence had been a family friend and mentor of both he and his father. His nerves were shaken since he'd never been in the Council during an official meeting.

The younger Knighthawk stepped boldly forward to begin his address, but he could no longer hold the tears back, "Father, I respect the pomp and circumstance of our rituals, but right now Halie is hurt. She needs our help. There are Varangian soldiers in the fields around the Abbey and deep into the river pass. Myra, the Witch of Tintigal, is with them. Sarah Michaelson was killed when we were attacked by a Zephyrhawk, which was controlled by Myra. Sidney was with me when we were captured and taken to her camp. I think they still have her."

Justin Knighthawk rose from his seat placing his blue cloak on the seat. He stepped down in front of his son placing a hand upon the boy's shoulder, "What did you say? What was that about Myra? We knew of the small Varangian group camped at our southern gate, but no one had informed me about Myra's presence here."

"She knows you," Skylar said looking deep into his father's eyes. "She forced me to spend the night in their camp. She tried getting me to stay with them, and to get me to tell her where Halie was. She talked about you as if you'd been close. Then she gave me drugs and I couldn't stop her from causing me to sleep in their camp. I had nightmares from when I was younger. When my mother died."

Justin knelt in front of his son and placed his arms around him hugging him tightly. Skylar grabbed hold of his father and began to sob on his broad shoulder. The others in the room sat silently, as some bowed their heads.

Brother Lawrence waited a few moments before stepping down and placing a gentle hand on his friend's shoulder, "Justin, what should we do?"

Justin continued to hold Skylar looking around the room at the other Council members, "We'll need to consult with the Knights Security Service to see if we can spare anyone to attempt to rescue Halie and Sidney. We must also make sure to guard all of the secret entrances since she knows many of them."

"Father, that is how we managed to get inside the Abbey. We went through the passage from the Pan's Oak to the Labyrinth."

Justin kept an arm around his son and smiled looking toward Kendall, who stood silently at the far end of the room, "Kendall Pastore, it has been a long time my old friend. You have helped to return my son to me."

The old woman slowly approached where Justin now stood next to his son," Your Excellency, he needed help, and my oath to the Elite Guard remains until I die. He told me of his ordeal, and I knew I must return him to your side as soon as possible. It has been a pleasure to be of service to the Order once again."

"I am grateful for your loyalty and your service," Justin replied smiling at the old woman. "Your place among the elders is always secure, and you should never feel unwanted here."

"I know that I could remain a part of the elders and pass on my wisdom to the Young Ones. We both know that I've always enjoyed my times alone and quietness of the woods."

"Alone, but never forgotten," Brother Lawrence added smiling at his old friend.

Justin looked around at the other council members, "I'll take Skylar for a walk, and discuss where he left Halie and the Varangian encampment. Then I'll meet with the Security Service and determine the best time and way to send some of our soldiers to retrieve them. The addition of Myra here has me very concerned. We need to bring her in and hold her accountable for her terror that she's unleashed on the entire system. I want her brought to justice."

"Yes, Justin," Brother Lawrence agreed and looked around the room at the others, "We all have things to do. Let's get busy. Kendall, please join us. We'll find you some food and you can rest here at the Abbey until it's safe for you to return to your home. Perhaps you can give some of our Security some guidance in facing the soldiers outside."

"Thank you for your hospitality. I am available to help you in any way I can," the Old knight replied, " However, I would like a word Your Excellency in private."

"Of course," Justin replied, "Skylar, please go with Brother Lawrence and sit at the Council table."

Brother Lawrence escorted the boy back to the table where he sat down in his father's chair and waited. Justin and Kendall stepped to the front of the room, where they could talk more privately.

Kendall took a deep breath and looked seriously at her friend, "Justin, I believe that the young girl, Sidney, has been corrupted by Myra."

"Why would you say that?" Justin was puzzled by her words.

"I didn't want your son to worry more, but I saw the girl. She was with Skylar when I found him in the woods. She was holding his head and crying. She was speaking of not wanting to hurt him or to see him hurt. I offered my help and asked her to come with us to my home, but she said she wanted to return to the Abbey for help. However, after I told her the way to go, she left us and went off toward where Skylar later told me the Varangians camp had been."

Justin's brow furrowed, "Sidney has shown the top aptitude as a student and Pledge. I can't believe she would easily be swayed to help the Varangians or Myra."

"That may be, but as Skylar said he was drugged by her to dream of things long forgotten. Myra may have used drugs or other powers to force her to help them."

"Do you think Skylar suspects anything?"

"Possibly, he thinks that she is still in their encampment, as a prisoner. I am worried Justin. If she is under Myra's influence, she could be used to do further harm to Skylar."

"Thank you, Kendall. Your perceptions have always been very great, and I'll heed your warning as we proceed. Please, go and get some food to renew your strength. Enjoy the hospitality of the Abbey and pray that this will all be over soon."

She reached out a hand to him, "You know my prayers are always with you."

Justin took her hand, and then hugged her with his other arm, "You are a dear and loyal friend."

"Always," she replied.

They walked to the table where Skylar sat silently watching his father and Kendall. Brother Lawrence nodded at Justin, as he stepped forward to lead Kendall out of the room

Justin reached a hand to Skylar, and the boy stood in front of him. He placed his hands on his son's shoulders holding him at arm's length looking him over, "Now my son, are you truly okay?"

"Yes, but Halie is in the rocks above the falls. There are some caves there where we hid the night before I crawled down the waterfall. She has a broken ankle and other injuries. She needs our help right away. The camp, where Myra was at, is just below the waterfall. That's where they should be holding Sidney," Skylar answered.

"I am glad that you're safe," Justin said pulling the boy back into his arms. "I'll take the information to Major Krueger. We must pray that they remain safe, as we try to come up with a way to save them."

Skylar eventually stepped back from his father and wiped his eyes, "But everything will be okay, right?"

"Skylar, we have to hold onto hope that everything will work out. Have faith," the man encouraged his son. "Come now, why don't you take some time and tell me more about your meeting with Myra. We'll go to our apartment and you can get cleaned up? You'll feel better and I can go speak to the Major about all of this. You also need to get some rest," Justin led the boy into the outer hallway.

"What is this I've heard about Myra?" a woman asked walking toward them. Her long Auburn hair flowed over her shoulders.

"Aunt Dara!" Skylar ran to embrace his aunt. "I thought you were on Caspian taking care of Commonwealth business."

"I was, but your Uncle Bern and I wanted to be here when you returned. We didn't want to miss the ceremony celebrating your completion of this level of your training. Now what is this about Myra?" she asked, turning to look at Justin, as she held the boy in her arms.

"He was about to tell me what happened when he ran into her in the mountains a few days ago," Justin placed a loving hand on the boy's shoulder. "Perhaps we should finish this conversation in the privacy of our home."

"I agree," Dara said kissing the boy's dirty forehead. "Let's go back to our home and talk there.

"But where is Uncle Bern?" Skylar asked.

"He's helping some of the others to secure the Abbey," Dara replied. "Now, let's go get you cleaned up and fed."

The three walked across the short garden between the Council Chamber and their home. They were soon seated in their living room in front of the fireplace, as Skylar recounted the details about Halie's injury and Sarah's death. He shared how he had been forced to go with Myra to the camp, and about Sidney being captured with him.

"What could she possibly want here? And, why now?" Dara asked.

Skylar looked up at her, "I'm not sure why. I do know she was researching some of the plants and minerals and mentioned their value."

Justin leaned close to his son and looked him deep in the eye, "I am less concerned about that right now. I need you to tell me what Myra told you about herself and her connection to Avalon One."

"Halie told me about her. How she'd left the Fidelian Order," Skylar explained. "Myra said she knew me, you, and my grandmother. She seemed to have been close to our family at some point."

Dara looked at Skylar fighting tears and trying to hide her concern, "Was there anything else that she said to you?"

"Not really. She was pretending to be nice, for someone who was supposed to be our enemy. She said she was concerned for my safety. However, I could sense that there was something that she was hiding. I also think she was controlling the Zephyrhawk that attacked us on the mountain."

Dara could no longer hide the worry in her eyes, "So she never told you how she knew you or your father?"

Skylar thought a moment, "No. She just said I had my grandmother's eyes. She also sang a song to me when I was falling asleep. I think you or grandmother must have sung it to me when I was a baby because it sounded so familiar."

"I'm sure we did, "Dara said, knowing the truth. "Skylar I'm so glad that you're safe. I'm sure the Fidelian Knights will find Halie and protect the Abbey. Now, I think your father was right, you should go get cleaned up. I'll find you some food. Besides I need to speak to your father for a minute."

Dara waited for the boy to leave the room before speaking, "Justin we must tell him the truth."

"It could destroy his trust completely. I fully intend to tell him at some point. I've always planned to tell him, but I'm not sure that now would be the right time."

"Look, my dear brother-in-law, we both know that he needs to know. In the end, it will protect him from her lies and manipulation. You know she'll use all of this to pull him away. I feel very deeply that he will be able to handle this. He needs to know the truth about Myra, for his own good."

Justin sighed and lowered his head, "You're right. Maybe I'm the one who isn't ready for all of this. He needs to know. I just wish we could protect him from the pain, but he is getting older and the truth is bound to come out eventually. I pray that he'll understand why we choose not to tell him before. I promise when this is done, I'll explain everything to him."

Dara hugged him, "God will help us through all of this. I'd better get him some food before he comes back down here."

"Right, and I should go speak to Major Krueger about what we know."

"I think you should take Skylar with you. Besides, you need some food to keep your strength up too. The universe will not fall apart, because Justin Knighthawk took a five-minute break."

"Fine," Justin said sitting back in his seat and watching the fire.

After several minutes Skylar returned to the main room of the apartment. He was cleaned up, and now wore the brown vestment of a Pledge. He sat down with the two of them for a much-needed meal. They didn't talk much, because they were all concerned about the future. They remained hopeful that they would soon have Halie home and put the danger of the Varangians behind them once more.

21

Justin and Skylar finished eating. They walked
to the garden. They followed the main walkway with
several moving sections, which ran the full length of
the Abbey. They passed several patrols as they rode
through the grounds. They were soon ascending the
steps at the front of the Command Center and walked
inside the mammoth structure. They walked past the
security officers at the door, and up the first flight of
stairs to the Administrative offices. Justin had an
office at one corner of the building and two of his
aides waited in the outer office, as they entered.

"Call Major Kruger," Justin ordered as he
walked through the outer office with Skylar at his
side.

"Yes, Sir," one of the aides said pressing a
button on the communication link.

Justin and Skylar entered the large office,
which had a desk beside the window and a conference
table at one side of the room. The took a seat near one
end of the table and waited for the Major to arrive.

Major Krueger was a large man. He stood six-
foot-five with his broad shoulders. He appeared to
tower like a giant in the room. Several advisers
accompanied him and took seats around the table.

"Major, I know you're all very busy with the
Varangians, but I need a favor. This is my Son Skylar
and he just arrived here a short while ago from his
Pledge's Quest."

"A wonderful experience, congratulations," the
major replied looking down the table at Skylar.

Justin nodded at the Major, "It's good that he has finished, but unfortunately my niece is injured in the mountains, and one of our other Pledge's has been captured by the Varangians in an encampment by Quest Falls. We need to see if you can spare a rescue party to go and save them."

The major motioned to one of his assistants, who pressed some buttons on the table as a holographic image of the area came into view, "Our reconnaissance has shown a smaller camp of Varangians, here," the Major highlighted the area next to the waterfall.

"Yes," Skylar said leaning forward to look at the map.

"Where did you last see your cousin?"

Skylar stood and walked down the edge of the table, stopping next to the mountains. He pointed to the pass where the creek began, "It was in this area."

One of the soldiers adjusted the image and closed in on the pass, "Is this better?"

"Yes. You see the three caves here. We were in the cave at the center. I think she planned to return there."

"Thank you," Justin said looking at the map. "What do you think Major?"

The Major took a deep breath and looked down the table at him, "Chancellor, I know this is your niece we are talking about. However, there is no way to offer help currently. I also regret to inform you that our last satellite images from an hour ago show a small group of people working their way around the far side of the mountain. They are likely working their way toward the upper pass."

Justin leaned back in his chair and sat silently for a couple of minutes, "How long will it take that group to make their way to the caves where my niece was last seen."

"If they keep moving at a regular pace, they could reach the area before late in the afternoon."

Skylar leaned forward filled with anger, "And, you don't have any ships to spare to save her before then?"

The Major looked at the boy, "I'm very sorry. We only have a few ships available, and with the Varangians forming an attack on our southern wall we can't rescue anyone right now."

Justin turned to his son, "We'll keep trying. Maybe we can get help from somewhere else. Maybe the Major will find some way. Give us some time, Skylar."

Skylar shook his head and stood, up from the table, " But there isn't time. That's what he just said. Time is running out. Why don't we call for help from the Alliance? Why can't they help us?"

Justin looked at his son somberly, "Son, the Knights have cared for this moon for many generations. We will not call on the help of others unless it is the last resort to saving us."

"Well, I don't know how much more desperate we have to be. We can't wait. We have to do something," Skylar started for the door.

"Skylar please," Justin said trying to grab the boy as he walked out of the room.

One of the men looked at the Chancellor, "Would you like me to go after him, Sir?"

"No," Justin replied. "Let him cool off a bit."

Skylar left his father, Major Kruger and the others in the strategy room, within the marbled walls of the Avalon One Command Center. He descended the long flight of stairs leading down to the ground of the Abbey's Citadel. He could see the lights of the Cathedral above trees of the park. He walked into the wooded park and sat down under a tree looking at the Command Center. Since they were unwilling to help he knew that he had to figure some way to save Halie and Sidney.

He listened to the water running down the stone fountain that sat in front of the Command Center. The painful thoughts continued to work on his heart and mind, as tears began to flow down his cheek. In time the sounds of the flowing water and the exhaustion of worry overcame him, and he drifted off to sleep.

Skylar slept for nearly two hours before drops of rain woke him from his slumber. He sat for several minutes watching the fountain, contemplating all that was happening.

"I can't just sit here and do nothing. If the Knights Security won't act, then I'll have to find a way to force them to help."

He jumped up and started to walk toward the fountain at the bottom of the Command Center steps.

"Skylar," an old monk and groundskeeper approached him.

"Hello, Brother George."

"I'd heard that you were going through your Quest. I also heard of enemy forces lurking about our tranquil moon. I am so glad that you and your cousin arrived safely back here at the Abbey."

"I'm here, but Halie isn't safe. She was hurt and is alone in the mountains. The Security Service is refusing to rescue her. They say their priority is to keep the Abbey safe. It's my fault she was hurt. If I hadn't been on the Quest, we wouldn't have been out there."

"That is not true, Skylar. You shouldn't blame yourself. Your training is a part of growing in the Order of Knighthood, and sometimes people are hurt."

"Yes, but now the Varangian Guard is at the gates of the Abbey, and she's trapped in the mountains."

"My young friend, we cannot possibly know or control every situation in which we find ourselves. Our goal is to remain calm and work patiently through the circumstances."

"That's easy to say, but they're going to try to destroy this place. They may also hurt or kill my cousin. How can I sit here and do nothing?"

"Evil always rears its head. How we respond to evil matters more than the power it tries to wield."

"This isn't some lesson from a book, Brother George. It's a reality. They have weapons and are outside the gates. Halie is hurt and defenseless against such an army of soldiers."

"The Knights Security Service is in place for just such matters. Halie has been trained to face any situation and to keep her wits about her. She is more than capable of handling this situation."

"I hope your right," Skylar said turning toward to face the Command Center.

"I am right, and deep down you know I am. Beware, of rash thinking, my young friend. Consider your thoughts well."

"I have considered them, very well," Skylar said walking away from the old man.

He passed several Pledge's wearing traditional brown vestments with their hair buzzed short. They were sparing with training swords on the other side of the fountain. Skylar had never fully complied with the hairstyle of his peers, and only wore the traditional dress when he was at the abbey. He didn't want people outside the Fidelian Order to know that he was a Pledge.

"Skylar!" a boy a bit bigger than Skylar ran up to him with a hand extended.

"Joel," Skylar smiled and shook his friends' hand.

"I thought you were still out on your Quest. They said they hadn't heard from you or Sidney in a couple of days."

"That's because we ran into a lot of trouble."

"Like what?"

Skylar spent the next several minutes sharing about Sarah's death, Halie's injury, and Sidney's capture. He told him about Kendall helping him into the Abbey, and about the refusal of the Knight's Security Squadron to act.

Joel listened carefully as Skylar shared, and waited to add in, "So, the Security Service is refusing to send any help at all."

"Major Kreuger said it wasn't possible with the Varangian's outside the walls."

"Skylar, I know you're thinking about something. What are you planning? Are you going to try to get out the way you came in and offer help."?

The boy looked off toward the Cathedral, "I thought about that, but they are guarding the entrances to the tunnel system now. Besides, there are more troops in the field outside the Abbey, and we'll soon be at war. I think I have another plan, and I'm going to take care of things right away."

"Skylar, be careful. Consider what you are doing, because getting yourself hurt or in deep trouble will only make things worse."

"I can't sit here and do nothing. I've got to go. Take it easy."

"You too. Keep the faith and grace be with you," Joel said, as Skylar turned to walk up the stairs to the Center.

22

Rain fell steadily. The cool damp morning air engulfed the Abbey. Skylar could see the fog forming on the mountains beyond the Command Center. He could make out several soldiers moving equipment behind the Command Center, out from the underground storage area onto the tarmac. He could see groups of four or five dark dressed security guards moving toward the edges of the walled compound surrounding the Abbey. He knew they were preparing for battle with the Varangians outside the Abbey.

He walked swiftly up the steps, invigorated with the pressing need to save his cousin. When he arrived at the top of the steps leading into the Command facility several heavily armed guards stood actively watching the entire area around them. The glass doors of the facility were now covered with metallic blast shielding, as they prepared for the coming battle.

The boy walked past the first two guards standing at the top of the stairs, without incident or thought. When he was younger, he was a regular fixture around the Command Center, since his father had been in charge for most of his life. Most of the guards knew him well and he was hoping that he could use this to his advantage now.

"Halt!" a guard standing next to the door ordered, as Skylar reached for the handle.

"What's up?" Skylar asked.

"The building has been secured. You can't just walk inside."

"Well, I thought my dad might be inside. I just wanted to talk to him a minute," Skylar said appearing disappointed.

"Wait one minute," the large man replied pressing his earpiece, "Yes, Chancellor Knighthawk's son is wishing to get in to see his father. Right."

The loud sound of metal locks could be heard as the massive door slid open revealing the glass doors underneath. Skylar took a deep breath, sighing with relief. He was glad that this part of his plan was working, but now he knew things were going to get more difficult.

"You may proceed," the guard replied.

"Thank you," Skylar said walking into the building. He could hear the metal shielding locking behind him, as he stood in the open center of the command facility. He looked around the four stories of offices that ran the administration and security of the Fidelian Order. He knew his father's office was on the second floor, and that the entire fifth floor above was the communication center monitoring the flights and security of the small moon.

"Well, stage one was easy. Let's see if I can get to the fifth floor just as easily," he said, as he walked toward the elevator.

He knew that he couldn't just press the button and go to the fifth floor, because it was secured, and only those with the correct security clearance could make it into the communication center. Since he couldn't use a retina scanner to get in he would have to find someone with a pass-badge and try to sneak past other levels of security.

He pressed the number four and got off the elevator. He stood at the railing across from him watching people moving about on the floors below. He had to wait several minutes before he watched the elevator indicate that it was on the fifth floor. Then he pressed the button to go down.

The elevator opened, and two security officers were standing inside, he recognized the young woman who had worked for his father for some time.

"Skylar, what are you doing up here?"

"I got off on the wrong floor," he said stepping to the back of the elevator and looking at the floor.

"So, two then?" she asked turning and pressing the button.

"Yes."

He watched the two officers who continued their conversation. He found exactly what he was looking for. The second officer, a young man, had a security badge clipped to the side of the bottom of his jacket. Skylar looked deeply at the badge and concentrated with all his might. The elevator was slowing to stop, and Skylar kept staring. The badge slowly lifted from the man's coat. Just as the doors opened Skylar reached out and took the badge out of the air and walked out of the elevator toward his father's office.

The doors closed, and he stepped to the railing watching below, as the two officers left the elevator on the ground floor and headed to another elevator that went to the underground facility. Then he returned to the elevator and swiped the badge over a scanner pressing five on the control panel. The elevator began to move up to the fifth floor.

The forbidden domain of the high-security communication center was buzzing with activity. People were speaking into their headsets and communicating various movements of guards and ships around the planet. The map on the wall indicated where the Varangian troops were positioned at the southern side of the Abbey. It appeared that the northern side of the Abbey was clear of any enemy combatants.

Skylar calmly walked around the room. He carefully ducked behind some of the empty cubicles trying not to be noticed. Then he moved again until he saw an open communication station, at the far edge of the room. There were very few people working around the area since they were monitoring maps and troop movements. He slowly slipped into the high-backed chair and slid down trying to remain hidden.

He swiped the card which he had taken causing the computer screen to activate. He then began to type in the needed information for subspace communication, which he'd learned from helping Halie and Ariel on the Pegasus. He was quite familiar with the protocol and very relieved that they hadn't changed much during the current crisis. Soon enough he had opened a sub-communication line within the Alliance network.

"This is Avalon One, to Avalon Prime Space Command," Skylar tried to speak in his deepest tone hoping no one would realize it was a twelve-year-old kid.

"This is Avalon Command, what can we do for you Avalon One?"

"I am trying to reach the Commonwealth bomber Pegasus, Lieutenant Nash Braveheart. He told us that he was staying at the Grand on Avalon Prime. I need to speak. This is urgent."

"One moment Avalon One... Yes, we have the ship registered at the dock here. We'll patch you through to his com-link."

Skylar watched the room around him hoping no one would notice a kid sitting at the console. Everyone was too preoccupied to notice him.

On the planet of Avalon, Nash was sitting at the back of one of the Videoplex clubs. Lights flashed on the stage, as a band played music. However, his interests weren't on the musicians. He was focused on the cards in his hand and the pile of Commonwealth Credits sitting in the center of the table.

A rough-looking man with a beard, wearing green coveralls threw down a few credits onto the pile, "I've got you now, Flyboy."

"Is that so," Nash said still leaning back in his chair. "I'll see you, and..."

The conversation was interrupted by the beeping of Nash's communicator.

"You are playing, or folding?" the large man leaned toward the table.

"I'm calling," he said laying his cards down, as he pulled his communicator out of his pocket and opened it up. "This is Nash, what do you need?"

"Sir, this is Central Command. There is a communication link from Avalon One. They say it's urgent and confidential."

The man across from the table threw his cards down, and Nash pulled the pile of credits close. He pressed the communication link in his ear and closed the communicator, "All right, I'm listening."

"Hold for the link, Sir."

"Nash, it's Skylar. I need your help right away," the boy's voice surprised him.

"Urgent comm-link, eh? Kid, I thought that you were someone from command trying to call us into duty or something. You gave me a little scare."

"Nash, this is important."

"I take it you're finished your test, and they want to throw you some party or something. You can count on Ariel and me to be there."

"Nash, you have to listen. I don't have a lot of time, and if they know I've contacted you I'll be in a lot of trouble," Nash could hear the fear and frustration in Skylar's voice and knew the boy was disturbed by something.

"Okay, you've got my attention kid. What's going on? What's so urgent?"

"Nash, it's Halie. She was hurt while we were training in the mountains. She needs someone to help her."

"Well, I am assuming that since you're contacting me through formal channels, you must be at the Abbey. Why don't you talk to your father or one of those monks and get someone to help you there?"

"Don't you think I've already tried that. Nash, they are all too busy to offer help. They think she'll be okay in the mountains. But I know better. She broke her leg in a fall. Then we were attacked by a crazy Zephyrhawk. There are more dangers there, and she needs to be rescued."

"I don't understand why they wouldn't send out a rescue party?"

"They have some pressing business to attended to and refuse to help."

"So, they allowed you to call me then?" Nash knew something wasn't right, by Skylar's approach.

"Not exactly. I knew you'd want to know. I knew you'd help."

"Well, I can see if Ariel and I can get clearance to come to Avalon One and offer help."

"No, Nash. You have to come. Look, I don't have a lot of time. Promise me you'll come."

"Okay, we'll meet you at the Abbey as soon as we can."

"No, you can't. They don't know I've called for help. Meet me a few miles north of the Abbey. There is a clearing about halfway to the small village, of Harbordale. I'll be waiting for you there."

Nash knew the boy was afraid, and he knew that he shouldn't go without orders. However, he also felt responsible, since they were his crewmates, "Okay, I'll get Ariel. We'll meet you there. I'm not sure how we'll find you, but we'll get there as soon as possible."

"I'll have a short-range communicator with me. When your close enough I'll be listening on channel one, seven, five."

"All right, we'll be there soon. Just keep yourself safe."

Nash reached out and began gathering his winnings from the table, as the large man across from him leaned forward and put his hand on top of his own, "Now, you wouldn't leave without giving me a chance to win some of this back, would you Flyboy?"

"I'd like to stay and play, my friend, but duty calls."

"Duty? There ain't nothing going on around anywhere right now. You owe it to me to let me try to win some back."

"Another time, Wil. I'm serious I've got to go, and, so do you?"

"Me? I'm not on duty for two days."

"I need a favor, old friend. I need you to go get my ship prepped for flight. I want to leave in about an hour."

The large man leaned back, "You're serious. She must be quite the lady, for you to leave our game so abruptly."

"Wil, one of my crew needs my help. I can't tell you more, because the less you know the better it is for you."

"Off the record then?" the big man smiled at Nash.

"Very off," Nash stood up from the table.

"I'll get your ship ready, but next time you're on Avalon for a break I get a chance to win some of my credits back."

"Of course. Now, go get the ship ready, I've got to find my partner, so we can get going," Nash quickly left the Videoplex to find Ariel.

Skylar turned from the communication board and looked carefully around the room. Everyone still seemed preoccupied with their work. He quietly walked to the elevator and pressed the button to go down. He made a small scan of the room around him, as he waited for the elevator, hoping no one had spotted him yet.

"You there!" an older officer at one of the nearby stations yelled at him.

Skylar turned to face the man and quickly turned away.

"Security, we have a Pledge on the communication floor. Request assistance immediately," the man's voice ordered.

Skylar knew he couldn't wait for the arriving elevator, so he turned and ran several feet to an emergency stairwell. He pushed the door open, as a buzzer sounded an alarm. To save time he jumped over the railing and swung to the next level. He was prepared to run down the stairs but saw two security officers at the bottom of the stairwell heading up. He opened the stairwell into the fourth-floor hallway, as another alarm sounded. He then ran for the open main stairway at the center of the floor.

He managed to run down another flight of stairs but could see another officer approaching from the floors below. He ran a few feet down the open area, and then laid over the edge of the railing and lowered himself to the second floor. He swung onto the floor and took a deep breath. Then he repeated the maneuver landing safely in the lobby of the main floor.

Skylar knew the blast doors were over the main doors, so he ran to the stairway leading to the underground levels. He'd been through the two underground levels many times. This was where all the armament and main hanger for the Fidelian Order were kept. He knew that if he managed to get to the main hanger, he could get outside. They were openly moving equipment in and out, so that would be easy. All he needed to do was get to the hanger.

Several guards continued their pursuit chasing the young boy down the descending hallway into the underground. Everyone was so busy in the hallways of the underground that he was able to run in and around people quickly. His size aided him in gaining distance from the guards pursuing him. He was just approaching the door to the main hangar when four guards came through the hanger door.

"End of the line, kid," one of the guards said as he held out his hand for Skylar to stop.

Skylar saw a cleaning cart sitting beside the wall next to him. He quickly took the cart and shoved it toward the two men on his front right, and the cart tipped over. It smashed to the ground and the smell of chemicals filled the hallway. Skylar then ran as fast as he could and fell to the ground as one of the men tried to grab him. The chemicals on the floor made it very slippery, and he slid past the large man and hit the closed door hard. He quickly swiped the security badge he still carried, and the door slid open. He tossed the badge onto the floor and ran through the doorway.

Now inside the main hanger, he ran toward the railing of the catwalk that surrounded the entire room. He jumped over the edge onto the main floor. The guards at the door managed to get inside and continued their pursuit. Skylar ran into the busy hanger, where people were driving equipment out onto the main landing tarmac. Everyone was too busy to worry about some kid, running through.

Skylar had run about halfway across the hanger, but he could hear the feet of the guards closing in on him. A maintenance truck was parked just in front of him, and he could see the barrel of oil on the back. He jumped high toward the barrel, toppling it onto the floor. Then he spun around pulling his sword from his side. He ignited the plasma looking directly at the two guards with a smile.

"It's been nice, but I've got to run," Skylar said with a laugh, as he hit his plasma sword onto the floor igniting the oil. A barrier of fire separated him from the approaching soldiers and gave him the ability to run toward the open door of the hanger.

"Now what do we do?" one of the guards asked as she stopped to catch her breath.

"Don't worry about it," the man with her said.

"What? We were told to stop that kid."

"I know who he is. I'll just report him to his father."

"So, who was he then?"

"Skylar Knighthawk. His father is going to be very displeased that he was in a secure area without permission. I'm sure he'll deal with him. Let's get back to our post. There are more pressing issues right now."

"The Chancellor's son?"

"You know what they say, the children of the leader are sometimes the worst."

"Shouldn't we get him then."

"Trust me it's better to report who it was and let his father deal with him. Now, let's go."

23

Ariel had been sleeping in her hotel room, at the Grand, when the beeping of the door alarm woke her up. She turned on the light moving toward the door.

"Can I come in?" Nash grinned at her.

She glared at him, "Somebody better be dead. Do you realize it's the middle of the night?"

"Well, something like that," Nash replied, as he stepped inside and shut the door. "Skylar just contacted me."

"So, the kid contacts you in the middle of the night and you think it's okay to wake me up. I need my rest. Couldn't this wait until morning?"

"Well, I don't want to interrupt your beauty sleep. Not that you need it. But he was very upset."

"What do you mean? I figured Halie would the one to tell us when they made it back to the Abbey."

"He says Halie's hurt and lost in the Central mountains. He wants us to come and help rescue her."

"Why would he request our help. The Fidelian Knights have their own forces and ships. There's even a small battalion of Commonwealth troops stationed at their disposal."

"He says that the leaders of the Abbey are claiming to be too busy at the moment and are refusing to help."

"Nash, your letting that little kid get to you," Ariel snickered at him, " You know kids overreact and exaggerate things. It can't be that bad or someone would be helping."

"I know that, but he sounds very sincere. Besides, if he's telling the truth we are obligated to help. She's a member of our crew and more important she's our friend. We need to help her. We owe it to the kid to believe his story."

"You know going without orders or getting clearance at least will get us into a lot of trouble."

"I know, and you don't have to come if you don't want to. If you do come, I'll take the blame if we're caught. After all, I'm the one in command of the Pegasus."

"No."

"All right. I understand and I'll talk with you when we return."

"I don't mean, no I'm not coming. I mean, no, you won't take the blame for me. I'm going on my own free will. When do we leave?"

"Can you be to the hanger in half-an-hour?"

"Sounds good, I'll meet you there."

Ariel walked through the door into the hanger twenty-two, and she could see the first rays of the breaking dawn over the Pegasus, which was sitting just outside the hanger on the tarmac. Wil, the large mechanic, was unhooking several plugs from the ship.

"Morning," the large man said smiling as the beautiful woman approached the ramp of the ship.

"Good morning, Wil. I don't suppose it'd do any good to ask how the two of you managed to get clearance for us to depart so quickly."

The burly mechanic laughed, "Well on quiet nights like this it's pretty easy to get a personal favor through."

She stepped into the rear crew quarters and stowed her bag under her bunk. Then she walked into the cockpit of the ship, where Nash was checking his computer controls.

"Good morning," he said with a grin. "I've taken the liberty of setting our course, but you can double-check the coordinates. Then we can be on our way."

"All right," she said, sitting in the copilot's seat and checking over the flight plan. "Wait a minute. This shows us landing north of the Abbey, closer to the village that is on the moon. Why aren't we going to the Abbey?"

"That's where the kid said to meet him," Nash said flipping switches above his head and then hitting the ignition switch turning the engines on.

"Did he also tell you what was going on outside the Abbey?"

"Just that Halie was hurt in the mountains. He said he wanted to meet us outside the Abbey to avoid being in trouble. I assumed with his father. Why? What's going on outside the Abbey?"

Ariel laughed a bit, "So, you think we can just stroll onto the moon unnoticed? The kid asks for help and we are just going to fly over the Abbey and meet him secretly out in the woods?"

"No, but we can come up with a story when we get closer. Then we can meet him where he asked to meet up."

"Well, you should know that there is a small skirmish going on outside the Abbey right now according to what I'm reading on the Alliance communication report."

"What kind of skirmish?"

"It looks like a band of Varangian forces are at the south side of the Abbey. The Knights began countermeasures about two hours ago, and a small battle is raging."

"What are you talking about?"

"Well, being the daughter of an Admiral sometimes gets you information no one else hears about. This is top secret. The Fidelian Order has a small force of Alliance soldiers under their command stationed at the Abbey. They feel that they and that force should be able to deal with this situation without alerting anyone else in the Commonwealth."

"That's ludicrous. If the Varangians are operating in the open at one of the most important sites in the Alliance, the entire fleet should be headed there."

"It may be honor. or the feeling that fear could overtake others in the Commonwealth if word got out. I don't know. What I do know is that it's been deemed a secret for now. That may be the real reason the Fidelian Security officials were hesitant to help Halie."

"Well, I guess we'll have to be on our guard, but we've faced worse situations," he replied as he checked his engine gages.

"I just figured you should know what we were flying into before we arrived."

"Thanks. And, now I think we need to get going, because our friends may need more help than I thought."

"Agreed."

"Then it's off to Avalon One," Nash said pushing the engine control forward, and pressing the communication control, "Avalon Control this is the Pegasus, we are taking off."

"Pegasus, you are clear on flight path one out of the atmosphere."

"Acknowledged," Nash responded pushing the throttle forward.

The triangular ship flew off toward the rising sun over the large capital city below. Within minutes they were out of the atmosphere setting an orbit to slingshot toward the moon of Avalon One.

Ariel hit a few buttons on her computer terminal, "The course for Avalon One is set. It will two and a half hours to our descending orbit there. I'd suggest you try to get some sleep."

"Who says I'm tired?"

"Please. I know you weren't sleeping when Skylar contacted you. I'd say you were probably at the Videoplex with Wil all night, as usual. We don't know what we are going to be facing when we arrive. I think we'd be a lot safer if you caught some rest. Besides, there isn't much to do here until we start our descent onto the moon."

"That's true. I guess you're right. I'll catch some sleep. Wake me when we hit orbit," Nash said heading back to the crew quarters.

Skylar made his way across the tarmac, dodging around several vehicles being prepared to defend the Abbey against the enemy outside the wall. He followed a roadway that led along the northern wall of the Abbey. He could see his duplex far down the roadway as he turned toward the main northern gate.

A dozen soldiers stood around the inside of the gate, and more beyond. He knew he had to find a way through the gate to the field where he planned to meet Nash and Ariel. An armored transport Vehicle turned toward the gate and stopped. Skylar saw that no one was seated in the rear gunner's spot, so he quickly climbed up the vehicle and found a communication helmet in the seat. He put the helmet on and hoped it would allow him safe passage.

The armored transport moved ahead several feet closer to the gate, and Skylar watched the movements around him carefully. Soon they were stopped at the gate.

"Is the northern border still clear," he heard the driver ask one of the guards.

"Yes, I think our forces are gathering a couple of miles toward the west."

"Right. Then we join them, so we can crush those Varangians once and for all."

"Safe maneuvers," the guard replied.

The large vehicle began moving ahead slowly. It followed the road about half a mile to the north of the Abbey and turned left at the first crossroad. Skylar looked around and saw the bushes, as they were starting to speed up. He quickly jumped out from his hiding spot and onto the ground. He ran into the bushes and laid watching the area to be sure he hadn't been seen. He still had a couple of miles to go, but he knew Nash wouldn't be there for some time. He began making his way toward the open field where he had arranged to meet Nash.

Once he was at the field, Skylar took the shortened sword blade and cut some branches to create a covering for himself. Then he crawled inside the shelter. He was now protected from sight and the weather. He was able to get some sleep, as he waited for his friends.

In the command center Major Kruger escorted the two-security officer, who had been pursuing Skylar into Chancellor Knighthawks office, "Sir, we've arrived."

The large chair behind the desk turned slowly revealing the older worn Knighthawk. He leaned forward motioning for them to come closer, "Come, and share what you have for me. Corporal Jarvis, I am told that my son used your identification badge to gain access to the communication level."

"Sir, I apologize. Had I any idea I would have acted quickly. I am not sure how he was able to do it."

Justin smiled at the young security officer, "No need to apologize. Relax Corporal. When my son gets an idea in his head, he makes his way. I asked you here to apologize to you for his young and irrational behavior and to return your badge to you. Major will you give this young man his badge back, so he can return to duty?"

"Yes Sir," Major Kruger said trying to fight a smile.

"Thank you, Sir," The corporal replied.

"That will be all Corporal, return to duty," the Major ordered.

The young man left the office quickly to return to his work.

The major turned to the two security officers and sternly looked at them, "And, what have you two to report to the Chancellor?"

"Corporal Jefferies, Sir. I am sorry Chancellor Knighthawk, we couldn't stop your son. He managed to slip away," the young man reported.

"Sir, I'm Corporal Gregory," the young female officer said, "We accept full responsibility for this failure, along with whatever consequences you deem fit."

Justin smiled and leaned back in his chair, "Neither of you has anything to apologize for. The boy is quick on his feet and very shrewd. If he didn't want to be caught. It wasn't going to happen. He'll turn up soon enough. I assure you that I will deal with him on this matter. Carry on in your duties."

"Yes, Sir," they answered mutually and turned to leave the office.

"Andrew," Justin said looking at the Major, "I may have erred in my advice to you about waiting to rescue my niece. Perhaps we should have tried to save her, and then confronted the forces. I thought I was taking care of the needs of the whole."

"Sir, it was the right call. We must stand firm against this small invasion outside our doors. I have a contingency plan to make a rescue of your niece within the next two days as well."

"Very good. See to it. I would hate if anything were to happen to her. I also don't think Skylar could bear that kind of pain right now."

"Would you like us to keep searching for the boy?"

"No. It would be wasted resources and time. Put the forces to better use against the enemy."

"Yes, Sir."

"Carry on and keep me updated."

"Yes, Sir," the Major said departing the office.

24

Nash brought the Pegasus down in the field, as Skylar ran through the tall grass. The boy ran up the ramp as it closed behind him. The Pegasus maneuvered just above the treetops to avoid being detected by the Abbey Command Center or the Varangians. The stealth design of the spacecraft would only help if they didn't get caught by the more sensitive radar system east of the Abbey.

"Welcome aboard kid it's good to see you," Nash looked back at the boy. So where are we going exactly?"

"The mountains. There is a waterfall. Halie is above the falls in a cave."

"Are you okay?" Ariel gently smiled at the boy.

He tried to smile at her, "I'll be better when we get to Halie.

"I understand," She said reaching back to the boy, "Come here."

Skylar stood up and she pulled him in and hugged him, as he started to cry, "I'm sorry. I'm just so scared."

"It's okay, Sky. We understand. Now, can you show me on the map where we need to go?"

"Sure," he said.

The woman kept an arm around him as he stood next to her. She navigated the map as he soon showed her where he had last seen his cousin. She smiled at him, "All right, kiddo, have a seat. Let's go find her."

"Let's do this," Nash said steering the ship to the west around the Abbey.

"So, what do we do, once we rescue Halie?" Ariel asked as they skimmed over the far western side of the mountain range. "I mean we all want to get Halie to safety, but are we planning to stick around the moon to help?"

"I'm not sure," Nash replied, "I'm kind of flying by the seat of my pants here. I guess we'll have to ask Halie what she thinks. My first response would be to take her to the Abbey and offer to help them. But these crazy knights and their honor may not be to open to more help from a Commonwealth bomber."

"Then why wait for them to ask?" Skylar asked. "We all know that they need more help than they have now, or they would have rescued Halie. They're being stubborn and we should just give them the help they need."

Nash smiled at the boy's boldness, "Well kid, it ain't always that easy. We push too hard in the wrong way, and your father calls an admiral somewhere. Then instead of piloting a bomber, I'll be piloting a garbage scow on the backside of the system. I don't think I'd enjoy that much."

Ariel laughed, "Neither would anyone assigned to work with you."

"What's that supposed to mean?" Nash asked. "Are you trying to say I'm hard to work with?"

"No. I just know that you wouldn't be able to 'fly by the seat of your pants' if your hauling garbage. I think it would be so routine that you'd find yourself a lot more trouble to get into. Anyone working with you will end up in trouble too," She replied.

Skylar laughed at Ariel's leaning forward in the seat, "Hey, I hate to interrupt, but there's the clearing in the rocks up ahead of us. We're here."

"We sure are, kid. Let's swing around to make sure we have the right approach then we'll sit down right in the center of those rocks."

"It looks a bit rockier than the map indicated," Ariel pointed out.

Nash looked out the cockpit window and rechecked his instruments, "I'll take it down nice and slow. Drop the landing gear. I'm sure we'll be okay."

The triangular ship slowly descended into the dark rocky opening. The engine fans blew dust to the sides of the ship, as it softly touched down on the rough rocks below. The dust died down and the rear door dropped down to touch the ground.

Nash walked back to the crew quarters and opened a storage door near the exit ramp. The door slid open revealing an array of weapons. He grabbed a holster and two hand lasers and put them on, and then grabbed a laser rifle. He pulled a smaller hand laser and holster from the wall and turned around, "Here kid. Just in case."

Ariel looked over Skylar at Nash and rolled her eyes. She wanted to tell him that Skylar shouldn't be armed, but she knew it wouldn't do any good. She also knew that they had no idea what they were getting into, and it might be better to arm him for his own protection.

"Ariel, he used one on Hyperborea. I'd feel better knowing he has some defense with him."

"I have my plasma sword," Skylar smirked and pointed to his side.

"You need something with a bit longer range," Nash held the weapon out to the younger boy. "Your part of this crew and we aren't going unarmed. We don't know if that troop of Varangians has reached the pass yet. Keeping ourselves safe is a priority."

"Okay," Skylar answered taking the weapon and locking the belt and holster around his waist "I hope that we don't have to use these though."

"So, do I Sky," Ariel replied as she picked up a sidearm and smaller rifle from the wall before they exited the ship.

Dampness filled the dark, predawn air, as they stepped onto the dry rocky riverbed. Nash pressed the electronic lock on his communicator causing the ship's door to close behind them. A low humming noise followed, indicating that the ship was now shielded from anyone unwanted intruders.

Skylar began to lead them along the rocky path, through the mountain pass. It was nearly an hour of walking before they arrived in the area near the waterfall. The sun was starting to break over the mountains to the east of them. They stopped to look around the open area near the caves above the falls. Making sure to keep themselves hidden near a couple of large boulders.

Ariel pulled out a hand scanner and held it up for several minutes looking around the area in front of them, "The scanner shows a couple of people down near the base of the waterfall, but I'm not getting any readings of anything up here. I think we are safe for the moment anyway. Unfortunately, I'm not seeing any sign of anyone hurt or laying anywhere nearby either."

"I'm not sure if we can fully trust the readings?" Nash said looking over the area. "There are some guards below at the encampment. The rocks may be shielding the scanners preventing us from knowing if Halie's in one of the caves. We may just have to investigate them one by one until we can confirm if she's still here."

"No, we will find her," Skylar replied.

"Okay, kid," Nash replied. "You think she's still in the cave where you were at earlier?"

"No," the boy replied. "We were in the center cave, and the opening is bigger than the others. I don't think she would return there. Just in case one of us told someone else where she was. I also only see two caves right now, but I know there were three here before."

"So, what's your plan, Sky?" Ariel asked.

"To ask for help," he replied sitting down on the ground closing his eyes. He calmed himself before taking a few deep breaths, "God, we need help here. We need you to help us find Halie safe. Show me which cave she's in and keep the Varangians away."

He sat in silent meditation for nearly half-an-hour. Nash continued to watch the area and Ariel continued to scan for any movement. She determined that there were several soldiers at the foot of the waterfall. She still could find no other life signs on the mountain near them.

"We must go to the cave on the right. Straight across from this opening," Skylar said breaking the quiet morning air.

"Are you sure? Didn't you say you had been in the middle cave?" Nash asked.

Skylar looked directly at his older friend, "Yes, I'm sure she's there. Now let's go."

"You heard him," Nash smiled, "Let's go save her."

"I never would have thought you'd listen to the kid," Ariel smiled at Nash and needled his arm. "You always make fun of their ways and think you have all the answers. Maybe you're finally maturing a bit"

"Well, maybe this whole testing and knighthood thing is a good thing. And maybe the kid is just starting to grow up a bit," Nash grinned at her. "Whatever it is, it seems to have made the kid more confident in his decisions. So, I'm willing to follow his lead. Besides, he has such a deep connection with Halie that it would be stupid to discount his opinions on this."

The three friends made their way over the rocky terrain, of the dry riverbed. They found a small indentation in the rocks, which was partially blocked off by rubble. Nash and Skylar began pulling the rocks from the wall, as Ariel scanned for any sign of life from within the dark cave.

"Nash, I'm getting a faint reading from inside,"
Ariel reported, as she knelt to help them dig away at
the crevice.

They finally managed to make the opening
large enough for Skylar to crawl inside. He could see
that the narrow cavity went back about fifteen feet,
before opening into a larger cavern of darkness
beyond where he could see. A faint light glowed in
the darkness at the end of the narrow entry, as Skylar
slowly worked his way inside.

"Nash, I see a small light ahead," Skylar
shouted back to his friends. "The passage is narrow,
but if you move a couple more rocks the two of you
should be able to get in here. I'm going to move on
ahead to see if it's Halie."

Nash looked in at the boy's feet, "All right, but
take it slow. You know from your experience that
glowing in a cave can also come from some other
sources, not all of them are friendly."

"I'll be careful," Skylar said, wiggling around
as he descended into the darkness of the cave.

"Well we'd better get busy," Ariel said pulling
at the fallen rocks. "Even if it is Halie, he can't pull her
out alone."

"It may take some time, but I think we can get
through," Nash agreed to throw some of the stone off
to the side.

The narrow entry was easy to maneuver
through. Skylar had moved past the initial debris. He
came to the larger cavern. He looked below where the
floor dropped a couple of feet and could see Halie
asleep on the cold damp floor. She was wrapped up in
her coat, her broken and splinted leg lay was raised on
a rock. A glow stick illuminated the area near her
head.

Skylar leaned back over his shoulder, "She's
here, guys! She's here.!"

"Is she conscious?" Ariel shouted into the
cavern.

"I'm not sure," Skylar replied. "I'm working my way to her now."

"Be careful," Nash instructed. "Try not to disturb any loose rocks or dirt."

"Okay, I'm going to reach her. The cave opens in here. There's a lot of room," Skylar said sliding out of the narrow entry toward his cousin's motionless body.

Skylar knelt next to his cousin, "Halie. Halie, can you hear me?" He asked trying to shake her just a bit, hoping she was asleep.

"How is she?" Ariel asked sliding down next to them.

"She's not awake. She's not answering me."

"Nash is clearing the rest of the rubble so we have a bigger entrance out of here," Ariel said opening her medical kit. "I'll see how she's doing. Can you use your laser on low to warm some of the nearby rocks? And, help get me some light, too."

Skylar ignited his plasma sword and pressed it between a couple of rocks, lighting up the cave. He then pulled Halie's sword from her side and sat it at another point to help light up the cave even more. Then he piled some large rocks and fired a constant pulse into the rock on low until they glowed with heat.

Ariel quickly knelt on one side of Halie and placed a bio-scanner on her forehead. She read the readings, as Skylar returned to kneel on the other side of his cousin, He held onto her unbroken hand, and said a prayer. Nash laid down the pack, with the bio-regenerator and knelt beside Halie's feet. He pulled another blanket out and tossed it over her frail form, and Skylar helped cover her.

"She's unconscious," Ariel reported. "I'm showing signs of dehydration, shock, mild hypothermia, and some loss of blood. Any or all of them could be causing her unconscious state."

"Can you fix her, Ariel?" Skylar tears running down his cheek. "I mean can you help her?"

"I'll do my best, Sky. You know I will. It may take a little while though."

"What should we do first?" Nash asked feeling a bit helpless under the circumstances.

"We need to get some heat on her. The blanket is helping, but it will take time for the heat of the rocks to warm her up. We also need to get an I.V. going right away to get her fluids back up. I can start to work on her arm and leg after that. Hopefully, that is where the bleeding is occurring. If we don't get fluids and heat going the rest won't matter."

"You get on the I.V., and I'll see if I can warm it up a bit," Nash said shining his flashlight around the small cave.

"What can I do Ariel?" Skylar asked as he kept holding his cousin's hand.

"Keep doing what you're doing. Your prayers and letting her know we are here are just as much help and maybe more," Ariel said, as she reached into the medical kit and pulled an I.V. out of the bag.

Nash moved slowly around the cave and carried three more large granite stones near to where the others were gathered. After stacking the third large stone onto the pile he knelt and pulled out his laser pistol and shot another steady low beam, as the rocks began to glow, and the cave warmed up even more.

"How long before we can try to move her out of here?" Nash asked looking nervously toward the cave entrance.

"I'm not sure. I want to use the bio-generator to regenerate the broken bones and heal the internal bleeding. Then it will be safer to move her, whether she is conscious or not."

"How soon can you start that?" Skylar asked looking up at the young woman.

"I can get started soon. I just wanted to be sure to get this I.V. going first. It would do no good to heal her up if she dehydrates on us before we get her out of here."

"Okay, give me the area scanner you were carrying," Nash said standing up. "I'll go wait by the cave entrance and make sure none of the Varangians come this way. Especially, since we know they were sending a patrol this way last night."

"Sounds like a plan," Ariel replied, handing him the small hand scanner from her utility belt. "Skylar can help me here."

"Whatever you need," Skylar said still holding Halie's hand tightly.

"Here," she said handing Skylar an antiseptic wipe, " I need you to clean that arm your holding onto, so I can put an I.V. in."

Skylar opened the pack and washed off Halie's good arm, causing her eyes to roll around a bit, "She's responding."

"That's good news," Ariel smiled trying to remain encouraging. "Now squeeze her hand tight, so I can get this needle into her arm," she instructed, as Skylar complied and soon, she was able to have a back of saline dripping into her arm.

Ariel then pulled out the large box with the bio-generator and removed the lid. She pulled out the arm of the mechanism and then moved the wand from the side of the device. She pricked Halie's finger and the machine began processing the information. It took about five minutes before a buzzer alerted her that the device had matched to Halie's DNA.

"Alright, step one is done," she said, smiling to reassure Skylar that things were going to be fine. "Now, we run the arm of the device over her broken leg, so that it can take the scan to determine what needs to be repaired. In about another five minutes it should start the process of speeding up the healing process."

Skylar closed his eyes, as he held his cousin's hand. He was starting to relax for the first time in days. He had hope that they would soon get his cousin to safety.

"Skylar," Ariel roused the boy.

"What? I'm sorry."

"It's okay, I'm done with her leg. Now I need to move her over a bit to make room, so I can extend the arm, and let the machine start its work on her arm."

The two of them gently slid Halie closer to Skylar. Ariel repositioned the bio-generator and began scanning the arm. Then she checked the hand scanner on Ariel's head and read the vital signs once more.

She smiled at Skylar, "She's going to be fine. She seems to be responding to the process quite well."

"I wish I could be so sure."

"I was trying to be reassuring before, but the newest vital readings are showing improvements already. She'll need fluids for quite a while because if we bring them up too fast it could throw her into shock again. However, the bleeding has stopped, and her blood pressure and temperature are returning to normal."

"When will she wake up, Ariel?"

"She may need a bit more fluid before she wakes up. Her body's still in recovery mode. We just have to give it the time it needs to build her energy back up. We'll just have to wait and see how things go. I know it's hard, but sometimes waiting is still the best medicine."

"Sure," Skylar replied. " I just hate waiting and wish things could happen faster."

"I know, but the good news is that we should be able to move her to the ship soon."

The scanner buzzed alerting Ariel that the bio-generator was finishing the process of repairing her arm. She folded up the device and returned it into the large medical backpack. She looked at the first I.V. to see that it would soon be empty. She ran another scan over Halie's body and sat silently looking at her friend for several minutes.

Ariel made another scan and leaned across Halie's still motionless form, "Skylar, I want you to go get Nash for me. I need to speak to him a moment."

"Okay. Are we going to get her out of here soon?"

"Please just go get Nash," She gently encouraged, as the boy made his way up the narrow entry.

Nash and Skylar soon returned and knelt next to Halie waiting for the report from Ariel. "The broken bones and internal bleeding are fixed. She has stabilized and seems to be coming out of shock. She's still dehydrated, so we'll need to keep the I.V. flowing. However, if we think we can safely find a way to move her I think we should get her back the Pegasus. There is better equipment to monitor and help us there."

Nash looked around, "I think the hardest part will be getting her through the entry out of this cave. We need to crawl ahead to pull her on a transport board. Once we are outside, we can activate the anti-gravity device on the board and walking her back to the ship will be easy."

"We have to move her as carefully as possible," Ariel encouraged. "I know it'll take some work getting out of this cave, but I still think it would be better to get moving."

"We will take it soft and slow," Nash said. "First, we move her onto the board, and then I'll attach a rope to the end. I'll go out ahead and pull the board, as you two guide it out of the small cave entrance. Start packing up, kid."

"Sounds good to me. I'd rather get her out of her than stay any longer than we have too," Skylar agreed.

"Ariel will need your help kid, so you're staying inside when I go out. Just help her along."

"Like I said the plan sounds good," the boy replied anxiously, as he began packing things up into their backpacks. " Now, let's get Halie out of here."

Nash pulled a small three-foot-long hard mesh board from the medical kit. He pressed a few buttons, as the mesh and metal board expanded to six feet in length. Ariel and Skylar rolled Halie's body on to her side, as Nash lay the board tightly beside her. Then they rolled her softly back onto the board. Nash pressed the side button causing nanites in the fabric to form the bed to the edges of Halie's body. Ariel tightly secured the four straps over Halie's form, as Nash tied his rope to the end of the transportation board.

"Are we all ready?" Nash asked.

They shook their heads in response, and Nash helped them position the board so that Halie's head was at the edge of the entry canal leading out of the cave. Then he crawled toward into the entry and pulled the board, as Ariel and Skylar lifted it into the narrow passageway. Nash pulling while Ariel and Skylar pushed. It took some time, but when they reached near the mouth of the cave they stopped. Nash made another scan of the area to be sure they were still alone. Ariel and Skylar positioned themselves at Halie's sides and waited for Nash to give the go-ahead.

"Alright," Nash said, "We're almost clear of the cave. Ready?"

"Okay, we got it," Ariel replied.

"One. Two. Three. Push," Nash pulled as they lifted, and the emergency lift board slid to the edge of the cave entrance.

Nash now stood outside the mouth of the cave holding the rope tightly, as they continued in slow movements of pulling and pushing to move Halie through the opening. Nash could see the edge of the transportation board just inside the dark cave. He held the rope tightly, but suddenly the rope snapped, and Halie and the board slid back into the darkness. Nash jumped forward into the cave reaching out trying to grab hold of anything to keep Halie from slipping back into the depths of the cave.

Inside the cave, the board suddenly jolted toward Skylar and Ariel, as they tried to stop the board from sliding any further. The board managed to slip back about five feet and shoved Skylar onto his back against the wall. Ariel managed to stop the board and held it tightly as Nash quickly grabbed the opposite end.

"Is everyone okay?" Nash asked.

"I think I'm okay," Ariel replied. "Sky, are you, all right?"

The boy sat in the dark silently biting his lip, trying to fight the pain in his foot which was pinned beneath Halie's body.

"Skylar," Ariel repeated. "Are you okay?"

"Hey kid, we need you to talk if you can."

Skylar took a slow deep breath to try to fight the tears, "I'm fine, let's just get Halie out of here."

Ariel tried to look at the younger boy in the dim light of the cave, "You're definitely, not fine. But I guess we'll have to worry about that when we can take a better look at you."

"Okay," Nash replied. "I've reattached the rope, so we can try again."

It took several more pulls, pushes, and twists before Halie was of the cave. Nash managed to slide the board carefully onto the flat ground, in the open-air morning air. Ariel pushed Skylar up out of the hole and tossed out the remaining gear, which they had been pulling behind them.

Skylar sat on the rocks trying to let his eyes adjust to the bright late morning sun. Ariel ran a quick scan over Halie's body, as Nash adjusted the blankets and straps to be sure she was safe on the transport board.

"She seems to be doing well," Ariel reported turning to walk back toward Skylar. "Now, let's look at that leg and see how you are."

"I'm fine," Skylar said forcing himself onto his feet, as he winced from the pain.

"Look your tough little monster. You're going to sit down and let me look at that leg. I'll determine if you're fine."

"Whatever," the boy rolled his eyes at her.

She stared into his eyes, "I don't recall giving you a choice in this," she said sternly. "Now sit your butt down."

Skylar sighed and complied with her demands. Ariel ran a scanner over his leg and read the indicator. She then pulled out some gauze and wrapped it around the deep scratch on his leg.

"So, how's his leg?" Nash asked as he watched the rocks around them.

"It's not broken, but he has a good bruise. It might be a sprain, so he may limp around for a few days."

"Like I said. I'm fine," Skylar snapped attempting to stand up again.

Ariel glared at him and he sat back down. She finished dressing the wound, "Now, you may get up. You need to listen."

"I'm fine. Can we go now? I don't like this place, and I don't want to stay this close to the Varangians?"

"I'll agree with that," Nash smiled and stood to his feet. He bent over and pressed another button on the emergency board. The edges of the board glowed with bluish light, as it slowly rose about three feet off the ground.

Nash positioned himself at her head and grabbed the end of the cot with one hand, as Ariel and Skylar each took a side to help guide the emergency board along the way. They slowly began to walk over the rocky ground toward their waiting ship. The spinal board stayed level as they walked along.

"Where am I?" Halie's weak voice asked as they came into the clearing near their ship.

"Well Sleeping Beauty," Nash smiled. "There wasn't a prince available to wake you from your beauty sleep, so we three dwarfs thought we'd move you from your cave of rest on our own. I mean we wouldn't want to stress your highness' sleep or anything."

"Funny," Halie said fighting a laugh, "It still hurts to laugh. Seriously, where are we?"

"We're almost to your chariot, my lady" Ariel joked. "Skylar called us to rescue you because the Abbey was a little preoccupied with your Varangian friends."

"How long was I in that cave?"

"I left you up here in the pass, about four days ago," Skylar said as a tear rolled down his cheek.

"Hey, don't you go getting all serious on me now," she chided him. "I'll be fine. I saw you get away from Myra and then went back into the caves. I knew they might follow me, so after filling my canteen I closed off the cave entrance. I remained hopeful that you or Sidney would find your way to the Abbey and bring help."

"We tried, but they cut us off. They captured Sidney and threatened her to try and make me cooperate with them. However, I escaped. I guess that's when you dropped the rocks to distract them."

Halie smiled at him, "Yes. I couldn't do much, but I thought it might help."

Skylar leaned over to give his cousin a small hug, "Then I fell into the river, and an old knight helped me find my way to the Abbey. Unfortunately, the Varangians had called in reinforcements and surrounded the Abbey before we got there."

"So, how did you make it inside?" Halie asked

"Kendall, the old knight, helped me inside through the old hidden passage, by a tree."

"Pan's Oak," Halie smiled. "Kendall? Kendall Pastore?"

"Yeah, you remember her?"

Halie smiled, "She used to guard us when you were a baby. She was there when..." she paused not wanting to bring up any more of the past.

Skylar smiled at her knowingly, "I know. She was there when they bombed the Abbey. She helped take us to Caspian."

"Yes. She was a very kind member of the Elite Guard. So, you made it inside, and your father had you call them for help?"

"Not exactly," Sky pursed his lips. "When I got inside the Abbey and tried to explain everything to my father, Major Kruger convinced him that we needed to worry about the Varangians first. That's when I decided to take matters in my own hands. I borrowed a security pass from one of the communication experts. Then I visited the communications center and called Nash for help."

"So, you just borrowed a security pass from a specialist. That was quite nice of them," she smiled.

"Okay, I might be stretching the meaning of borrow a little bit. But I had to do something."

"Sounds like a pretty wild adventure. You'll have to share the details with me sometime."

"Maybe when you're healed up," Ariel suggested, as they reached the ship. "Let's get you onboard."

"Then we need to figure out what to do from here," Nash suggested as they walked up the ramp of the Pegasus.

They pulled the emergency transport cot next to Halie's bed in the crew quarters. She managed to pull herself on to her bed. Ariel hooked a second I.V. above her bed. Then she checked her vitals once more.

"So, am I going to make it?" Halie jested.

Ariel smiled, "I think so. You may need one more I.V. to help bring your hydration back up fully. We need to get some food in you too. But you're looking pretty good."

"What can I make you, Halie," Skylar asked, excited to be of help to his cousin in any way possible.

"Whatever you bring me will be fine," Halie said smiling at the boy.

"Skylar just get her some chicken or vegetable soup. Her body is still recovering and may not be able to handle anything too heavy for a while," Ariel suggested. "You don't want to overdo it, so just rest."

"Okay," Skylar said opening a packet of soup and putting it into the microwave.

"So, not that I'm not happy to have us all back together," Nash said sitting down at the small crew table, "But, I don't want to risk attracting any Varangian attention. We should decide where we should go?"

"What are your suggestions?" Halie asked.

"That's new," Nash smiled, "We come to you for the advice usually and you want my suggestion?"

"You're the captain of this crew, aren't you?" the young woman said looking at him. "That means we go where you decide. Our opinions just help along the way."

"Well, we have a couple of options. We could go to the Abbey and let them know you're okay. That means facing the music about breaking protocol and misusing the communications center. We could go to the village and hide out a while and hope that the Varangian's move away soon. Then there's also leaving the moon to Avalon Prime."

Ariel looked at her friends, "Look, I've done a good job with Halie and all, but she needs to be checked out by a real doctor. We can't just fly off the planet, without attracting the attention of the Knights security anyway, or worse the Varangians."

"Then it's to the village," Nash said standing.

"No," Skylar said, handing a cup of soup to his cousin. "We must go to the Abbey."

They all stared at the younger boy a bit amazed at his suggestion.

"Are you sure kid?" Nash questioned.

Skylar looked at his friends, "Yes. We have to, 'face the music', as you said. Besides, the Abbey could use our help. The small force of Commonwealth foot soldiers and Knights would be able to push those enemy forces away far easier with the power of a bomber on their side."

"I appreciate your enthusiasm, Sky," Ariel took a breath, "But, the Knights haven't been open to the help from the Alliance. They may not want our help."

"I'm not so sure I want to face the trouble we might be in quite yet, either," Nash said.

"But, you won't," Skylar insisted. "I will. I'm the one that disobeyed the Council's instructions, stole a security badge, called you here, and led you to save Halie. I'm the one who will need to face the Council's punishment."

"No kid, we are a team. I knew what I was doing when I came here," Nash replied.

"He's right, Nash," Halie said. "The Knight's Council will not hold you responsible but will hold him responsible for involving you in their affairs."

"Then why go to the Abbey? We can go back Avalon Prime, and then on to the Excelsior," Nash answered.

"No, Nash. In the end, it will be better if he's honest and faces the Council and his father. They won't destroy him. In returning to tell them the truth of his actions he will earn his freedom and grow in his training. Honesty and responsibility are a core of what we hold dear. Set course for the Abbey, so we can end all of this."

Nash took a deep breath, before continuing, "Alright, we head for the Abbey then."

"One problem," Ariel said. "Skylar also said, that another Pledge was being held in that camp."

"Sidney?" Halie asked.

"They used her to try to get to me. We can't leave her there," Skylar replied.

Halie thought for a minute, "Skylar, she left the camp and returned the day after you left. I kept watch, to be sure you had gotten away. She was gone for a few hours and then returned on her own. Then they sent out their drones again."

"So, what," Skylar replied. "She's my friend. Myra probably forced her to return. They were looking for me and she's there because of me. We have to try to save her."

The others sat silently for a few minutes each waiting for the other to say something that would help them out of the situation. When no one answered, Nash finally spoke up, "All right. There can't be too many soldiers in that camp. We have enough room to land the Pegasus at the base of the falls, beside the camp. We go in hard and we see if we can find the girl, and then we head for the Abbey."

"Skylar," Halie looked up at her cousin, "the consequences of this action could be dire. It could cause a full-scale reaction from Myra and the Varangians."

Skylar stood up, "We can't leave anyone behind. No matter what, we have to try."

"Then, let's make this happen," Nash said with a grin.

"Father, protect us from our own plans. Help us in this endeavor," Halie said, as the others moved into the cockpit.

24

Nash turned on the engines of the Triton Bomber, dust flew around the rocks as they ascended into the air. He kept the Pegasus turned on to silent mode, trying to keep the engines as quiet as possible. The element of surprise would be needed if they were going to be able to make any attempt at saving Sidney from her captures.

"Okay, kid," Nash instructed. "You're going to move into one of the gunner towers, so we can have all the firepower available. We need to take out the Varangian defenses, so we can find the girl. But we don't want to destroy the whole camp in the process."

"Right," Skylar said moving toward the rear crew quarters, and then dropping through a small side door that led into a lower gun.

"I'll take the upper gun," Halie's voice surprised them all.

"No way," Nash replied, "You can't risk your own life."

"I'll keep the I.V. in my arm if that will make you feel better," Halie said with a smile, as she opened the small door leading to the upper gun.

"There's no sense in arguing," Ariel replied. "Besides, like you said last night, I'd rather have her on my side than against us."

"Fine," Nash said as he directed the ship over the waterfall. "We go in hot and heavy. Try not hitting the tents, just guns and anything they try to throw at us."

"Right," Skylar said into the com-link he now wore.

"Roger," Halie said from her perch in the upper gun.

"I'll leave the front guns and scanning to you," Nash looked over at Halie.

"Sounds good."

The Pegasus dropped quickly over the waterfall and hovered just outside the encampment. Five soldiers ran into the open area firing lasers and bullets at the large bomber. Skylar and Halie aimed and fired at the soldiers knocking them to the ground. Several small armed drones flew out of the woods toward the ship firing small cannons and lasers around the ship, but one by one they managed to destroy the entourage.

Nash set the ship down, only a few yards from the first tent, as debris flew around the camp. Skylar crawled up into the main cabin and stepped toward the rear of the ship. Halie remained in the gunner's tower hoping to offer her friends cover fire if needed.

"Where do you think you're going?" Nash asked as he stepped toward the exit ramp.

"I'm going to save my friend," Skylar replied.

"You stay here and give me cover," Nash ordered.

"No, you're not going alone. She's here because of me, now are you going with me or staying here?" Skylar pressed the button opening the ramp and started down.

"Keep us covered," Nash shouted into the ship, "And Ariel, if we are killed, get out of here."

Skylar had already entered Myra's tent but found it empty. Nash stepped inside, as Skylar turned toward back toward the guards' tent. Two soldiers stepped out of the tent, and Nash unleashed several rounds at them. They fell to the ground allowing Skylar to run into the tent.

Skylar saw his friend laying on the bed at the rear of the tent, and ran to her side, "Wake up Sidney. Wake up."

Nash ran in behind the boy, "Let me get her. We can't stay here too long."

"I'm sorry Sidney," Skylar's tears ran down his face. "Wake up, please wake up."

"Wake up," Myra's mocking voice came from the shadow at the edge of the tent, "Oh please wake up."

"You are a sorry child, my boy. If you've come to rescue her. She's already told us where your cousin is, and now she's nothing more than a vegetable."

"No!" Skylar swung around pulling the plasma sword from his side and igniting it as he ran toward the woman.

Myra spun around and wielded her scepter toward the boy. She flashed plasma and electric shock waves that tossed the boy across the tent knocking the table over as his body flew away from her. Nash used the opportunity to pick up the girl and carry her out of the tent. Skylar jumped to his feet and ran toward the woman once more.

"Stop!" the woman once again used her scepter to throw him back to the ground. "If you were to kill me then you'd never know my secret, my boy."

Skylar stood again, "I don't care about your secret or anything you think you might have for me." He pulled the handgun from his side and shot toward the center of the roof above them causing the tent to collapse. Then he jumped and slid out the door leaving the woman caught heavy canvas.

Nash ran toward the ramp, as Halie fired a few shots behind them making sure they had a safe lead. Skylar followed Nash into the ship and shut the ramp. Ariel took the ship quickly into the air and headed above the trees.

Nash laid the younger girl on a bed and returned to the cockpit to help Ariel, as Skylar knelt next to his friend. He could see bruises on her face and hands, as she struggled to breathe.

Halie was soon sitting beside him, "Let me see what I can do?"

"No!" Skylar cried. This is all my fault. She's hurt and it's all my fault."

The ship shifted slightly, as Nash increased speed, and Ariel stepped back into the crew quarters, "Thought maybe I could help."

"What about Nash? Doesn't he need some help?" Halie asked.

"He said he can manage. He's returning to the field where we landed this morning to try and reevaluate our next move," Ariel replied. "Now, let me get a look at your friend here."

"Sky, Sidney's in the best hands I know. I think I'll go up and offer Nash some help with the ship."

"You aren't in much better shape," Ariel replied, "You should be resting."

"There's no time for that now," Halie said turned to go to the cockpit. She staggered a bit as she walked forward.

"Will she be okay?" Skylar asked tears rolling down his cheeks, as Ariel ran her scanner over Sidney's body. "This is all my fault. I should never have run away from the camp."

"Skylar," Ariel stopped and looked into the boy's eyes. "Stop talking like that. This is Myra's doing and not yours."

"But she wanted me. I mean she was trying to get me to stay, Ariel. She made me dream of the day my mom died. There was something about Myra. If I would have cooperated with her then Sidney wouldn't be hurt right now."

"You know that's not true," Ariel said, as she put an I.V. into the girl's arm. "If you would have stayed, you'd be hurt just like her. And, worse yet Halie would be dead. That witch is pure evil, and you are good."

"But, part of me wanted to stay with her."

"Skylar, she was manipulating you. Now, we need to try to help Sidney. I'm going to run a blood sample through the computer and see what I can figure out. You sit here with her and keep her comfortable."

"Okay," Skylar said, as he placed a blanket on his friend and held her hand.

Nash looked at Halie as she sat in the co-pilot's seat, "What do you think you're doing? You should be back there resting. You've already been through way too much."

"We need to get this ship to safety, and the last time I knew it was better to have two of us at the helm. Besides, Ariel's going to be busy with Sidney. She's in bad shape."

"Yeah, I just hope Ariel's able to do something to help her."

"I know she'll do her best, and that's all that can be asked," Halie said wincing from the pain in her body. "So, what's the plan?"

"I was going to land in the field north of the Abbey, where we met Skylar early this morning. I figure we can regroup and then head to the Abbey."

"I'm not sure that we'll have much time after all Myra's not going to sit back and rest. She'll probably move on the offense," Halie replied, as she grabbed her stomach and doubled up in pain.

"Halie. Halie!" Nash flipped a couple of switches, as the ship stopped and hovered above the trees. "Ariel! Get up here! Now!"

"Stay with Sidney. Keep her comfortable," Ariel said smiling at Skylar, as she walked toward the cockpit.

"Hurry up!" Nash shouted again.

"What's going on?" Ariel asked entering the cockpit.

"It's Halie, she just doubled up in pain. I'm not sure if she passed out?"

"Oh no," Ariel said kneeling in front of her friend. She quickly ran a scanner over Halie's head and stomach. "I'm not sure. She could be having an allergic reaction to the pain med's or there may be something more serious going on?"

"More serious, like what?"

"I don't know. We need better equipment and more time. It could be from not eating. It could be internal bleeding that didn't register."

"So, we need to get her to the Abbey. We need their help."

"That would be best, but we need to get her onto a bed right away," Ariel said.

"Okay," Nash said standing and wrapping an arm around Halie, as he and Ariel helped to guide her back into the crew quarters.

"What's going on?" Skylar cried as they laid Halie on the bed across from Sidney.

"She overdid it," Ariel said.

Skylar began bawling, "What do you mean. We were saving her."

"And we are," Nash said, placing his hand on Skylar's shoulder, as he turned to go back to the cockpit. "We're taking you all home, back to the Abbey where you belong."

25

     Nash guided the ship over the tree line to the west of the Abbey. He was more worried about avoiding the Varangians now than being detected by the Abbey Command Center.

     Ariel managed to get adjust the I.V. in Halie's. She ran the scan on Sidney's blood and sat at the table looking at Skylar. "I don't know if I can do much more."

     "You've done your best," Skylar said tears continued to run down his face.

     "Stop the waterworks, Bud," Halie said raising her head and grabbing Skyler's arm.

     "Are you okay?" Ariel asked as she knelt and scanned the young woman.

     "I'm starting to feel a bit better. I don't know what happened."

     "Maybe we tried to get the food and water in you too fast," Ariel said. "I told you to take it easy."

     "I guess I should have listened."

     The sun was setting as Nash directed the Pegasus over the plains, "How's everything going back there?"

     Halie was now sitting up again, with an arm around Skylar, "I'm feeling quite a bit better."

     "Her vital signs are returning to normal," Ariel replied. "I think she just overdid it and needed a bit more rest."

     "That's good news. What about the girl? How's she doing?" Nash asked.

Ariel opened her scanner, "I can't imagine what they did to this poor kid. The chemicals are off the charts. It contains high levels of Avalonian Nightshade. I'm not sure why she isn't dead yet. And, I'm not sure there is anything that can be done to save her. I know we can't do anything more than to try and keep her comfortable."

"Thank you for trying Ariel," Halie said squeezing Ariel's hand. "You've tried your best, and that's all anyone can do."

"Well," Nash looked out the window, "We'll need to make some plans."

"So, I take it we haven't arrived at Abbey?" Halie asked.

"I decided we should take a moment, before walking into something we aren't prepared for. I've been monitoring communications while trying to remain as silent as possible throughout our flight."

"What's the news, Nash?" Ariel asked bracing herself for the worst.

"It seems Myra and the Varangians are set on trying to take the Abbey over. They've called for backup forces and there is a Varangian destroyer in orbit awaiting their orders for help."

"What about the Knights? Surely the Order was given to call for help from the Alliance?" Ariel inquired.

"They have kept them informed of the situation, but they haven't formally made any request yet. They are still deciding if they should or not."

"They won't," Halie interrupted. "The Fidelian Knights are the sacred protectors of all that is holy and the history of all our people. They take their role so seriously that they often feel they cannot rely on others for help."

"I assumed that too," Nash agreed.

"I don't see the problem," Skylar interrupted. "We need to get to the Abbey to get Halie fully recovered, and to get the help Sidney needs. The Knights need a bomber since there are only a handful of fighters available on the moon's surface. So, let's get going."

"It ain't quite that simple, kid. There are a lot of things to consider. First, we can't just land whenever we feel like it. I'll have to break the communication silence, so they can drop part of the shielding to allow us to land. And, I'm not sure what the reaction of the Varangians will be when a Commonwealth bomber lands at the Abbey. Especially, after our attack on her camp."

"Good," Skylar said hitting his fist on the table. "Maybe the surprise will make them think twice and then they'll retreat. Maybe they'll see us and think the Alliance is sending help now."

"Or," Halie said putting her arm around her cousin, "Maybe it will force their hand, and they will feel they need to attack with the full force they have available."

"Sometimes it's better to fight," Skylar pushed.

"Sometimes," Halie said. "But like you said there are only a handful of fighters on the moon. A Varangian Destroyer can carry up to sixty fighters, and twenty-five bombers. Not to mention the power of their laser cannons, which could pound the Abbey defenses."

"Right," Nash agreed, "The laser cannon fire would reduce the shielding in less than an hour, leaving the Abbey vulnerable to fighters, bombers, and foot soldiers."

"So, we're just going to sit here and do nothing," Skylar pouted.

"No," Hallie said. "We are going to the Abbey. Nash just wanted us to know what we were getting into, and the consequences we'll face. The choice is very clear. We must let them know I am okay. Then we offer aid."

"She's right," Ariel said. "We may be here without orders, but to know what we know and to ignore the situation would be worse than what has already been done."

Nash rose to his feet, "We go to the Abbey then."

"Everyone to their stations," Halie said, picking up the I.V. from above her head. "We're in this together."

The four young people took their places in the cockpit, Nash and Halie in the pilot and co-pilot position, Ariel in the navigation and communication control, and Skylar in the research and backup control. Nash turned the ship and they could see the lights of the Abbey a couple of miles ahead of them across the forest below.

"Alright Ariel, turn on the com," Nash said.

"Right."

"Avalon One, this is the Pegasus. We are coming your way. We have the Knight, Halie Ambrosias, requesting permission for landing at the Abbey," Nash said, as he continued to rise into the lower radar zone, and turned the engine silence off.

"Pegasus, this is Abbey Command, please hold your current position."

"We're heading your way Abbey Command," Nash said moving the ship forward slowly across the sea of grass below.

"Roger that Pegasus continue your present course."

"They just dropped the northern part of the shield near the Command Center," Halie reported.

The v-shaped ship was soon descending onto the tarmac, beside the Command Center. Nash turned the engines down and looked out the window toward the hanger at the base of the Command Center. Dozens of troops were moving around the hanger area transporting supplies around and loading ships with weapons.

"Well, it looks like we'll have to face the music right away," Nash said watching a small group of people walking toward them from the hanger. Three armed guards led Justin, Dara, and Bern, along with two medics riding a small transportation cart behind them.

Skylar leaned forward to look out the window at the group approaching, "They don't look happy."

Halie reached over and patted the boy's shoulder, "Just tell the truth, kiddo. It will go better if we are all just honest with them. The truth always sets you free."

"Here we go," Nash said pressing the switch to open the ramp.

The four young people walked slowly down the ramp. Ariel escorted the floating emergency board with Sidney's body. Nash stood out in front of the others, and Halie leaned on her young cousin for support. The group of officials stopped a few feet from them, Justin stood a bit in front of the others.

"Lieutenant Nash Braveheart, reporting in, Sir. I've come to return your niece and son to you, Chancellor."

"Lieutenant Braveheart, I do not recall receiving any orders for a Commonwealth mini-cruiser, and I don't recall requesting one."

"No, Sir. I want you to know that I take full responsibility for my ship and my crew. We are indeed here without orders or permission from anyone. We used deception to allow us onto the moon, so that we could conduct maneuvers for personal gain, of sorts," Nash answered.

"Personal gain?" Justin asked studying the young man.

"It's beyond the capacity of this crew's dedication, to leave anyone behind," Nash replied.

"I see," Justin said stepping to the side and looking over the bomber, "So, what you're saying is that it's okay to take matters into your own hands when you're aware of the injustice of those who should have taken action or sought help from their friends."

Nash swallowed hard and glanced down at Skylar, who had a look of surprise, "Yes Sir. And, I have no regrets. I further offer the Pegasus and her crew to help in whatever way you deem necessary to face your current situation."

"I'm not sure you can offer services when your ship is under the command of the Commonwealth Alliance. This matter is a matter for the Fidelian Order to deal with."

"That is very true, Sir," Nash said looking toward President Ambrosius and her husband. "However, as part of the Commonwealth force, I am obligated to protect the highest members of the Alliance's officials when I find that they are in danger."

"Lieutenant Braveheart. It is still Lieutenant, and not Sergeant or corporal, correct?" Dara smiled as she stepped around Nash to hug her daughter and nephew.

"Mother, I am so glad to see you."

"And, we are all glad to see all of you," she said turning back to Nash, "Even if you came here without proper authority."

"As for help," Justin said extending a hand to thank Nash, "I appreciate that you came to save my niece. Even if you were covering our weaknesses. We would like to invite you to join our discussion in the Command Center, as we decide our next move with the Varangians. Your help is greatly appreciated."

"Yes, Sir."

"And as for you, young man," Justin said stepping toward his son. "You know better than to disobey not only my instruction but the decision of the Council and other leaders of the Order. You were irresponsible in your actions, even if your motives were in the right place."

"I'm sorry, father. I know I let my emotions drove me. I also realize that I'm not in good standing any longer. But, saving Halie and Sidney is worth it."

Justin hugged his son and then knelt in front of him, "I'm glad that you fought to save your cousin and your friend because loyalty is very important. However, you owe a lot of people an apology."

Skylar swallowed hard, "Such as?"

"To start with the communication specialist, whose badge you stole. The head of the Knights Security Service. Not to mention the several guards who you put to the test. Then, of course, your aunt and uncle who you've worried to death through all of this. You've already apologized to me, and I accept your apology. Now, let's get going inside."

"After I start my apologies," Skylar said as he ran to his aunt and hugged her, "I'm so sorry."

"It's okay," Dara hugged him tightly. "We are family, and we'll always forgive and stick together."

Bern smiled and put his hand on the boy's shoulder, "Young man, we all owe you an apology too. The Knights are not supposed to leave their own in harm's way. There are times when we senior members of the Order forget the zeal that brought us to where we are. We overthink and analyze things and forget that sometimes action is the right thing."

"But dad we are taught to remain in control and not let passion drive us," Halie said with a smile.

"We're not robots, my dear. We must not be overly rash in our decisions, but zeal and emotion are not our enemies," he smiled at his daughter.

"There's still the matter of the Varangians," Dara said, "I think we need to get to the Security Council and figure out our next move."

"Agreed," Justin said, "They're in my office waiting for us now."

Bern escorted Halie to the medical transport cart, "I'm not needed in the meeting, so I'll accompany Halie and her friend to the infirmary. They can give her a good checkup and look into what they can do to help Sidney."

"I think that's a great idea," Justin agreed. "I think we'd all feel better if one of us were with her. Skylar, I want you to accompany your uncle as well."

"But I want to listen in on the meeting with the security council. It's educational, after all."

Justin smiled at his passionate son, "While it may be educational, I think it would be better for you to stay with your uncle Bern and Halie. You haven't had any rest from your testing and run-in with the Varangians. Then you were off saving your cousin. It's time to let others handle things for a while and get some rest for yourself. Besides, it wouldn't hurt for you to get checked out too."

Skylar took a deep breath, "Yes, Sir."

"Have you been checked out, or rested at all since you left me?" Halie asked, him as they sat next to Sidney on the side of the medical cart.

"I rested with Kendall one night. I've also taken a couple of naps."

"But," Dara scolded, "No, you haven't rested or been checked over yet yourself."

"Then I think you'd better go with me. Besides, you haven't officially been recognized as completing the Pledge's Quest yet, and as a simple Pledge Trainee you are required to remain with your mentor." Halie said with a grin.

"I think I've met the requirement for the test and then some," Skylar said glaring at his cousin.

"But, technically," Bern said with a smile, "your cousin is correct. Until the ceremony officially recognizing your advancement you are required to remain with Halie."

Justin put a hand on his sons' shoulder, "Besides, I don't recall saying this was up for debate. I want you to accompany your cousin. There is no more discussion."

"Yes, father."

The small group walked through the hanger and then into a hallway, where there was a security transportation elevator. This elevator was only available to security and high-level officials. A guard opened the elevator, as they walked up to enter.

"Level two, and three," Justin instructed as they entered."

"Yes, Sir," the guard answered, pressing the communicator on the side of his helmet," Levels two and three."

The door shut, and the elevator soon arrived three levels up stopping two floors above the ground. Dara, Justin, and Nash stepped out and headed for Justin's office. Then the elevator continued up to the third floor. The medical cart rolled out of the elevator, with Bern, Halie, Skylar, and Sidney. They moved off to the medical infirmary, medical labs, and experimental design labs of the Fidelian Knights.

26

Justin led the others into his office. Six of the twelve members of the highest council of the Fidelian Knights were already seated around the table, with Major Krueger and three other military men seated together at the table as well.

"Ladies and Gentlemen," Justin addressed the room as he assumed his chair at one end of the table.

His sister-in-law Dara took the chair opposite him. Brother Lawrence was already seated at his side. Nash and Ariel took open seats along the wall where several other people were observing the meeting.

"We all know the situation. The Varangians, under the command of Myra, have been holding a position at our southern wall. While we've debated about proper procedures and what might be best for the traditions, they have been calling in help. Major what is the latest update."

"Sir," Major Krueger leaned forward. "A Varangian Star Destroyer is hiding in the asteroid belt just past the outer moon of Avalon. We began procedures to move the children, most of our teachers, and part of our leadership away from the Abbey to ensure their safety. Many of them are safe in the village as we speak."

"Very good," Justin said. "How soon will we have transport ready to take them off the moon?"

"Sir?" the Major looked bewildered and disturbed.

"Major, the continuation of the Order of the Fidelian Knights is paramount. We have faced wars and trials before. We cannot risk losing those young people in training. Nor can we risk losing a whole generation of leaders and teachers."

"That was why we started moving some them out of the Abbey and into the village."

"When the Varangians begin a full attack the village and anywhere else on this moon will fall under their power. We must remove them from the moon to a safe location on the planet, or somewhere else. How soon can you make it happen, Major?"

"Captain Thomas?" the major asked the woman sitting next to him.

"Sir, I will get right on this. However, we'll need assistance. We can't send the few fighters we have as escorts or we'll be left vulnerable if they attack."

"It isn't if, but when Captain," Justin said sternly. "We have waited too long, and that is our own doing. We must seek help immediately. Use the transports and fighters we have and get everyone off this moon that you can. The ground forces will need to step it up until the Alliance can send aide."

"I concur," Dara said standing up from her chair. "The Commonwealth Alliance and the Knights have been together too long to allow the Varangians and that woman to destroy our greatest knowledge and treasures. I will send a secure call for the Alliance to give aide."

"And, Justin said, "You'll be on the first transport off of this moon."

"My place is here with the Order in this desperate hour," she replied sitting back in her chair.

Brother Lawrence now stood, "Begging your pardon, Madam President, but your place is back at the capital on Caspian. The entire Commonwealth needs solid leadership, and you must return there right away."

"Dara, he's right," Justin urged," Captain make sure the first transport is headed for Caspian and be sure the President and her husband are on board."

"And, what of the Council of Twelve," Dara asked looking at Justin.

"My place is here leading the Fidelians to protect our history."

"And, if the Abbey should fall?"

"That is why six of our members will be escorted away from the moon, along with you. They'll ensure the continued direction of the Order if destruction should befall the rest of us."

"It would be a travesty to lose such a great leader," she said sadly.

"It would be a greater travesty to ignore our responsibilities. The matter isn't up for debate. Let's make this happen."

"Yes Sir," the Major agreed.

Brother Lawrence leaned forward, "I request to remain here."

Justin shook his head, "You've always been a trusted adviser, my old friend. I would hate to risk such wisdom."

"I feel that I can best serve by leading a vigil in the Cathedral. We know, after all, the true power source of our faith."

Justin looked intently at the older man, "Very well. As always you are wiser than we are in such things. You will go to the Cathedral. We'll gather the children and leaders left, as well as the old ones who are less able to fight."

Brother Lawrence smiled, "Then the true powerhouse will be working for the greater good of all."

"Everything is set. Let us go with mercy and strength. The meeting is adjourned," Justin said standing to leave the room.

Everyone left the room, leaving Dara and Justin alone. She walked up and took his hands in her own, "I am worried."

"Do not worry. For who of you can change even one hair of your head?"

She smiled at him, "Don't quote the ancient texts to me. I have them memorized. And, while I know that greater love is to lay down one's life, I don't see this as a need for you."

"Your place is at the capital, and mine is here Dara. We both know this to be true."

"I know. I will go, but I wish you were with me."

"We can stay in constant prayer that this Abbey will stand, and if it's God's will that I perish then I am ready."

"What of Skylar?"

"He and Halie are a part of the crew of the Pegasus. If the Commonwealth is joining the fight, then they will serve where they are called to be. Now, go and check on your daughter and get on the next transport off Avalon One."

"Take care," she said embracing him, hoping it wouldn't be for the last time.

Doctor Jennings ran the scanner in her hand over Halie's leg, "Well, it appears the medic on your crew is trained quite well. Your vital signs are looking good. The bio-generator has produced about a ninety percent recovery of your leg and arm. They'll be tender for a week or so, but you should be okay to go with some rest."

"How much rest?" Halie asked.

"I'd say you should be good to go in the morning."

"I'm sorry, I'm not staying here in the infirmary until tomorrow."

Bern looked sternly at his daughter, "You will do what the doctor recommends. You've been through a lot, and your body needs time to recover."

"Your father is correct," the doctor continued. "If you don't rest you are likely to relapse to a worse state."

"Okay, what if I promise to rest, can I be released. I mean I'll likely rest better in my own quarters than in some infirmary bed."

"Well, I guess I could allow that. You must promise to go and get the needed rest. I will not clear you to return to duty until tomorrow afternoon, so you'll need to follow my instructions either way."

"Sounds good to me," the young woman said, putting her long black jacket on.

"I mean it," Doctor Jennings said, "the computer will not register you as released for duty until noon tomorrow. I don't care if this whole facility is under attack, you will not be doing anything."

"I understand," Halie replied as they left the room.

"So, now what?" Skylar asked.

"We go to your father's office to find out what they've decided," Halie said.

Bern looked down at his daughter, "I Believe Doctor Jennings was quite clear. You're to rest until tomorrow. I think you and Skylar should return to our apartment and rest there for now. Besides, we don't know how long we'll have before the Varangians decided to attack, and you two need to get some rest while you can."

"We will be okay, dad," Halie said hugging her father.

"That won't work this time," the middle-aged man said with a smile. "Your mother would kill me if I didn't make sure the two of you went back to the house. Now, I want you to go back to our apartment. I am sure that we'll be along shortly. Then we can update you."

"Yes, father," Halie agreed, as Bern went to the elevator, and they walked toward the main stairway leading to the front door of the complex.

"Are we really leaving?" Skylar asked.

"He's right Sky. We both need to get some rest. The Varangians outside I don't think we'll have a lot of time before our help will be needed. We should rest while we can. It's not like anyone is going to listen to us in the committee meeting anyway."

"But we can't just sit around doing nothing."

"No, we can get rested, so we can help. Now, let's go back to the house and see if we can find some food. We haven't been home in a long time," the young woman said putting an arm around the boy and escorting him toward the guards at the door.

27

A fire was burning in a large fireplace, as Skylar and Halie entered their apartment. The stone fireplace had a dark wood mantle and both families' coats of arms hanging above an ancient wooden pendulum clock. Since both families had been a part of the affairs of leadership and state for many generations.

Skylar had joined Halie over a year before to work on his training in the field. It felt strange to be sitting in the empty home where he had grown up and spent so much time as a younger boy. A part of him relaxed in familiar surroundings. Another part of him felt a bit out of place as if he no longer belonged here.

"Why don't you go to your room and rest awhile," Halie said.

"And, what are you doing?"

"I'm seeing if I can find some food. I'm starving."

"I doubt it. My dad's the only one living here most of the time. He probably eats in the cafeteria. I mean he's not gonna cook just for himself."

"Well, I'll see. You go get some rest."

"You should rest too."

"I will. Don't worry, now go lie down and get some rest," she said smiling at him, as she sat down on a chair beside a stone fireplace.

"I'm not going to my room. If you're not going to be neither am I."

"Skylar Orion! I said go to your room and get some rest."

"Fine," the boy said heading up the stairs.

Skylar went into his room, which was quite sparse. There were several models of spacecraft hanging from the ceiling. The window overlooked one of the garden courtyards between the neighboring duplexes. His mind was running with all the things he'd been through in recent days. He figured he wouldn't sleep but decided to lay on his bed. The familiarity of the room helped him to lower his guard and he was soon sound asleep.

Halie fell asleep watching the flames of the fire flickering in front of her, as she relaxed on the overstuffed sofa. The home was warm and comfortable especially after traveling for over a year. Fighting wars and facing the trials of the past few days had exhausted her. Even with the threat of the Varangians outside the gates of the Abbey. Their home was always a place of security and it made the rest even easier.

Halie had been asleep for a little over an hour when the door leading toward the central courtyards of the Abbey opened. Bern and Dara walked slowly through the door and saw their daughter asleep in front of the fire.

"Don't disturb her," Dara said, "She needs her rest."

"She'll be very upset if we don't speak to her before leaving. You know she'd never let us live that down."

"I know, but their friends are joining us in a bit, and we need to pack up to leave. Let's just let them sleep a bit while we get our things together."

Bern looked at his daughter, "I don't like the idea of their involvement in this skirmish. She's still recovering, and Skylar's been through too much lately. The battle on Hyperborea, the testing, and running into Myra. I think they need a break."

"I'll admit that leaving them here scares me too. I'd especially like to get Skylar as far away from her as we can. I'm not sure he's ready to face her again yet."

"Is Justin sure that Skylar hasn't figured it out yet? I mean if he realizes the truth about her, it could set him down a path that he'll never recover from."

"I know, but Justin feels that letting him see the truth of her evil will help him understand the truth about her."

"About who?" Halie asked looking over the couch at her parents.

"Oh, Sweetheart we didn't want to wake you," Dara smiled. "You need your rest."

"No, it's okay. I wanted to see you anyway. I didn't have much time earlier."

"We don't have much time now either," Bern said looking at the old clock above the fireplace. They're taking your mother and me back to Caspian in about an hour. They feel it would be safer to have her away from this battle."

"That makes sense. Who were you talking about when you came in?"

Dara took a deep breath and looked at her husband before looking again at her, "Myra. Your uncle and I were discussing earlier if it was time to tell him the truth about Myra. We aren't sure what she said to him, and with all the other commotion going on we hadn't had the time to figure out what he knows about her. He said she spoke with him and knew his father. However, he never said that he knew who she really was."

"I don't think he knows yet," Halie said. "He may suspect, but if he knew I think he would have told his father right away. I also don't think it would have been easy to get him to go get some sleep if he truly knew who she was. He'd be wanting to fight her or go to her."

"That is our feeling, too. We're also afraid that he has suspicion and if the truth is revealed in the wrong way it will turn him not only away from his father but the whole Order as well."

"I won't let that happen, mom. I know I can keep him on the right path."

"We hope so," Bern said with a smile of approval, "It's a great responsibility you took on in being your cousin's mentor."

"I knew what I was getting into. Besides, he's my cousin and no one else should have to deal with his issues," the young woman snickered.

"You're a great kid," Dara said hugging her daughter. "I just wish we had time to enjoy a longer visit."

"So, do I. If you are leaving in less than an hour, I'd better get Sky up or he'll never forgive me. He misses you a lot," she said getting up and walking toward the steps leading to the two bedrooms where Skylar and his father slept.

"We'll go pack, and see you in a minute," Dara said, as they headed up the set of steps to their room on the opposite side of the home.

"Sky," Halie said knocking on his bedroom door. "Sky, it's Halie, get up."

"Go away," the muffled, grumpy voice growled from inside the room.

"Sky, my parents are getting ready to leave. I know you'll want to see them, so get up."

"Leave me alone," his voice growled a bit louder.

Halie sighed, before knocking again, "Skylar Orion Knighthawk, you have twenty seconds to open this door or I'm coming in and dragging you downstairs." She waited a moment, "Did you hear me... One... Two..."

The door slid open and Skylar stood glaring at his cousin, "What do you mean leaving? Why are they leaving?"

"They decided since she's the President she should be in a safer place. They're leaving on the first flight to get back Caspian. I knew you'd want to say goodbye. So, get downstairs."

"I do. Sorry, I yelled at you."

"Look, Bud, I know you're tired. I can overlook it this time," she said giving the boy a nudge forward toward the open stairway leading to the main level.

The back doorbell rang, as they reached the bottom of the stairs, "I'll get it," Skylar shouted, as he ran past his cousin toward the back door.

"Check out who it is, before you open that door," Halie instructed.

Skylar hit the video communicator and saw Nash and Ariel, so he pressed the lock button to open the door, "Come in guys."

"Hey, hope we're not intruding," Ariel looked at Halie, "I know you two are supposed to be resting."

"No, it's okay. My parents are getting ready to leave soon anyway. Where are you two staying?"

"On the ship," Nash replied.

"We have a couple of extra rooms, you're welcome to stay here, " Halie invited pointing to the stairs. "There's plenty of room."

"No, we just wanted to see how you were doing," Nash answered. "I'd rather stay on the ship, so we can be ready to move if needed."

"Then maybe we should all stay on the ship," Skylar suggested.

"We'll be back together soon enough," Ariel said musing the boy's hair. "They won't clear Halie until tomorrow afternoon anyway."

"That may be," Halie said, sitting down at the counter looking into the kitchen. "If things do break out don't plan on leaving without us. Whether I'm cleared or not I'm going to help to defend my home. There's no way I'll sit around here while others are fighting."

"Me too," Skylar said, "And, it doesn't matter what the Council says. Nobody's stopping me from fighting when the time comes."

"Oh really," Dara said walking up behind the boy. "No one?"

"Um..."

"That's what I thought, tough guy," she said with a smile leaning to hug the boy. "You'll follow the rules given to you, young man, or you'll have us to deal with. As for defending our home, the Council has already said that you'll continue to serve with your crew if things come to that. So, if they determine that they need you in the air, you'll both go with Nash."

Halie smiled, "Glad to know that we haven't been taken completely off this assignment. They're like family to us now."

Dara smiled at Nash and Ariel, "I could see that in their determination to save you. I'm very pleased that you're serving with such loyal friends. It's not always easy to find such loyalty. I am sure you'll all be blessed in this friendship for many years."

Bern sat down two cases, as he entered the room, "The luggage is ready. We thought the doorbell might have been one of the aides coming to get our things."

"No Sir," Nash replied. "Just a couple of pesky Commonwealth troops."

"No, young man," Bern said shaking Nash's hand, "Family. You two are very close to our children, and that makes you, family to us. You'll always be welcome in our home."

"Your children?" Nash was puzzled by the statement since his own family had never been very close. He still had a hard time with the close-knit family that Halie and Skylar came from.

Halie smiled, "I've told you that our parents have raised Skylar and I together since we were born and that we are more like brother and sister than cousins. Everyone is a part of the family."

"That's right," Dara said hugging both Skylar and Halie, "And, none of us would have it any other way. Bern is right, you both are welcome in our home anytime. "

"That's right," Justin's voice surprised everyone since no one had heard him enter the room. "Family is deeply important, and as far as I am concerned you both are now part of our family."

"Dad," Skylar said stepping to hug him. "I have missed you very much. I know I don't always tell you, but I do miss you when we're gone."

"I've missed you too, son?" Justin replied as he held his son tightly.

"I don't get it?" Nash asked, "When we saw all of you, and back on Hyperborea I thought you were some hard-nosed, stuck-up knight. Everyone was afraid to see you coming, and you stood sternly waiting for us when you came off the ship. Now, here you seem relaxed. I mean even the kid here was afraid to speak to you on Hyperborea, and when even when we first returned to the Abbey earlier."

"I was afraid," Skylar said. "That doesn't mean I don't love him. He's my dad. It's just that he's also in charge of the whole Order of Knights. When we saw him on Hyperborea he wasn't just coming as my dad. He was coming as the leader of the Order. When we first returned today it was the same thing. I knew he was coming as both my dad and the person in charge. I was a little afraid on both accounts."

"Both accounts?" Nash asked.

"I knew I'd went against the instructions of the Elite Guard and the Council. I also went against his wishes, stole an I.D., and snuck into the Communication Center to call you. I knew I was in trouble, even though I thought I was doing the right thing."

"Besides, this is my home," Justin added, " and you and Ariel are now a part of our family. Skylar has been taught the ways of the order since he was a child. However, he also knows that I am his father before I am the Chancellor of the Fidelian Knights. When we are in this house and the pomp and circumstance of my job are not allowed here. Here he is just my son and I am his father."

Nash smiled, "Well, thanks for making us a part of your family and all, but I've never had a close relationship with others. I'm kind of a loner, but this crew is closer than any family I've ever known."

Dara smiled at Nash and gave him a small hug, "Everyone needs close friends, Nash. Everyone. And, we are glad you are here."

The doorbell rang again, and Skylar ran toward the front door this time, "I'll get it."

"That will be our ride to the shuttle," Dara said turning to hug Halie one more time. "I'll miss you. My prayers are always over you."

"I know," Halie as tears welled in her eyes.

"It's your aide," Skylar said walking back to the group.

"I'll miss you too," Dara said, hugging the boy, "Our prayers are ever over you as well."

"Thanks," Skylar said, with tears running down his cheek.

Justin gave his sister-in-law and Bern a hug, "God be with you."

"May His face shine upon you," Bern replied.

It was quiet for a few minutes after Dara and Bern had left, and finally, Justin spoke, "Did you invite your friends to stay?"

"Yes," Halie said, "But, they are insisting on staying with their ship."

"You can get to your ship in a matter of minutes, through the emergency tunnels," Justin replied. "I wish you'd stay with us. Besides, I'd feel safer knowing that my family will have you with them when the attack begins."

"You said we could get back to our ship faster?" Nash asked.

"The tunnels," Skylar said. "We don't use them normally, but there is an emergency tunnel system connecting the Cathedral and Council Chamber with some areas outside the Abbey grounds, as well as to the Academy and Command Center."

"And," Justin, said smiling, "Even a couple of offshoots to places like the labyrinth, and our home."

"Our home?" Skylar asked.

"Yes," Justin said looking at the fireplace. "After the attack when you were a toddler, the Elite Guard insisted on adding a passage that comes out behind the fireplace and into the main underground passage system leading throughout the Abbey."

"That's good to know," Nash replied. "It will be nice to rest a bit."

"Dad, how long do you think it will be before Myra and the Varangians make a move to attack us? Do you think she's going to wait long?"

"No. I have a strong feeling that she's just making some final preparations, before unleashing her forces on the Abbey?"

Halie sat down staring at the fire again, "Do you think the Abbey can stand against an all-out attack?"

Justin looked at her sadly, "We must stand. We can't allow her to gain control of the Archives and the wealth of knowledge stored here. The entire past and knowledge of our people have been entrusted to us. We can't risk losing anything. The shield should protect us and give us time for the Commonwealth to send us backup troops. I know we should have requested them earlier, but I am still confident that the Knights will be able to stand firm until they arrive."

"What if the shield fails?" Skylar asked.

"We will fight to the last knight if necessary. Now, enough of this. I am going to prepare you all my specialty for dinner."

Skylar smiled, "Chili. I miss having your and Aunt Dara's home-cooked meals."

"I'll get on dinner. Why don't you all rest here by the fire," the older Knighthawk said leaving them all sitting by the fire, as he went to the kitchen to prepare a meal. He needed to cook. He needed something to do, rather than continue to ponder on the inevitable fight that loomed over their heads.

28

A Varangian troop mover rolled through the edge of the woods. They rolled on large tracks and could hold twenty armed soldiers. It rolled to a stop at the edge of the field south of the fortified walls. The rear door opened, and four troops stepped out forming a barrier, as Myra and Lieutenant Reed stepped down behind them. They could see their troops lined through the center of the field.

A small band of soldiers sat around a fire in front of them. One of the men stepped forward, "Ma'am, I was told that you were coming."

"Commander Cheung," Myra stepped past her guards, "You have your special forces assembled?"

"Yes Ma'am," the man with a heavy beard and wearing his flak jacket replied. "I picked twenty of the best from the."

"Very good. You'll be accompanying me into the Abbey."

The Commander looked toward the fortified walls, "Ma'am? I was told that we'd have difficulty taking the forcefield down. The Scythian's bomber force won't be ready for another day or two."

Myra smiled looking past the commander at her old home, "We are going inside tonight."

"Tonight?"

"Across the field over there is a large tree. There is a secret entrance into the Abbey that leads under the field. Several tunnels lead to the most important parts of the Abbey. You and your troops should be able to infiltrate the Command Center basement from the tunnels. That's where the power supply for the force field is housed. Once you drop the power our troops can attack."

"Wouldn't they be guarding the tunnels?" Commander Cheung asked.

"Yes, but the tunnels aren't used very often. They shouldn't be expecting a visit, which should be to our advantage."

"Yes, Ma'am."

"Very good. Get your troops and follow us inside."

"Yes Ma'am," he replied, turning to collect his troops.

They entered the passageway under Pan's Oak and were moving quickly through the narrow tunnel leading into the Abbey. They moved slowly and cautiously forward for about twenty minutes, as they came to a cross passage. They stopped for a moment, as Myra motioned them to continue forward in the dimly lit tunnel.

"Ma'am, there is a light approaching," Lieutenant Reed said stopping them all.

Myra stepped forward past the troops, "It should be all right, but stand ready."

A moment later a brown cloaked man approached, carrying a glowing plasma sword. The Commander tensed and raised his rifle.

"Brother Torrance," Myra smiled at the tall thin man.

"Good evening, your Highness," the tall monk said shutting his sword off and uncovering his head.

"Have you made our way clear?" she asked.

"Yes, Your Highness. I've waited for years, for your return. It is time for you to take control of knowledge and power. It will allow you to become the rightful ruler of the entire system."

Myra smiled, "I knew I could count on you, my faithful friend. I assume that you've arranged safe passage for these troops?"

"Yes. They can reach the Command Center. I've assigned troops to other areas and the main passage is clear. They should be safe until they emerge from the tunnels."

"Excellent. And, the other passages?"

Brother Terrance looked down, before responding, "Your Highness, it will not be easy. He will not let you near him. He'll die before he allows you to find the boy."

"Let me worry about that. You've done your part. You'll be richly rewarded in time. Return to your duties before you're missed."

"Very well. Be safe and have success, your Highness," the middle-aged man replied as he turned and quickly went back down the passage.

Myra turned and walked back to her troops, "Our friend has helped clear the passage ahead of us. You should move quickly."

"Yes, Ma'am," the commander replied motioning the troops forward into the passage ahead.

An hour later Myra and twenty-five troops had reached the main passageway leading through the center of the Abbey from Cathedral to the Command Center. The tunnels were dimly lit, as they stopped at a cross path. They stood silently for a few moments watching in all four directions, trying to be sure no one had seen them.

"Everything is going as planned," Myra whispered. "From here we can get to any part of the Abbey. To the right is the Great Cathedral, and to the left is the Command Center. Commander Cheung, I want you to take your unit and go to the Command Center. When you come up inside the Center, you'll be at the rear of the underground hanger. There is a hallway behind the hanger that leads to the main power center. If you drop the power the entire Abbey will be in the dark and force field will deactivate."

"Very good," the Commander replied motioning his troops around them down the passageway. "Ma'am, may I ask where you'll be going."

"I have some business of my own to attend to. Carry out your orders, Commander."

"Yes Ma'am," the large man replied as he followed his troops down the hallway leaving Myra, Lieutenant Reed, and four troops.

"Ma'am, which way will we be going then," Lieutenant Reed inquired.

Myra smiled, "We'll be going the opposite way. My business is on that end."

"The Cathedral?

"That direction, yes," Myra replied turning and walking down the passageway to the right.

"If you don't mind my asking, what are we looking for in the Cathedral?" Lieutenant Reed asked.

"The tunnels lead to several areas, not just the Cathedral. It's not what I am after, but who. Now, let's get going."

"Yes, Ma'am," she replied, motioning her troops ahead of them into the dim passage ahead.

"Lieutenant, I want you and your troops to move ahead to the Cathedral. Inside there are two items of power hidden at the altar in the front of the Cathedral. There is a small door built into the rear of the altar. Inside you will find a flat rock, which you must retrieve. A wooden box sits at the center wall of the platform, under a stain glass picture of Moses carrying stone tablets. You'll find two long poles that fit into the wooden box, so it can be carried. You and your troops must take this box with you as well. My ship will be back at the foot of the falls. Get those items and meet me at the ship."

"A box and a rock?"

"Not just any rock, the Messiah Stone. And, inside that box is the power of ancient Israel, which has been passed down to the Fidelian Knights since they were formed."

Lieutenant Reed looked puzzled, "They sound quite important."

"Very important. The stone is from the rock beneath the cross of the Messiah. It was filled with his blood, and it contains the center of the power of the Fidelian Knights. They have believed in the power of the stone for over two Milena. The Ark within the box is considered to be the center of the power of God. And now it will all be mine," Myra smiled at the young officer.

"If that's what you came for, why are you staying here in the tunnel?" the Lieutenant asked.

"I didn't come just to get the power of the Knights. Taking their power will destroy them. I came for something far more valuable and more personal to me. I'll be fine, and once I've retrieved what I've come for I'll find my way back to the ship."

"What about the attack on the Abbey? I thought you were leading us to take the moon?"

"Captain Alvarez is capable of heading up the attack. It's far more important to protect my treasures. Whether the troops succeed or not, I'll have what I've come for. Now, you have your orders and time is short."

"Yes, Ma'am. We'll see you at the Intrepid then," the Lieutenant replied moving forward through the corridor ahead.

29

"Dinner was great, Uncle Justin," Halie said as she carried her bowl into the kitchen. Skylar was helping to clear the table, but she stopped him, "Hey, why don't you go rest by the fire, I'll take care of this stuff and load the dishes in the washer."

"I don't mind helping," he answered.

"No kiddo, you need to rest up."

"Okay," Skylar said walking toward the couches by the fire, where his father was reading his hand communicator and his friends sat. "So, any word about the enemy troops?"

"Yes, they just let me know that they're moving troops to our western flank. They're at the edge of the forcefield."

"So, it'll be soon," Halie said sitting down beside Skylar.

"Yes," Justin replied staring into the fire, "I sense that it will be sooner than we think. We should get some rest, so we are all ready."

"Sure," Halie agreed, as she leaned back and put her arm around her cousin.

"Yeah," Skylar added as he snuggled down watching the fire.

They sat silently watching the flames of the fire for a while, Skylar had almost fallen asleep when an alarm blared outside the home. Skylar jumped, nearly falling off the couch. Halie squeezed him.

"Looks like the wait is over," Justin said, rising from his chair. He stepped to the right of the fireplace and turned the last square on the decorated mantle. The fireplace slid back slightly and then to the side revealing the secret passageway into the tunnel system. "Let's go. We need to get you to your ship."

"Yes Sir," Nash agreed.

"Thanks again for your hospitality, Chancellor Knighthawk," Ariel said.

Justin smiled, "It's been my pleasure to host you here. Now, let's get moving. That alarm means that someone has breached the security somehow. We need to move fast to get to the Command Center. If there's a breach, we need to prepare to act right away."

They walked quickly to the bottom of the stairway leading into the tunnels, as the fireplace door closed behind them. They were in one of the dim passageways following Justin toward a brighter light near the end of the corridor where it met with the main passage leading through the heart of the campus above.

"Right this way," Justin encouraged. "We'll come to the main passageway right up there. We can follow that straight to the Command Center. We'll be right behind the hanger, so getting to your ship will be quick."

"Sounds great," Ariel replied.

"Yeah," Nash agreed, "Right now I want to be in my ship ready to go."

"I'm sorry we can't allow that," Myra's voice brought them to a stop as they came around the corner.

Justin quickly drew his plasma sword igniting it as he motioned the others to stay behind him with his arm, "What are you doing here? How did you get into the Abbey? Nash get them back."

Nash listened and put an arm up guiding the others back a few feet into the passageway they had just come from.

The woman smiled looking into Justin's eyes, "Oh, you think you have everything so under control, Justin. You've always thought that you could manage everything. Meanwhile, the universe is chaos all around us. I have control within the chaos, and the tighter you hold the more it all slips away."

"Yes, you are at the heart of this evil. I've known that from the start. When you tried to destroy the Cathedral and disrupt the power of the Knights eight years ago, I realized how evil you were. Why can't you just be satisfied with what you've already taken? Why can't you leave people to live in peace? Why are you so filled with hatred and the hunger for power that you can't remember the good that once was?" Justin asked.

"You know why I'm here. I only want what belongs to me," she replied, as the end of her scepter began glowing with power.

"You can't have what you want, because it doesn't belong to you. You can't have any of the relics, and you definitely can't have him. You gave up your rights when you left here. Now leave this place before you regret this intrusion."

"He's a part of me, and I want him with me. He'll rule at my side right where he belongs."

"No," Justin answered staring at the woman, "You destroyed yourself and that past long ago. And, you're not going to destroy him. You will not destroy the foundations of the Fidelian Order either."

"Always so dramatic, Justin," the evil woman replied looking past Justin toward where the younger foursome stood. "He knows. And, I will have my way."

Her scepter fired a blast toward Justin, as he dodged and reflected the blast away with his plasma sword. Justin turned and lunged toward Myra. She moved to the side defending with the scepter causing sparks to fly around them. Justin again pushed in toward the woman, intentionally forcing her to turn into the passageway leading to the Cathedral.

"Get them out of here Nash!" Justin instructed as Myra tried to reposition herself. He managed to hold the evil woman away from Skylar and the others. They now had an opening into the main corridor leading to the Command Center.

"You have my word," Nash replied as he watched for an opportunity to take the others to safety.

Myra shot another blast toward Justin. He again moved and deflected the shot. Opportunity for escape came as the lights in the tunnels flickered and went out. Nash slowly guided Skylar in front of him into the main corridor, and the others stepped around the corner after him.

Myra smiled in the glow of her weapon, "It would seem our team has reached their goal. Give up now Justin. I will win. Power, true power always wins."

"No Myra, faith, and justice always win. Run Children. Run!" Justin swung his sword toward the woman, as she pushed him away. Halie ignited her sword for light, and Nash turned on a light connected to his laser pistol, as he guided them down the dark corridor. Flashes of light continued behind them letting them know the battle between the two forces of good and evil continued.

30

Lieutenant Reed waited with her four soldiers at the door leading into the Cathedral, for the right moment to move into the Cathedral. Suddenly the lights flashed off and the corridor was dark.

"Now is the time," the young officer said opening the door, "Move in."

The five troops moved slowly into an empty hallway where a single emergency light was shining at the end of the hall. They moved cautiously toward the light. Once at the light they turned around the corner where the entry into the Cathedral was. They stopped at the edges of the door. Lieutenant Reed silently motioned for them to stand at the sides of the large wooden door.

Once they were in place she stood at the center and motioned for them to pull the doors open. The door opened and candles burned across the front of the room around the altar. Several dozen people were kneeling in the prayer at the altars.

"Let's move in," the Lieutenant smiled. "It looks like a couple of kids and old people."

They slowly walked up the center aisle but stopped just before the first row where people were sitting. Lieutenant Reed looked around, "Two of you move to the outside aisle so we can cover the entire room. Then we'll move to the altar to get what we've come for."

Two of the soldiers moved to the outside aisles and stood ready to shoot. Just as the others started to walk forward Brother Lawrence stood up from the center of the prayer altar and turned toward them, "You'll not bring destruction to this place of peace."

"Have a seat old man. I don't see any need for anyone to get hurt, right now anyway. We are here for the Messiah stone."

"You can't have anything from this sacred place," Brother Lawrence replied. He put his hands into his pockets and stood calmly at the center of the aisle. Everyone else remained silent in prayer.

"Look, I don't want any trouble old man. This is your last chance. Get out of my way," the Lieutenant ordered raising her gun toward the man.

"I would recommend that you leave here. Your evil will not be allowed in this place. You see young lady; our power is not in the relics here. The Messiah stone, the Ark, and many other items are within our possession. They are not the real source of our power. The One we serve is the source of our power and not the items we hold."

The Lieutenant aimed her rifle at the old monk, "Enough. Move aside."

"I cannot help you," Brother Lawrence calmly replied.

"Then you leave me no choice. Let this be an example to the rest of you!" Lieutenant Reed shouted. She pulled the trigger on the rifle. Several shots went toward the old man reflecting away from him into the walls.

She stared at him, readjusted the power of her rifle, and aimed once more. She held the trigger down. Several more blast went out from the weapon and deflected toward the soldiers standing at the sides of the room killing them.

"Kill them all!" she ordered as the other two soldiers raised their weapons.

"Please stop for your own sake," the old monk replied sadly.

"Never. Kill them," she said as all three of them began firing into the people around the room.

Flashes of lights flew around the room as if a force field surrounded the people who remained in prayer. Soon, the laser fire bounced back toward the soldiers and the Lieutenant stood alone silently looking at the old man.

"How did you do that? Where is your force field?"

Brother Lawrence shook his head at her looking sadly into her eyes, "I told you. The One we serve is greater than the Witch you've allied yourself with. We're seeking his help, and we are willing to die for our cause. However, the Creator has chosen to protect us. You're now alone. We won't harm you. You can lay down your weapon and join us or you can leave this place now."

"I won't join you," the young officer said sternly, as she lowered her weapon. "You may have won this small battle, but this Abbey is going to fall. Our troops will overrun this place. Until we meet again old man," she replied walking out of the Cathedral and into the outside courtyard.

31

Justin managed for several minutes to keep himself between Myra and the children. Allowing them to make their way down the passageway leading to the Command Center. Flashes of light now and then caused Skylar to look back hoping to see that his father was defeating the evil woman.

"Give up Justin the battle is over," Myra sneered shoving her scepter toward his face and knocking him down.

"Sorry, my dear. I'll never let you take this Abbey. Good shall prevail. It can be knocked down, but in the end, I know who wins," he replied pushing Myra back down the tunnel, as he jumped to his feet.

"We shall see," she said raising her scepter and powering it up. Bolts of electricity flashed toward Justin.

Justin repelled the bolt of electric with his sword once more.

The bright flash lighted the entire passageway briefly and Halie looked back sadly, "We can't leave my uncle in here alone."

Nash looked back at her still holding Skylar in front of him, "Somehow I don't think he needs any help. I promised to get you out of here. Now Let's go. With the power, out the entire Abbey is going to be in danger. We have to keep moving."

"But my dad," Skylar begged.

"No," Halie turned and started following Ariel and Nash again, "He's right, Sky. We must think of the greater good. The entire Abbey's in danger and we have to reach our ship to offer help."

Justin reflected the electricity toward Myra, as she jumped out of the way, "You can't have him, Myra. You gave up that right when you left here. When you chose the dark arts over truth and light. You won't threaten him or the Order any longer."

Myra sneered at him, "I will not be stopped. You can't stop me," she reached a hand out and used power to shove Justin down the hallway ahead of her.

"Let's keep moving," Ariel said, as she shot a blast back at Myra's dark form standing in the light of her scepter.

Myra reflected the shot into the floor, "Nice try, young one, but you're no match for me."

"No," Justin shouted as he jumped to his feet once again and crushed his sword against Myra's scepter. "This is between you and me."

"Enough!" Myra's shout echoed throughout the entire tunnel as she shoved her pointed scepter into Justin's chest. "You have no power over me. And, I have won!"

"No!" Skylar cried as Nash wrapped his arm around the younger boy keeping him in front of him as they moved down the passageway.

"I'm coming my dear one," Myra shouted from behind them.

Halie started to turn back wielding her sword in front of her, preparing to run toward Myra. Ariel grabbed hold of her arm, "No. We aren't losing you too. We have to get out of here now. We have to honor him by saving this moon."

Halie took a deep breath and looked into her friend's eyes, "She just killed my uncle."

"Which is why you have to keep going. If not to save yourself then for your cousin."

Halie looked at Nash forcing Skylar on ahead of them, "You're right. Let's get to the hanger and save the Abbey. The time for mourning will come, but right now we need to push this evil from my home."

Ariel grimaced, "Let's do it then."

They soon reached the end of the passageway and ascended steps. They had to push a steel door open that led into a hallway behind the hanger.

Skylar started to turn back toward the door. Nash knelt next to him and held him by his arms, "NO! You can't go back in there."

"She killed my dad," Skylar sobbed.

Halie knelt next to them crying, "Skylar, we can't stay here. The Abbey's defenseless. The Varangians will be overrunning the campus and we can help more from the ship."

"But, dad."

"I know, Sweat Heart. I know. He would want us to save the Abbey. We need to get to our ship to help out."

"Stand back," Ariel instructed as she aimed her pistol at the door and shot several times melting it shut. "That should keep her down there. Now, let's go."

The foursome ran across the dimly lit hanger toward their ship. Troops ran in various directions moving equipment and loading ships outside the hanger. They were sure to reach the goal of their ship, but now everything had changed. They only thing they knew for sure was that it was time to fight.

32

Nash pushed Skylar across the hanger in front of him. The Pegasus sat on the tarmac hooked to a plasma charger. The younger boy stopped crying. He walked in a daze toward the ship. Tears still ran down Halie's cheeks as Ariel walked beside her.

"Let's get aboard," Nash hit the security control opening the ship's ramp.

"I'll contact Central Command, so we can airborne faster," Ariel said.

"Sounds good," Nash guided Skylar's near-catatonic body up the ramp. Just as they reached the top of the ramp Skylar stopped nearly tripping Nash. "Kid, we need to get on board."

A tear rolled down Skylar's cheek, "He's dead. My dad's dead. I can't leave here."

"All right," Nash pressed, "We've got to get you on board. And, we have to leave here."

"No," Skylar began to sob again.

"Not now kid," Nash leaned down and picked up his younger friend. He carried the boy onto the toward the cockpit, "It's not that I don't care kid, but since I do care we have to go now."

"Nash chill out," Ariel urged him as she leaned over to give Skylar a small hug.

"He's right Ariel," Halie interrupted. "We can grieve when this is over, right now we have to get the ship airborne. We need to stop that Witch from her plans. Now contact the Command Center and get our clearance.

Ariel sat down in her seat and turned on the communication link to the Command Center. Halie knelt in front of Skylar and hugged him. "I am so sorry Sky, but we can't let her get off this moon. And, I can't let anything happen to you, especially now."

"Halie," Nash said turning his chair back to face her, "What was Myra after. She was willing to kill your uncle to get what she wanted."

Halie bit her lip, looked at the floor, and then back at Nash, "Well, she likely wants a few of the special items that she knows the Fidelian Order hold dear."

Ariel looked over the computer screen, "Halie, it's us. She was after something very specific. What was it?"

"She was after me," Skylar answered staring into her eyes.

Halie bit her lip again as a tear rolled down her cheek, "Yeah she wanted you."

"Why?" Ariel asked. "Is it just that she wants to corrupt him and destroy all your uncle's hopes and dreams?"

"Oh, I'm sure she'd love to do that, but she wants Sky, because," Halie stopped as the tears began to flow, "He's...He's..."

"Her son," Skylar said leaning into Halie. She wrapped her arms around him, as he cried.

Nash looked at Ariel, "Get that clearance. Then patch us through to the Excelsior."

"The Excelsior?" Ariel asked.

"The transport that Halie's parents left on was headed for the Excelsior. Captain Joseph will see them to Caspian safely. We need to contact them on a secure channel. They need to know about the Chancellor."

"True," Ariel agreed watching her friends and wishing she could take their pain away. "This is the Pegasus to Abbey Command. We're requesting clearance for takeoff."

"Pegasus, this is Command. Things are very chaotic. You're clear when you're ready. Forces are moving in fast. There are ships overhead. All we can do is wish you a safe travel. May the grace of God be with you."

"Roger that," Ariel replied as Nash ignited the engines of the bomber.

They were soon in flight. Nash flew out away from the Abbey, hovering over the great woods away from the main battle. "Contact the Excelsior."

"I'm working on it," Ariel snapped.

"Sorry," Nash replied.

"This is the Excelsior," a voice came through a second later.

"This is the Pegasus," Ariel replied. "I have a secure message..."

"One moment Pegasus," the communication link went silent.

Ariel looked at her controls, "Excelsior?"

"Captain Joseph here, what can we do for you Pegasus?"

Nash took a deep breath, "Sir, we need to reach President Ambrosius right away."

"What is the problem, Lieutenant?"

"It's a very important message for her ears only."

"One moment. We'll patch you through to her quarters."

"Thank you," Nash replied. "Halie, do you want me to handle this?"

"No," she said holding her young cousin tightly. "I need to tell her."

"Holo-link is coming online," Ariel said turning on a holograph in the front the center of the ship. "It's your mother."

"Mom," Halie tried to fight the tears.

"Sweetie, what is it? What's wrong? Why are both of you crying?"

"Mom it's Uncle Justin."

"What is it, Halie? Just tell me."

"Myra came after Skylar. He fought her."

"I know, Honey. I know. I sensed it somehow. He's gone."

Halie began to weep again, "I am so sorry, mom. There wasn't anything we could do. He told us to get out and she killed him."

"Where are you?"

"We are on the Pegasus. We're still on Avalon One."

"Come to us. Let others fight this battle."

"She has the stone," Skylar interrupted.

"What," Halie leaned the boy back and looked into his eyes. "What do you mean?"

"I had a dream last night. I saw her with the Messiah stone. I know it sounds crazy, but I'm sure she was coming to try to take the stone too."

"What else can she do to us?" Dara asked.

"Not what she wanted," Halie said. "She was after Skylar, but we saved him. Uncle Justin saved him. I didn't know anything about the Messiah Stone."

Dara replied, "It makes perfect sense. The Stone is the central power that has held the Fidelian Order together for centuries. She believes that by taking that power she can destroy the order. However, she's forgotten that our true power isn't in some stone. At least you were able to get away safely and get Skylar out of there."

"Only because my father sacrificed himself for me," Skylar cried.

"He knew he had to protect you from her," Dara encouraged.

"How could my own mother be so evil?" Skylar asked running to the crew quarters.

"You told him?" Dara asked.

"No, he figured it out during their fight," Halie answered.

"I think you should join us right away."

"No," Halie replied. "I think we need to stop this right now."

"But you have your cousin to consider. I'm worried about you too."

"Sorry, mom. Just send all the help you can, and we'll stay and do our part."

"I understand Sweetie. I've already sent for more troops. They should be there soon. May grace and protection be with you."

"And with you."

"I love you, mom."

"And we love you very much. Both of you," she said as the transmission stopped.

They sat silent for a moment before Nash turned his seat to face Ariel and Halie, "We've been through a lot recently. Halie, you were nearly killed. Skylar's life was in danger, and now he finds out his mother is some witch. We were stranded on Hyperborea and nearly killed by that woman. Your uncle's dead. No one will think less of you or us for leaving this battlefront to others."

Halie stared past Nash through the cockpit window at the explosions around the Abbey far in the distance, "Friends and family have died, but many more friends are facing death right now. If we leave now it'll only be for a short trip to the Excelsior. We can drop Skylar off with my parents. Then we'll return to help the battle here on Avalon One."

"I'm not leaving," Skylar stood in the doorway leading to the crew quarters. "I may have been born to her, but she hasn't been my mother. She killed Sidney and my father. She'll continue to destroy people unless someone stops her. If I have to be the one to stop her, then so be it. She's not taking our home and all that we stand for."

"You sound pretty determined, kiddo," Ariel said, watching the boy's face.

"I am," he replied sternly.

"Sky, this isn't your battle to win," Halie said reaching out to take the boys hand in her own. "She isn't your responsibility. She's always had an evil heart. You don't need to let revenge fill your heart."

He looked into his cousin's eyes, "I'm not seeking revenge. I just can't leave here knowing more of our friends are in danger. There are no more transports left, so we need to help protect the others until they arrive to save them."

"Are you sure about this kid?" Nash asked looking from Skylar to Halie.

"Yes," the boy answered.

"Okay," Halie agreed, "It's settled then. We return to help in the fight and pray that help arrives soon."

"Then buckled in," Nash ordered, turning back toward his controls and locking his seat in place. "Let's go offer some help and save your home."

33

Myra couldn't open the door into the Command Center but was forced to return to the surface within the Labyrinth. A battle at the eastern gate, beyond the Cathedral, raged, as she emerged from the Labyrinth. Lieutenant Reed was crouched down beside a rock watching the battle. Myra could see her and walked toward her.

"Lieutenant," Myra whispered approaching the young woman.

"Ma'am, you made it out."

"Of course, I did. And, the tide has swung our way. The Chancellor of the Fidelian Knight is dead. Our troops are breaching the eastern gate, so it won't be long before the Abbey is in our hands. I assume you've sent your troops out with the Ark and the Stone?"

The Lieutenant looked at the ground, "I'm sorry Ma'am. My troops were killed. I was the only one to make it out of the Cathedral alive."

"They don't allow weapons in the Cathedral. It's a Sanctuary. How were they killed?" Myra couldn't believe what the young woman was sharing with her.

"It was amazing. Hard to explain. When we arrived, about fifteen people were kneeling around the front of the room. They were praying, I guess. Then this old monk rose and approached me. He put his hands in his pockets and stood calmly in front of me. When I demanded the items in return for his life he just stood there. I shot point-blank at him, but the blasts ricocheted off him and killed two of my men. Then we all began firing until only I was standing. None of them moved. They just kept praying, while my troops were killed by their own fire."

"That's the power they have, because of those relics," Myra said. "It won't matter, because soon enough we will control the Abbey and that power will be ours."

"No," the Lieutenant said staring still in amazement, "the old man said it had nothing to do with the relics. He said it had to do with the One they served, and that they would be protected. Then all of us were dead, except for me."

"Don't you see, it's all part of the way they work to manipulate people. They hold onto power and claim that they are in contact with some greater power that is inaccessible to anyone. The truth is that you can have power too. It's tangible, and someday I'll show it to you. Right now, we need to meet up with our troops. Then we'll take that Cathedral and watch the rest of this Abbey fall into my hands."

"Yes, Ma'am. It looks like they've broken through. I was listening earlier, and I think Commander Ortiz is leading them in."

"Ortiz?" Myra smiled, "Perhaps he'll not fail me as he did on Hyperborea. Can you raise him on your communicator?"

"Yes, Ma'am."

"Call him and let him know to meet us at the door of the Cathedral. We're taking the power away from the Knights."

"Yes Ma'am," Lieutenant Reed replied, turning to talk into her communicator.

It wasn't long before Myra stood with the Lieutenant and Commander Ortiz, at the door to the Cathedral. Laser fire and explosions could be heard outside, as the Fidelians fought against the Varangian soldiers.

"What will we do if they use their power again?" the Lieutenant asked.

Myra smiled, "They'll know that they have lost when I enter. They'll surrender without any fight. Now follow me inside."

Myra walked in front of the officers and ten soldiers down the main aisle of the sanctuary. The children and adults around the room continued to pray. Brother Lawrence rose and walked toward them with his hands in his pockets. He approached the evil woman. The Myra's scepter began to glow, as she neared the old monk. He calmly walked toward her.

"Brother Lawrence, I should have known you were leading the prayer gathering," Myra sneered at him.

"Why have you come to this place? This is a sacred space and there is no place here for evil."

"I've come to tell you that the Knights have lost. Your great leader is dead, and our troops are moving through the campus. Our ships overhead will prevent any reinforcements from arriving. It's now time to surrender and give me the Ark and the Messiah Stone."

Brother Lawrence took a deep breath, "I knew that Justin had fallen. I felt his loss. However, you know he's not the source of our strength."

"No, but your leadership will fall into chaos without him."

"And, that is where you thrive isn't it?" the old man smiled at her.

"I haven't the time for this nonsense," Myra said swinging her scepter. "Commander, restrain the good Brother."

"Yes Ma'am," Commander Ortiz replied motioning one of his men forward. The man walked past Myra and put restraints on the monk's hands.

Brother Lawrence calmly complied, "You can hold me, and you can desecrate this holy place. But you'll never win. In the end, the Knights will remain, because we serve a higher purpose."

"Lieutenant, take some of the troops and retrieve the relics. We need to save them before I have this building blown to bits," Myra ordered.

"Yes Ma'am," the Lieutenant and six of the troops moved past all the kneeling people to the altar area. She knelt behind the altar and opened the door where the stone was hidden, "You four go retrieve the poles to carry the box hidden there."

"Yes Lieutenant," one of the soldiers replied as they walked toward the stained-glass window of Moses.

The Lieutenant looked inside the empty cupboard and bit her lip before responding to Myra, "Ma'am, the Stone isn't here."

Myra's face became angry, "What do you mean?"

One of the soldiers whispered to Lieutenant Reed, and she looked at Myra, "I'm sorry, it isn't here. The Ark has been taken as well. The poles are missing and the box in the front is empty too."

Mya shook with anger as she put her glowing scepter near Brother Lawrence's face, "What have you done with them? You've lost and I want the Relics."

Brother Lawrence smiled, "You can have me. You can destroy this entire Abbey. But you won't ever win."

"The Relics old man!" the woman demanded.

"They are gone," he replied calmly. "I had a vision that they were in danger weeks ago, and they were removed from here to keep them safe."

"How did you repel the soldiers earlier?" she asked

The old man smiled, "You never understood. It was always fake for you. The true power isn't in buildings, relics, or any man-made thing. Some trust in chariots, some in horses, but we trust in the name of the Lord."

Myra twirled around in anger, "Stop quoting the ancient text to me. Tell me where those relics are, or I'll start killing the children."

"They're not on Avalon One. We assigned a small group of Knights to take them somewhere safe. Only those who took the relics will ever know where they are. They left here three days before you arrived on Avalon One."

Myra smiled, "You, smug old man. I was here nearly a week before those troops arrived at your door."

"You arrived the day that the two Young Ones began their Pledge's Quest. I tell you we've known you were here, and you are under the impression that you'll win. We know that we will win in the end."

She looked at the commander, "Gather everyone in this place in the courtyard outside. We'll use them to stop the fighting and win the Abbey."

"Yes, Ma'am," the Commander replied as the soldiers began moving throughout the sanctuary pushing people toward the door.

34

Nash maneuvered the Pegasus toward the Abbey, "It looks like the battle is in full swing. Are you two up to manning the turret's?"

"I'm ready," Skylar said walking back to climb the ladder to the upper turret.

"We'll get to it," Halie added taking the lower ladder to lower turret. "We'll need the guns because we can't risk bombing the Abbey with the people inside."

"No," Ariel replied, "But, we can bomb the forces outside the walls. I'll man the front guns and bring the pulsar bombs on-line for you, Nash."

"Sounds great," Nash replied, steering the ship low over the treetops. As the trees cleared, he dropped two bombs onto troops at the southern entrance of the Abbey, before flying over the main campus.

Several fighters bore down on them from above. Skylar spun around shooting the turret at them. Soon one of the fighters spun out of control and hit the second fighter causing them to explode above them. Halie aimed at ground soldiers advancing on the walls shooting into the troops who were trying to fight back with their small rifles. Nash continued directing them over the campus, as they fought off several fighters, and continued to shoot at enemy troops moving through the campus below.

Nash made several passes over the campus, causing at least minor destruction of the enemy troops with each pass. They were making another pass over the Cathedral. Halie looked below, "No. They can't do it."

"What's wrong?" Ariel asked.

"They are escorting children and Old Ones out of the Cathedral into the courtyard. We need to do something. They'll kill them."

"Hold the fire," Nash said. "We don't need to provoke them. Keep your fire until we are over the field again."

"Roger that," Skylar said watching explosions from firefights above them in the sky.

"I'm getting some new readings," Ariel reported. "A yacht class ship is flying in from over the mountains."

"Myra's ship," Halie replied. "What is she up to now. Please help us, Lord."

Nash dropped a couple of bombs onto Varangians in the eastern field, as they flew away from the battle, "Everyone ready to make another sweep?"

"Wait for Nash?" Ariel answered. "Two more readings are coming in. The Excelsior and Washington have arrived. They are leashing full force into the air above. They think they can break the blockade shortly."

"The cavalry's arrived," Nash smiled.

"Wait something is breaking in on the com-link. I'll try to clear it up. It seems to be on all channels," Ariel replied patching the link through so the others could hear.

It was Myra's voice, "We hold one of the last leaders on Avalon One, Bother Lawrence, along with over a dozen children and so-called 'Old Ones.' I demand that the remaining Knights respect the lives of your most precious souls. Surrender the Abbey and the Relics. Then I'll release them. Cease your attack and consider my offer I will only make it once."

Nash and the others looked toward the Abbey. Laser fire began to cease everywhere, "What do you want me to do Halie?"

"Stand down," she replied staring at the smoke rising from her home. "Slowly make your way to the Cathedral. We'll meet with her. Perhaps we can help to get some of those children to safety. I mean we can fit four or five on board."

"It's a trap," Ariel said. "You know she won't honor any cease-fire. She's not going to let anyone go free."

"Yes, she will," Skylar spoke up.

"Skylar, the answer is no," Halie replied over their com-link.

"It will buy time for the others to get away. She'll be focused on me, and everyone else may have a chance to get away," he replied.

"Kid, you can't sacrifice yourself," Nash responded.

"Greater love has no man than to lay down his life for his friends. That's what we've been taught since I was a kid. She killed my best friend and my father. I can't let her kill anyone else," Skylar answered.

"Stop quoting the Ancient text to get your way," Halie smiled at her cousin. "Nash, I hate to agree with him, but it's the best chance to save the others. The power and future of the Fidelians are not in the Abbey, but in the One, we follow. We must try. Head to the Cathedral, and land in the garden outside."

"Since your set on this, I'll move us into position."

"Ariel, can you patch me through on all channels?" Halie asked.

"Yes," Ariel replied pressing several switches, "You're on an open channel now."

"This is Halie Ambrosias. Myra, your demands have been heard. We are coming to you with a greater proposal."

Myra stood with her troops, "Well, my dear. What do you think you can offer to change my mind?"

"I didn't say I would change your mind. I'm saying I have an offer to free the hostages," Halie responded. "I have someone who wants to speak to you." Halie turned off the main communication link and left only the ship's com-link on. "Skylar it's up to you know."

"I am listening," Myra responded.

"Mother," Skylar's voice shook. "I am the one thing you want more than anything else. You were willing to kill my best friend and my father, but I am still not with you."

"You know," the woman replied with a smile.

"I think I knew before. I can't let you kill anyone else. We're coming to land near you. Release everyone and call your troops back so that the Knights and Commonwealth troops can leave the moon. Then I'll come to you willingly."

Myra's smile broadened, "Very well. I'll call our troops back, so that you may land. When you're off your ship I'll release the hostages and make sure everyone's allowed to leave safely. You will come to see that joining with me will lead to a far more fruitful future than you could ever dream."

"I'm sure it will be filled with surprise," Skylar softly responded.

Dara and Bern stood with Admiral Pembroke on the bridge of the Excelsior. They'd been guiding the battlefront and monitoring the situation closely. They heard the entire conversation between Myra and Skylar.

"Should we comply with Myra's demands, and withdraw our forces?" Captain Joseph asked looking at the Admiral across a holographic image of the battlefronts around the moon.

Admiral Pembroke looked at Dara and Bern, and then back at the Captain, "Call the bombers and fighters back to a safer position. We need to make it look like we are complying with her wishes even if we intend to fight back in the end."

Bern stepped closer to the command table, "Have a transport ship prepared as well. Make sure to announce that an unarmed transport will be sent to land at the Abbey to pick up the Fidelians that remain."

"Can we trust her, to keep her troops from destroying an unarmed ship?" the Admiral asked.

"I think she'll honor the request," Dara replied. "However, she won't give long for anyone to leave. We'll accompany the transport to the Abbey to pick up the children and teachers."

"Ma'am," Admiral Pembroke looked sternly at her, "I can't allow either of you to go with the transport. You're too valuable to the Alliance. We can't risk our President being killed."

"Admiral, I wasn't bringing this up for negotiation," Dara replied. "The Commonwealth will survive with or without me. A new leader can be elected. My family and friends are down there. The future of the Alliance may be at stake. Bern and I will be going with the transport to make sure we can save the children and teachers from the Abbey."

"My wife's right," Bern answered. "I would prefer that she remain here. I also learned long ago not to argue with her, Admiral. Besides, I don't believe Myra will risk losing the boy again. She'll allow us time to leave, as long as she thinks she'll get him."

The Admiral took a deep breath and looked sadly down at the battle map, "How can you let that boy sacrifice himself to her? I couldn't be as calm as you are right now."

"Calm," Bern replied, "We aren't calm. We're controlled. Trust me, Admiral, every fiber within us would love to lash out or fly down and take our nephew with us. However, there are hundreds of lives on the moon and thousands of Commonwealth and Varangian lives at stake. This battle can be quelled and allow us a better time to react in a stronger way."

Dara's eyes welled up, "Sometimes what's necessary is very difficult. We don't do this easily, but with great pain, Admiral. Now, make the arrangements for the transport. We're going to the surface."

The Admiral shook his head, "I knew it would do no good to argue, but I had to try. Your ship will be made ready, we'll send six guards with you just to be sure that you're safe on the surface."

"Thank you, Admiral," the President replied, "May grace and mercy be with you."

"May you be the ones to be under grace," the Admiral replied, turning to walk to the communication station.

35

The Pegasus slowly landed in the open garden beside the Labyrinth, in front of the Cathedral. Myra stood in front of her troops and the children and teachers from the Abbey. Brother Lawrence remained handcuffed, standing beside Myra. Several Varangian soldiers were scattered around the edges of the eastern side of the garden, and a dozen Commonwealth soldiers and Fidelian Knights stood along the northwestern side of the garden.

Nash looked at the standoff outside the cockpit window, "You can't be serious about this?"

"He's right Halie," Ariel said trying to fight tears. "You can't do this. She's going to kill you and take your cousin. There is no way we can let this happen."

"We must cooperate with her," Halie stared out the window. "The lives of those kids and instructors are at stake. If we can get them safely out of here, then that is all that matters."

"I couldn't just give in so easily," Nash answered.

"It's my choice," Skylar replied. "It's my life and my choice. She's my mother and I won't let her hurt anyone else here. Now, let's get this over with."

"Two ships are approaching," Ariel interrupted. "One is a Commonwealth transport and the other is a Varangian yacht."

"The transport is here to take the children and instructors away," Haile replied. "The yacht is the Intrepid, Myra's ship."

"I thought she wanted this moon?" Nash replied, "Why would she want to leave?"

Halie watched the two ships slowly approaching, "She wants the moon, and what she thinks is the power of the Fidelian Knights. But she wants Skylar more. She'll leave troops here to control the moon and return here when it's safer. For now, she will likely take Skylar to her fortress on Tintigal."

"Let's get this over with," Skylar said sadly, standing to and walk to the back of the ship.

"Open the door," Halie said following her cousin. She stopped at the door of the cockpit and looked at Nash. "Once those kids and instructors are safely off the planet take off."

"You can't stay here," Ariel begged.

"I'll be fine. You need to make it look like your leaving with the transport."

"I don't like where this is going," Nash said sternly looking at his friend.

"Nash, I know I can rely on you," Halie replied holding the tears inside. "As you go over the Cathedral destroy it. Drop whatever it takes to wipe it off the face of this moon."

Ariel looked shocked, "It's been sacred to the Fidelians for so long. How can you ask me to destroy it? Besides this will kick the battle into full swing again."

"I'm counting on the battle restarting and hoping the element of surprise will help get the rest of our troops off the moon. As for the Cathedral, it's been a symbol of peace and hope for generations. In the end, it is only a building, a structure for use. Our source of power and strength are not in the structure but within our souls. I'd rather destroy the Abbey on our terms than let them think they have defeated the Fidelian Order. The reality is that the Knights were around long before this Abbey was ever built here on Avalon One. They will continue even without the Abbey long into the future."

Nash forced a grin, trying to be supportive, "I understand. You can count on us. Be safe, and as you always say, may mercy and grace be with you."

"And, with you," she replied turning to join Skylar at the rear of the ship.

Halie and Skylar walked down the ramp of the ship as the Excelsior's transport ship landed several yards behind them. Myra's ship, the Intrepid landed about fifty yards south of the two ships right next to the Labyrinth.

"Halie," Skylar said, "I don't want you to save me. Save the others, but don't worry about me."

Halie stopped and looked down at her younger cousin, "Sky, I love you very much. I admire your willingness. I also realize that I may have to let you go with Myra, but she won't get you without a fight from me."

"Your parents might have something to say about this too," Skylar said looking toward the transport ship, where Dara and Bern were now walking toward them.

"What are you doing here?" Halie asked. "Why would you come here knowing Myra is here."

"That's why we came," Bern replied. "To be sure she honor's her word. I do not doubt that Skylar will go through with this, but I doubt she'll keep her word."

"But you shouldn't be endangering yourselves," Skylar added.

"Sweetie," Dara said putting an arm around the boy, "If I am going to have to let you go with her, I at least needed the opportunity to say goodbye."

A tear ran down Skylar's face, "Yes Ma'am. I love you."

"And, we love you. We're very proud of you, young man," Bern added as he placed a hand on Skylar's shoulder.

"We'd better get this over with," Halie said. "We don't want to keep her waiting."

They walked about thirty feet from Myra and stopped. The evil woman smiled as they stopped, "Well, what a nice little family reunion this is."

"Myra," Dara replied sadly, "You've fallen from such great potential. It there was any decency left in you, you wouldn't do this."

Myra snickered, "My decency. My son has been kept from me for eight years. He didn't even know I was his mother. And, you dare to speak to me about decency?"

Bern stared at the woman, "You stopped being his mother when you left the Order. You tried to destroy the Abbey then. I guess it looks like you'll finally get your way."

"No," Myra replied with a smile, "I'm getting the Abbey, and all its power."

"You still don't understand," Dara shook her head, "I suppose you never will. The power of the Fidelians is not in things but the Creator of all things. You may force Skylar to go with you, but I'm convinced that he already has a solid foundation. He will not be moved from that foundation, even if he must go with you."

"Enough of this ridiculous banter," Myra said, looking at Skylar. "No matter what they've told you and no matter how bad this looks, you've always been my son. I've always wanted to return to be with you. You'll see that I love you and that I am not as evil as they make me out to be."

"I'm prepared to go with you," Skylar coldly replied. "I won't interfere with your plans. Just keep your word and let everyone go."

"Once you're by my side, they're free to go."

"No," Halie demanded, "You get him once I know these kids and teachers are on board the transport ships."

"This is not a negotiation, young lady," Myra glared at her niece. "We had an agreement."

"I'm staying here with him until they're airborne," Halie replied. "I assure you that he'll stay here, once they are safe."

"I've already promised to release them, and all of the Knights on the moon are free to go. Now, I want my son."

"Once they're safely away, you'll have what's coming to you."

Myra sighed, "Fine. Release everyone. Take them away from here quickly," she growled at Dara.

"My pleasure," Dara replied, "Everyone, quickly get to the transport." She turned and hugged Skylar tightly, "Never forget where you've come from."

"I won't," he answered.

"Halie," Bern looked at his daughter sternly, "Once we are gone, get out of here."

"I promise I will get off the moon. Nash will be taking the Pegasus with you, and I'll join the rest of the Knights at the Command Center and leave on the last transport."

"Be safe," Dara added.

"I will."

It only took a few minutes before the transport ship and the Pegasus were both rising into the air. Myra stared calmly at Halie and Skylar, "Your family and friends are safely on their way. Now, my beautiful niece, I suggest you join the remaining Knights and get to the transport at the command center. That is unless you plan to join me as well."

"I'll join them shortly. I just want to say goodbye."

"Make it quick, I'd like to get my son aboard my ship."

Halie hugged Skylar, "I love you, Bud. I will never give up."

"I know," Skylar said.

"It's time," Myra held out her hand, "Come to me, my son."

Skylar slowly turned away from Halie, "I'm coming. But don't call me that."

Myra smiled at the boy, "But, I am your mother."

"You're the person who gave birth to me," Skylar said as he stood in front of her, "But, that doesn't make you my mother."

"Skylar Orion," Halie said sharply, "Mind your attitude."

"Yes, Halie," Skylar said putting his head down and stepping next to Myra.

Myra put her arm around Skylar's shoulder, "Thank you, Halie. Thank you for being so honorable."

"My honor is for the Fidelians," she replied, as she pulled her sword from her side and ignited it.

"There's our sign," Nash shouted to Ariel. They had been watching the event unfolding, as they ascended.

"Let's do this," she smiled.

He quickly maneuvered the bomber over the Cathedral and dropped three pulsar bombs, as Ariel began firing the forward guns into the Varangian soldiers below.

The explosion knocked Myra to the ground, as Halie motioned Skylar to run toward the Fidelian Knights still standing in the bushes behind them.

"You little, brat! How could you deceive me like this?" Myra shouted as she stood to her feet. "KILL THEM ALL!"

Gunfire erupted around them, as the battle began again. Above their heads, several Commonwealth fighters began firing upon the forces around the eastern gate of the Abbey. Skylar ran across the garden toward the bushes where several Knights and Commonwealth soldiers were defending their position.

"I didn't make this deal with you, Skylar did. I never intended to give him to you. I said you'd get what was coming to you," Halie said as she ran toward Myra swinging her sword.

"Skylar Knighthawk," Major Kohler startled Skylar. "I'm getting you out of here."

"Major, my cousin. I can't leave."

"She put herself out there to save you. Now, I'm sending you to the Command Center. We have some fighters there waiting to take the last important people from the moon. I want you on one of them right away."

"I need to stay. I need..."

"Skylar, you and your family are too valuable to the Order of Fidelian Knights. Your father trained me, and you'll make a great Knight one day. But, right now you're going with Corporal Sweeny. Sweeny, you make sure he is on a fighter off this moon. Do you understand?"

"Yes, Sir," the young man standing next to them replied."

"We still control the west side of the campus, so you should be able to get him out of here, safely.

"But my cousin?" Skylar begged.

The major leaned down next to him and looked him in the eye, "I'll do everything I can to try to save her, you have my promise. Now, please go."

Skylar took a deep breath, " Yes, Sir."

Myra lifted her scepter to deflect the plasma sword and knocked Halie to the ground. "Why couldn't you just leave well enough alone."

"Why couldn't you just stay away from here and leave Skylar alone."

Myra swung her scepter toward Halie, as the crystal powered plasma glowed, "I don't want to kill you. But, I will if needed. Can't you see that my troops have this moon."

At that moment two laser blast knocked Myra away from Halie, as the Pegasus returned. Myra stumbled to her feet, "I will destroy you. All of you!" she shouted toward Halie.

Halie smiled standing to her feet, and backing away from the woman, "Not today. I'd suggest you and your troops retreat. I think the tide is turning."

The Pegasus sat down between the two women. Myra limped toward her ship. Halie ran to the Pegasus and was soon sitting with her friends in the cockpit, "I thought I asked you to escort the transport."

"We did until some fighter escorts arrived. Now, where's that little cousin of yours?"

"I'm not sure? I sent him to the Knights and troops. I assume they would try to get him to the Command Center to get him off the moon."

" Then let's go find, the kid," Nash said, as he raised the ship into the air."

They rose above the burning rubble of the Cathedral and watched the Intrepid fly over the battle in the eastern field. The sleek ship disappeared into the atmosphere quickly taking Myra away from the moon. Nash turned the Pegasus around and headed toward the hanger on the other side of the Command Center.

36

The Pegasus slowly glided over the Fidelian Abbey, as Commonwealth soldiers moved forward across the open spaces and around the buildings below. Two additional Commonwealth transport ships were landing on the tarmac as Nash landed behind the large Command structure. The ramp was still lowering at the rear of the bomber, as Halie jumped off and ran toward the hanger.

Soldiers were moving in formation, working their way around the command center. Several pilots and copilots were walking toward five remaining fighters that waiting on the tarmac. Halie stopped briefly to examine whether Skylar was with any of them.

"Ma'am," one of the grounds crew members asked as she approached her, "Are you looking for something?"

"Yes, my cousin."

The young woman stopped and looked at Halie, "I'm sorry Halie. I didn't realize it was you."

"Joanne. Joanne Sharoane?"

"Yes," the officer replied, "I'm in charge of the flight deck."

"I sent Skylar here. I was hoping he was still around. Please tell me he made it."

"Yes," Joanne smiled.

"Then, he's on one of the fighters."

"Yes."

Halie smiled, "I'll have to catch up to him on board the Excelsior then."

"No," Joanne laughed. "He's on that fighter right over there. I'll stop them." She pulled the communicator from her side, "This is Major Sharoane, Captain Lenard please stand down. I have someone here for your passenger."

"Yes, Ma'am," a man's voice responded."

"Thank you," Hallie replied as she ran toward the smaller craft.

Skylar jumped to the ground and ran toward her. She picked him up as she hugged him spinning him around and back to the ground, "I am so glad you are safe."

"So am I," he shouted.

"Good to see you, kid," Nash said grinning at his friends.

"That makes three of us," Ariel added, as Skylar ran and hugged her.

"What's the plan?" Nash asked. "Do we stay and fight or go."

Halie looked around at the soldiers running around and the fighters taking flight nearby. "I believe that it's time for us to go."

"But, the Abbey?" Skylar asked.

"We've done our part. The Alliance troops are arriving to help Major Kruger. He'll be able to lead them to victory and secure the Abbey. It's time we get you away from here, where you some real rest."

"Let's get going then," Nash replied as he turned back toward the Pegasus.

They were soon on board their ship rising above the fighting remaining in the field outside the Abbey. Halie watched the battle a moment and then turned in her copilot's chair, looking back at Skylar, "Why don't you take the copilot's chair, Bud."

"What?" Skylar was surprised. She had never offered to let him take the seat before. A smile crossed his face, "Yeah."

Halie helped get him positioned and then moved to the crew area at the back of the ship. Ariel soon followed her and found her sitting at the table leaning back with her head against the back of the seat and her eyes closed. "What's going on?"

Halie sat up and opened her eyes, "Just a bit tired I guess."

"Tired?" Ariel studied her. "No, you've been exhausted before and you wouldn't have let Skylar in the copilot's seat. Are you, all right?"

"I'll be just fine."

Ariel sat down next to Halie and pulled her friend's coat open. She could see her friend's thigh was bleeding, "Why didn't you say something?"

"Because, if all of you knew my injuries weren't healed up and getting worse, you wouldn't have let me face Myra. I had to face her to save Skylar and buy the time needed for our forces to arrive."

Ariel shook her head, "You could've been killed."

"But I wasn't. Now, are you going to treat this wound or let me bleed to death on the way to the Excelsior?"

Ariel smiled, "I'll bandage the wound. I don't think you're in danger of dying. They can put you on a bio-generator when we get on board the Excelsior. Then I'll call ahead to have them ready for us when we arrive."

"Thanks," Halie said leaning back again, as Ariel began to clean the wound out.

"So, you were hurt?" Skylar asked standing in the doorway

Halie looked at him, "I'll be fine. It's just a flesh wound."

Skylar looked at Ariel, who smiled at him, "She'll be okay kiddo."

"I thought you were going to help fly us to the Excelsior?" Halie asked.

"Nash said he had it under control," Skylar replied. "I knew something was wrong when you told me I could help fly. We're out of danger and should arrive soon. Then you'll be safe."

"No, we'll all be safe," Halie smiled at her cousin, thankful that they were putting the danger behind them.

They were soon walking across the hanger of the Excelsior, as Dara and Bern approached. Dara stepped forward and hugged Halie and Skylar, "I am so glad that you're both safe."

"And," Bern added, "that your plan worked. You managed to not only get us off the moon but allow reinforcements to be sent."

"We saw them arriving, dad. I'm glad it worked out," Halie said.

"But, you're hurt," he replied looking at his daughter.

"Its small gash left from my fall. I'll be fine. How is the battle going?"

"Admiral Pembroke says that we should have the moon clear within the next twenty-four hours. One of their two destroyers has already left."

"That's good to hear," she replied hugging her father. "So, we should be able to promote Skylar soon then."

Skylar looked up at her, "And, bury my father and Sidney properly."

"Along with some very good soldiers and knights," Bern hugged the boy. "But even in the midst of sorrow new life can come. Now, let's get all of you some food and some rest." He guided them toward the elevator.

"It's great to be back here, Nash said. "I can't wait to get to my quarters and get some rest."

"I agree," Ariel smiled.

Dara put an arm around Ariel, "You might want to report to the bridge. I think your father would like to see with his own eyes that you're okay, Corporal Pembroke."

The young woman smiled, "I agree. I'd like to see how he is too."

They all made their way to their respective places to begin recovering from their battle on the first of the three moons of Avalon. The Admiral's estimates were very accurate. The Varangian army was chased from the moon within a couple of days. Brother Lawrence and Major Kruger led a joint force to begin cleaning up the Abbey. Skylar and his friends finally got some much-needed sleep.

37

It had been eight days since the battle. The morning sun rose above the tree line, as dew glistened on the bushes surrounding the Labyrinth. The fountain flowed quietly, and birds chirped nearby. The peacefulness within the Labyrinth almost made it possible to forget the destruction of the Cathedral outside the maze of bushes around.

Brother Lawrence stood in front of the crowd gathered around, "Good morning, friends and family of the Fidelian Order. We have endured great hardship and loss in these past days. We come here today to honor the memory of those who have died defending our home. We are reminded in the Ancient words 'Greater love has no man than to lay down one's life for his brothers.' Our brother Justin Knighthawk willing laid down his life for his son and the future of The Fidelian Order against an evil that is dear to our hearts. We also mourn Sidney Morgan and Sarah Michelson who were taken from us at such a young age. We remember the twelve members of the Order of Fidelian Knights who fought to defend our home with their lives. We honor as well as the forty-three Commonwealth soldiers who gave up their lives to defend the peace of Avalon One. We now bring forth the ashes of our brothers and sisters, to their eternal resting place here within the walls of our hallowed Abbey."

Twelve of the Elite Guard stepped forward carrying boxes in their hands. Each of the boxes contained the remains of two of their fallen comrades. Dara stepped forward carrying a smaller box, as Skylar stepped next to her. They escorted the remains Justin Knighthawk. The Knights gathered around the central square of the Labyrinth all drew their plasma swords igniting them in unison. The ashes were placed in the ground under a large cross that sat at the edge of the square.

"And, now brothers and sisters let us pray. Our Great Father, we thank you for your deliverance from the forces of evil. We know that you will help us to rebuild our home once again. We ask that Your grace will fill us and heal our hearts and souls today, as we mourn. We look forward to one day joining our fallen warriors and friends in the eternal hope. Help us to live in grace now and forevermore. Amen."

The swords of the Knights were all holstered at their sides, and pallbearers all stepped back with the rest of the people gathered in the Square. Dara stepped forward and stood beside Brother Lawrence, "I want to thank each and every one of you for your love and for your service. Justin would have been proud of every one of you. The council of twelve will experience loss, but we as the Knights of faith and knowledge will persevere. May we all be blessed into the future."

"Thank you," Brother Lawrence said giving Dara a hug. "The council has voted a new member to the Council of Twelve, today we welcome former Major Kruger. He joins the council as a replacement for the seat created by the loss of one of our own," cheers rose from the crowd, as the Major joined the Council of Twelve standing beside Brother Lawrence.

"I thank you for this honor and promise to continue to lead with wisdom. I shall never be Justin Knighthawk, but I'll do my best to serve the Council and community well."

"Now, I would ask that Halie Ambrosius please step forward," Brother Lawrence said, as Halie stepped forward a bit bewildered by the invitation. "Hallie Ambrosius, we know your family heritage within the Fidelian Order. We've seen how well you've stood in faith through some trying situations in the past year. We've also seen your willingness to give your life to preserve our faith and traditions. It's the decision of the Council to extend the rare invitation to you. We would like to welcome you to join the Council of Twelve, as an adviser. You will not have voting power, but we believe your wisdom will be an asset to us."

Halie's eyes grew large with surprise. She'd only heard of one other person being given an advisory role to the Council of Twelve, and that was her mother, "I am extremely honored. I'm not worthy of such an offer."

"We see things differently," Brother Lawrence replied. "We look forward to your wisdom in future affairs. We also invite you to join us from time to time, as an instructor here at the Fidelian Academy. We understand that you wouldn't want to leave your friends and the work you do with the Alliance, but your service and wisdom will always be welcome here."

"Thank you, very much," she replied smiling at her mother who was looking on with approval. She returned to her place beside Skylar, Nash, and Ariel.

"Finally, we have one more act of order to complete while the full assembly of the Fidelian Knights is gathered together. Pledge Skylar Orion Knighthawk, please step forward."

"What's going on?" Skylar whispered to Halie.

"It's your turn. Now, step up there."

Skylar walked out in front of everyone and stood silently before Brother Lawrence and the Council of Twelve. He took a deep breath and said a silent prayer for help, as he waited what they might decide for his future.

"Skylar Knighthawk," Councilwoman Garcia looked at him, "What is life?"

"The Creator has given life. Life is, therefore, a gift and should be treasured. All life is important. Humanity shall be cherished no matter what their status or where they have come from."

"Very good," the beautiful woman replied with a nod and a smile.

"Skylar Knighthawk," Councilman Mercier a short older Councilman gave Skylar a stern look, "What is creation then?"

"All of creation has been given to us as a gift. We should respect every part of creation and work to live in harmony with creation in every way we can."

"You answer wisely," the older man said smiling.

"Pledge Knighthawk," the newest Councilman Krueger looked at the boy, "How does one earn eternity?"

Skylar swallowed hard and looked at the large man, "Salvation is a gift that must be accepted. The sacrifice has been paid for us. We are responsible to choose to accept the gift given. A gift that I shall always hold dear."

Councilman Kruger smiled, "Excellent. Your faithful training is proving you well."

"Skylar," Bern addressed his nephew, "What is the role of a Fidelian Knight?"

"To live faithfully. To act justly. To protect faith and knowledge for the preservation of all humanity."

"Your wisdom shows through," Bern replied smiling.

"Young Knighthawk," Brother Lawrence looked down at the boy, "You have survived great trials, and made it through the Pledge's Quest. You've answered the questions of the Council well. We stand in the shadow of a destroyed Cathedral and have mourned the loss of family and friends. Can you address how you will cope with all of this in your heart and soul?"

Skylar smiled at Brother Lawrence, "If you would have asked me a short while ago, I don't know that I could have answered so clearly. Today, while my heart breaks for the death of my father, I stand stronger. I know now more than ever that there is a Creator in control of all things. Even though I've experienced loss and suffering, I know now that I don't stand alone. I am from a long line of faithful Knights who have held faith and knowledge for generations. I also know that no one faces life alone. Even though we may stand by ourselves, we stand with the Creator and all the wisdom of those who have taught us. Our greatest strength is when we stand together in the power of the Creator. Then there is nothing that we cannot do.

Will I miss my father? Yes, I'll miss him very much. I hope to honor him every day. I will learn to the best of my ability. I'll always try to live honorably within my service to the Order of Fidelian Knights."

The smile on Brother Lawrence's face broadened, "Then I take the greatest pleasure in welcoming you to the Squire Stage of training. You will continue to work under the direction of your cousin Halie when you're not here working on necessary training."

"Thank you so much for believing in me," Skylar said smiling, as Brother Lawrence hugged him.

Brother Lawrence turned the boy around and kept a hand on his shoulder, "Everyone, I present the newest Squire in the Fidelian Order of Knights, Skylar Orion Knighthawk. May he remain faithful to the end. May he serve justly. May he live wisely always."

Brother Lawrence placed a necklace with the Fidelian cross around the boy's neck and then turned him around. Everyone cheered for the boy.

Skylar ran to his aunt and cousin hugging them, "Thank you for believing in me and for being there for me."

Dara smiled at him holding him tight, "That's what family does."

"Just remember, your family is bigger than you think," Nash said as he and Ariel stepped up and hugged their friend.

Skylar smiled, "Together we'll continue to protect the Commonwealth and the Fidelian code of faith, justice, and wisdom."

The Fidelian Coat of Arms

About The Author
D.G. Shipton

I grew up in Northern Michigan, graduating from Marion High School, in 1988. I received my Bachelor's Degree from Indiana Wesleyan University, in 1998, and a Masters of Divinity Degree, from Asbury Seminary, in 2012.

I have been an avid reader since early childhood, reading many classical writings from Mark Twain to H.G. Wells. Early on I became especially interested in Mystery and Science Fiction. I continue to enjoy reading and watching Mysteries and Science Fiction & Fantasy.

To keep up with my writing projects and new releases please visit my webpage
https://dgshiptonblog.wordpress.com/
You can also sign up there to receive a newsletter of my works and activities. If you signup you can receive a free short story.

www.ingramcontent.com/pod-product-compliance
Lightning Source LLC
Chambersburg PA
CBHW020247180626
46810CB00006B/2403